The Belles Dames Club

By the same author

Maid of Honour
The Bargain
Lady Vengeance
The Dream Chasers
The Highclough Lady
A Lady at Midnight
Dance for a Diamond
Gentlemen in Question

The Belles
Dames Club

Melinda Hammond

ROBERT HALE · LONDON

ISBN 978-0-7090-8272-9

Robert Hale Limited
Clerkenwell House
Clerkenwell Green
London EC1R 0HT

2 4 6 8 10 9 7 5 3 1

Typeset in 10¾/14½pt New Century Schoolbook
by Derek Doyle & Associates, Shaw Heath
Printed and bound in Great Britain
by Biddles Limited, King's Lynn

CHAPTER ONE

'Well, Miss Clarissa, another hour or so will see you safe back with your stepmama.' As soon as the maid had uttered these prophetic words, the carriage slowed to a halt. Miss Wyckenham's dark eyes gleamed.

'Becky, you wretch!'

'What, miss? I didn't do nothing!'

Seeing that her maid was truly alarmed, Miss Wyckenham merely patted her hand.

'No of course not. But if *you* did not cause us to stop, I must find out what did. Gibson, the door.' Miss Wyckenham scarcely waited for her footman to let down the steps before jumping down on to the road and making her way towards the coach-man, who was inspecting one of the horses. 'Well, John?'

He straightened up.

'One of the wheelers, Miss Clarissa: cast a shoe, he has, and no way can I carry on, not on this rough road.'

'Oh dear. And are we near a village – a smithy?'

'As to that, I don't rightly know.' He broke off and looked round as three young boys came crashing out of the trees on to the road.

'Hi there – not so fast, young feller-me-lad!'

The coachman waved his whip towards them and the three boys stopped, looking back at him warily. One of them hurriedly put his hand behind his back, but not before Clarissa

5

had seen what she thought was a sling-shot in his grasp.

'How far is it to the village?' asked John. 'Is there a smithy there?'

One of the boys, the largest and, thought Clarissa, the eldest, nodded.

'Aye, mister. You'm not a mile away from Tottenham, and there's a smith near High Cross.'

As the coachman turned back to Clarissa, the three boys took to their heels.

'Well that's a bit o'luck, miss. I'll get the horse unhitched and be on my way. If Tottenham's as near as they say then it'll take about a half-hour to get there.'

'Lord love us, you ain't suggestin' we walk there?' cried Becky, who had come to the carriage door and only heard the last half of the conversation.

Clarissa glanced at her maid's ample figure and her lips twitched.

'No, no, Becky. You and I can remain in the coach. John shall take the horse to the smithy and we shall be back on the road again in no time. Am I right, John?'

'Aye, miss. I'll pad it to Tottenham and get a new shoe for the poor nag, if you are sure you don't mind waiting here? Bramley and Gibson will stay with you, so you'll be safe enough.'

Clarissa thought of the two burly footmen that her sister had insisted should accompany her on the journey to London. She nodded as she climbed back into the carriage.

'Very well, John, off you go now.' She handed him a small purse. 'If you cannot get the animal shod today, then perhaps you can hire another team. I am determined to reach London tonight.'

The coachman smiled.

'Don't you worry, Miss Clarissa: we'll get you home right and tight.'

'I do hope he's right,' muttered Becky, making herself comfortable in one corner of the carriage. 'There's only a few hours of daylight left.'

'And that is all we need,' returned Clarissa, determined to be cheerful. 'Besides, it is almost a full moon tonight, and once we reach London the street lamps will be sufficient to guide our way to Mama-Nell.'

While Becky closed her eyes and prepared to sleep, Miss Wyckenham looked longingly out of the coach window at the grassy bank. It dropped gently away from the road towards a tumbling stream that glinted in the afternoon sunlight. They had been travelling since dawn and the idea of strolling across to the stream was very tempting. She glanced back at her maid, now snoring gently. It would be cruel to rouse her. With sudden decision Clarissa retied the ribbons of her wide-brimmed hat, opened the door and climbed out. Immediately the two footmen playing dice upon the carriage roof prepared to descend, but she raised her hand.

'No, no, do not disturb yourselves. I am going to walk down to the stream.'

'Then one of us should come with you, miss—'

'There is no need, I shall not go out of sight. I merely want a little air.'

Clarissa followed the rough path that ran diagonally from the road to the stream. There was a light breeze to offset the April sunshine, and Clarissa buttoned her tight-fitting riding jacket as she strode out towards a little wood a short distance ahead of her, glad of the chance to be moving after the confines of the carriage. There was a wider and well-worn path running beside the stream: a local right of way through the wood, she guessed, older than the turnpike road that ran along the higher ground, and much prettier too, she thought, for the ground was dotted with yellow spring flowers on each side of the path. Clarissa followed it towards the trees, enjoying the peace and solitude.

A little way into the wood the stream and the path turned

sharply. Clarissa looked back. The two footmen were still sitting on the roof of the carriage and she could hear their voices quite clearly. Smiling, Clarissa carried on, eager to explore a little way into the wood. It was too early for the trees to be in full leaf and she found herself in a dappled shade. Clarissa strode on to the bend in the path, curious to see where it might lead, but stopped abruptly when she found her way blocked by the body of a man.

CHAPTER TWO

Clarissa stared down at the figure at her feet, her heart and brain racing. The man was lying on his back, his eyes closed. There was no sign of blood and a quick glance around showed her no other person, only a rangy black horse standing a few yards away, quietly cropping the grass. Should she call her footmen? She decided against it. She knelt beside him and reached out a tentative hand to touch his neck. It was warm and she was relieved to feel the steady pulse beneath her fingers.

'Excuse me,' she murmured, untying his neck-cloth.

The cut of the close-fitting riding coat and brocade waistcoat proclaimed the town gentleman rather than a country squire, and a fashionable tall-crowned beaver hat lay close by. Clarissa ran to the stream and dipped her handkerchief into the clear water, returning moments later to bathe the man's forehead. Not a handsome face, she thought: too hawk-like, the jaw-line too strong. She paused to brush a stray lock from his brow. The hair was dark, glossy as a raven's wing and cut short in the modern style. It was matched by the dark, straight brows and the lashes that lay against his pale cheek. He stirred.

'Gently, sir.'

He opened his eyes. They were grey as granite, she noticed, and for a moment they gazed up at her blankly. Then he smiled and the austere lines of his face softened into something much warmer.

'Elizabeth?'

Clarissa instinctively grasped the hand he held up to her.

'No, sir, I am not she. My name is Clarissa.'

The smile died as his vision cleared.

'What happened?'

Clarissa sat back, releasing his hand.

'It would seem you fell from your horse.'

He sat up, groaning.

'The devil I did! Something frightened him.'

'Three young boys ran out of the wood a few minutes ago. One, I think, carried a sling-shot. I thought they had been hunting crows.'

'Hmm. Whether by accident or design they hit a bigger target. Little devils.' He turned his hard eyes upon her. 'What are you doing here?'

'One of our carriage horses cast a shoe. My coachman has taken the animal to the village to be shod.'

'And left you here alone?'

'No indeed. My maid and two footmen are here with me.' She saw his incredulous look and her smile deepened. 'They are within earshot, sir, believe me. But my maid is asleep. All I wanted to do was to take a short walk and I had not the heart to wake her.'

'You would have been better advised to do so, ma'am.'

'And what could she have done that I did not? In fact, the silly creature might well have fallen into hysterics, then I should have had two bodies on my hands.'

'It is not a matter for laughter, madam. Propriety demands you should be attended, for your own protection.'

The note of censure in his voice was unmistakable.

9

'Indeed?' she returned coolly. 'I think in this case propriety demands too much. I am in the habit of looking after myself.' She rose and watched him follow suit, a little unsteadily. 'Now, sir, if you are recovered sufficiently to mount your horse, I will leave you to continue your journey.'

'Please, don't go.' He did not look at her, but began to brush the moss and twigs from his coat. 'I apologize if I appear churlish, madam.'

'Frankly, sir, you do.'

He stopped and looked up, no sign of humour in his hard eyes.

'Then forgive me, and accept my gratitude for your assistance.'

He bowed. Clarissa gave him a slight curtsy before turning and retracing her steps out of the wood.

She knew a momentary disappointment when he did not call after her. He had not even asked her name. She shrugged. It was not important, after all. She would probably never see him again. Clarissa smiled to herself. If nothing else, it had helped to pass the time.

CHAPTER THREE

It was very late when Miss Wyckenham's carriage reached London. It had been necessary to dine on the road, but not all her maid's arguments could make Clarissa put up at an inn overnight.

'Lady Wyckenham has never stood on ceremony with me, Becky, and I would so much rather reach Charlotte Street

tonight. Mama-Nell knows I am on my way.'

'Well it's not seemly to go arriving at such an ungodly hour.' Becky sniffed. 'Lady Wyckenham could well be abed.'

When the carriage finally pulled up in Charlotte Street, Clarissa feared her maid had been correct. The house looked alarmingly dark with the shutters firmly closed at the windows of the main rooms on the first floor. Perhaps Lady Wyckenham had left Town.

'That cannot be,' Clarissa muttered, as if to herself. 'She told me she would be here for me, and that I should come as soon as may be.' She alighted and trod resolutely up the steps, rapping loudly on the knocker. The door opened a fraction. 'Ah, Simmons, good evening.' Clarissa stepped past the butler into the hall. 'You look surprised, and no wonder. I am sorry to arrive so late, but we were delayed on the road. Please have the footmen bring in the bags. Is my lady at home?'

'Miss Clarissa! No. That is. . . .'

'Oh. Is she dining out?'

'No – yes.'

'No, yes? Simmons, this is not like you.' She pointed to a little black page asleep on a bench against one wall. 'Ah, my lady has visitors.'

'Miss Clarissa, you should not be here. . . .'

She laughed as she removed her hat.

'And where else should I be? I know it is very late, but would you expect me to sleep in the street until morning? Now, if you will have my trunks taken up,' she stopped as the faint sound of laughter came to her ears.

The butler began to wring his hands.

'Miss Clarissa—'

She did not hear him. More shouts and laughter could be heard. She ran quickly up the stairs and opened the door to the drawing-room.

Her entrance went unnoticed. The room was a large one, illuminated by dozens of candles blazing from a central chandelier

11

and from the branched candlesticks placed about the room. The elegance of the room was enhanced by a series of large frescoes depicting stories from classical Greece, but on this occasion the scene that met Clarissa's stunned gaze rivalled anything she had heard of that ancient society. A roaring fire blazed beneath the ornate marble chimneypiece but all the furniture had been moved back to the edges of the room. A number of ladies were seated in a semi-circle facing the centre, their attention fixed on the only two men in the room: two wrestlers.

Two naked wrestlers.

A quick glance at the ladies showed Clarissa only two faces she knew: one was her stepmother, Lady Wyckenham, sitting next to a beautiful redheaded matron in emerald silk, and her stepmother's long-time friend, Viscountess Gaunt. Lady Gaunt was one of the more enthusiastic spectators, sitting forward on her chair and waving her arms as she exhorted her favourite to do better.

The combatants grappled together on the red and gold Aubusson carpet. The men fought energetically, the combined light from the fire and the candles gleamed on their sinewy limbs. Clarissa watched the men lock arms and cling together, muscles straining, shifting backwards and forwards as each tried to gain the advantage. Then it was all over. A sudden twist, a grunt, and one of the men was on his back. His opponent raised his arm in victory and a loud cheer went up from the ladies, some of whom threw their coloured scarves at him.

Only then did anyone notice Clarissa's arrival. The striking redhead looked towards the door, gasped, and quickly alerted her hostess. In a rustle of silken skirts Lady Wyckenham rose and flew across the room.

'Clarissa! Good heavens, I had quite given you up.'

Looking past her, Clarissa saw the victorious wrestler pick up Lady Gaunt's scarf and hang it about his neck.

'Mama-Nell, what—?'

Lady Wyckenham took her arm and whisked her out of the

room, shutting the door firmly behind her.

'Clarissa, what in heaven's name are you doing here?'

'I told you I was coming today – did you not get my letter?'

'Yes, yes, but I thought you had stopped on the road – I did not expect you to arrive here at eleven o'clock!' She guided her stepdaughter towards the morning-room, calling for candles to be lighted.

'Evidently. Mama-Nell, what is going on?'

'Oh, merely a little entertainment.'

'Entertainment?' Clarissa's eyes began to dance. 'Madam, those men were *naked*!'

Lady Wyckenham raised her brows.

'What of it? They were wrestling.'

'Do – do you make it a habit to hold wrestling matches in the house?' asked Clarissa, trying hard to keep her voice steady.

'No, no, this is the first one – it was Dorothea Gaunt's idea, and I must say it has been vastly diverting.'

'*Lady Gaunt* suggested this?' Clarissa stared. 'Mama-Nell, I cannot credit it.'

'No, no, how should you?' said Lady Wyckenham in soothing tones. 'My poor darling, you must be exhausted after such a long day. Let me take you up to your room, and I will ask Mrs Simmons to prepare a supper tray for you.'

'But you have not explained—'

'No, and now is not the time, my dear,' My lady ushered her towards the stairs. 'You need to rest, my love. Tomorrow we can talk. I will explain everything.'

Clarissa stopped and gave her stepmother a searching look.

'Everything. You promise?'

A small hand on her back propelled her onwards.

'You have my word.'

CHAPTER FOUR

The next morning Lady Wyckenham was surprised when Clarissa entered her bedroom carrying her morning hot chocolate.

'My love, are you up and dressed already? I vow you put me to shame with your energy.'

'I have never liked to lie a-bed, Mama-Nell, you know that. What an extremely fetching night-cap.'

My lady put one hand up to the snowy confection fastened over her golden curls.

'Thank you, my darling, it is one of the things I purchased in Paris last year. But you should not be waiting on me, my love.'

'I intercepted your maid on the stairs: I thought we could have a comfortable coze.' Clarissa put the tray down before my lady then sat down on the end of the bed, leaning against one heavily carved bedpost.

'So, tell me, how did you leave your sister?' asked Lady Wyckenham.

'Anne was very well – and very happy to have her husband home again.'

'No doubt you were sorry to leave Royston.'

'In some ways, but ever since the war ended Anne has been expecting Henry to return from America. Now that he has done so it is only right that they should have the house to themselves.' Clarissa smiled. 'Except for one short break, he has been away for four years – they are like a newly-wed couple. I was most definitely *de trop!*'

'Well, my love, you are very welcome here. Henceforth my home shall be your own. I know that after your father's death I could not comfort you as a mother should—'

'You were distraught, Mama-Nell.'

Lady Wyckenham studied her cup.

'Nevertheless, I was not a good mother to you in those days.'

'But Henry had just gone off to war, and Anne was alone, so it was natural that as sisters we should comfort one another.'

'But I should have looked after you both!' cried Lady Wyckenham, her pretty face crumpling.

Clarissa shook her head.

'You know that was not possible. I was desperate to stay away from town at that time. Besides, Anne was never close to you, as I was.'

'She dislikes me.'

'No, no, not now. It is true she resented you a little, when you first married my father, but she was so much older than I, and could remember Mama so much better. It was quite natural.'

My lady gave a little laugh.

'Both William and Anne thought your father had run mad when he married me. They thought I could not make him happy, but I did, Clarissa, I *did*!'

'I know it, Mama-Nell. I was very young, but I remember how he changed: he came alive again when he met you.'

Lady Wyckenham smiled mistily.

'We had some good times, Clarissa. I would wish to see you as happy in a marriage. And now you are come back to live with me I shall do my best to find you just such a husband.'

'Thank you, Mama-Nell, but I have not come to town to find a husband.'

'Oh? Is there a beau back in Royston?'

Clarissa's dark eyes were alight with laughter.

'Several!' she replied saucily, 'but none that I liked well enough to marry.' She grew serious. 'I have a very comfortable income, so marriage is not a necessity for me. I thought. . . .' She paused. 'I thought, if you would let me live with you, we could perhaps travel together: I do so long to see something of the world.'

'Well of course, my love, if that is what you want.' Lady

Wyckenham was rather startled. 'But, my dear, you have unfortunate memories of your first season, surely now—'

'My dear ma'am, that is not why I have stayed away from you. True, I thought myself bereft when Papa died, and Jack's betrayal was painful, but I have not been nursing a broken heart all these years, believe me. The truth is, I fear I am too particular. I want just such a partnership as you had with Papa, and if I cannot find that, I think I shall remain single.'

Lady Wyckenham was too wise to continue the subject, but silently made up her mind to find a suitable husband for her beautiful stepdaughter. Clarissa might be three-and-twenty, but with her luxurious dark hair, deep-brown eyes and a generous mouth that always seemed on the edge of laughter, Lady Wyckenham thought there were few men who would not take a second look when Clarissa entered a room.

'Well,' she said at last, 'I shall be delighted to have your company here in town, my love, and if you are of the same mind next year, then you shall come with me to Paris. You will like that, I think.'

'Indeed I shall, thank you, Mama-Nell.' Clarissa paused. 'About last night—'

Lady Wyckenham set down her cup with a clatter and pushed the tray to one side. 'Goodness, I can hear the church clock chiming the hour! Send for Polly, my love, I must get up.'

Clarissa leaned forward, imprisoning her stepmother's hands in her own.

'No, no, I shall not let you get up until you explain to me about last night.'

'But I have an appointment with my milliner.'

'You promised, Mama-Nell.'

Lady Wyckenham saw the determination in Clarissa's face and sighed.

'Oh very well.' She sank back against her pillows, as if considering where to start. 'When your dear father died, you know I shut myself away to mourn, as was proper, for a full

year. Since then I have travelled widely, as well as coming back to town regularly. There is so much more freedom granted to a widow than a single lady, but even so the conventions have to be observed, and I had become so very bored.' She looked up. 'You are not a babe, Clarissa. You know that in such cases many women amuse themselves by taking a lover. For a short time I thought—' She broke off, biting her lip, then said with a sigh, 'I found I did not wish to do so – it would insult the memory of your dear papa.' My lady's lips curved slightly and there was a mischievous twinkle in her eyes. 'Besides, I have never met anyone who aroused my passion for more than a month, and a mere infatuation would not do! No, I wanted no male attentions, though there were plenty for the taking, I can assure you.'

'I am sure there were, Mama-Nell.'

My lady glanced across the room to her mirror: even in the unforgiving light of the morning sun she was not displeased with her appearance. She was now approaching forty, but her skin was still smooth and the blue eyes as bright as ever. She continued.

'About a year ago, I paid a visit to my relatives in Norfolk: cousins, and kindly souls who invite me to join them for a few weeks each year. While I was there I met an old man, some sort of great-uncle. We got talking, and he was pointing out to me a portrait of one of our ancestors on the wall: an ancient picture of a jolly-looking man with a squirrel resting on the sleeve of his coat. He told me the painting had been done as one of a set. The sitters were all members of a drinking club called Little Bedlam, and each of them took on the name of an animal so that their identities should remain a secret from the servants.' Lady Wyckenham gave a little smile. 'I well remember the old man's words, *"Crack-brained idea, that. Never known a household where a man's servants didn't know everything that went on."*' She gave a little shrug and looked up at Clarissa. 'So there it is. I decided to start a little club for my friends – ladies

17

only, of course. At first I thought to call it the New Little Bedlam, but thought the Belles Dames Club more appropriate. We meet to drink, talk, play at cards – oh, anything we wish. We have gone disguised to Ranelagh and even to a public masquerade. The element of secrecy means we avoid censure.'

'And the scarves thrown out to the wrestlers last night? Was it like a medieval joust, the winner picks the lady of his fancy?'

Lady Wyckenham's cheeks betrayed a slight flush.

'Some of the ladies were very taken with the wrestlers. And the victor deserves some reward for his efforts, don't you think?'

'Mama-Nell, that is outrageous!'

'No more outrageous than the husbands spending the evening at Brooks's or White's before going on to some snug little house in Pall Mall. I do not wish to indulge in that way myself, but if others are so inclined. . . .'

'Lady Gaunt was definitely so inclined!' retorted Clarissa.

'Dorothea has always liked to set the world by its ears. I am sorry, Clarissa, have I shocked you?'

'No, no. A little surprised, perhaps, but even more intrigued. When is your next meeting? I should like to be there.'

My Lady sat bolt upright.

'Clarissa, the Belles Dames Club is for married ladies.'

'My dear madam, you can scarce prevent me from attending if these meetings are held here.'

'I can and will. It would be unseemly.'

'Oh? And why is that?'

'I have already told you: it is for married ladies only. We have to consider your reputation.'

'You have already told me that the club is secret.' Clarissa reasoned. 'How then could it damage my reputation?'

'You are too young,' declared my lady, a hint of desperation in her voice.

Clarissa laughed at that.

'How so? At three-and-twenty, I am as old as several of the

young matrons I saw last night – perhaps older.' She slipped off the edge of the bed. 'Come, Mama-Nell, you must let me attend the next meeting, or I shall write to William and tell him all about your little club.'

Lady Wyckenham stared at her.

'You would not – you know how much he disapproves of me already.'

'Of course I would not. I was only joking you, dearest. But the knowledge that my slow-top brother would disapprove of the Belles Dames Club makes me even more determined to become a member. Now, I will give you just an hour to dress and break your fast, Mama-Nell, then I have ordered the carriage to take us to King Street, for I must see the silk mercers. You tell me you have to see your milliner, and *I* am in desperate need of new gowns.'

CHAPTER FIVE

Lights blazed from Orpington House and, as Lady Wyckenham's carriage approached the impressive entrance, she laid one gloved hand upon Clarissa's arm.

'No need to be nervous, my love. You look very well, believe me. It is a pity Madam Marguerite could not find you a gown at such short notice, but your embroidered muslin suits you admirably, and besides, you will be among friends.'

Clarissa could not resist.

'Fellow members of the Belles Dames Club, madam?'

'Of course: that is why I was determined you should accompany me this evening. After your sudden appearance last night the other ladies would never forgive me if I had left you at home.'

19

No sooner had the ladies put off their cloaks than they heard a pretty musical voice behind them.

'So you have brought her.'

Clarissa looked round and recognized the diminutive redhead she had seen the night before. The lady was coming towards them, smiling. She was dressed in a cloud of primrose lustring, her shining red curls piled artlessly upon her head, and a welcoming smile in her huge green eyes.

Lady Wyckenham introduced her as Lady Sarah Matlock, but the redhead waved her hand dismissively.

'Don't you dare call me Lady Sarah – I am Sally to my friends, and I know you will be one of them, Clarissa – you will let me call you Clarissa, won't you? I have been so looking forward to meeting you.'

'I was only sorry Mama-Nell did not have time to introduce us last night,' murmured Clarissa with a teasing glance at her stepmother.

Lady Sarah gave a gurgle of laughter and tucked her tiny hand into Clarissa's arm. 'Your arrival caused a stir, I can tell you! But no matter. Helen has told us all about you, you see, so I know I shall like you. We are of an age, I think.'

'Yes, you are,' agreed Lady Wyckenham, adding pointedly, 'but Sally is now a married lady, and therefore has much more freedom.'

'But I am sure we shall find a great deal we can do together, Mama-Nell,' murmured Clarissa. 'Shopping, for instance, and joining clubs.'

Sally saw the mischievous look and clapped her hands together.

'I was so afraid you would be outraged by what you saw last night. I thought you might pack your bags and leave immediately, but Dorothea said you would not do so. She said you were always an unconventional child.'

Lady Wyckenham frowned.

'Lady Gaunt assumes to know my stepdaughter very well.'

'But she is right, ma'am. You know I want to join your little club.' Clarissa looked at Sally. 'Could you vote me in?'

Lady Sarah nodded.

'Of course we could.'

Lady Wyckenham opened her fan with a decided snap.

'That is quite enough!' she cried, much flushed. 'This is not the place to discuss such matters. Sally, I would thank you not to encourage her.'

'Oh fiddle, Nell! If you did not wish Clarissa to join us, then you should not have brought her here, for you know you will have to introduce her to all the other members of the club.'

Lady Wyckenham opened her mouth, then shut it again, unable to think of a suitable retort.

'There,' declared Lady Sarah, casting a triumphant look at Clarissa, 'I think it is safe now to assume that you will be joining us!'

'By Gad, Marius, why in heaven's name do you come out wearing that dead-and-done-for look?' Barnabus Norwell shook his head at his friend's sober mien. 'For God's sake man, *smile*.'

Marius Lexington, ninth Earl of Alresford, raised his black brows.

'I am not aware that I look so gloomy. It must be my nature.'

'That I cannot allow! I think it is that you have got out of the habit of being sociable. When we were boys together you were awake upon every suit, always ready to run a rig.'

'But I have grown up since then.'

'Grown old, more like. There is still much to enjoy in life, Marius. I vow you are my despair.'

Only someone as well acquainted with Lord Alresford as Mr Norwell would have noticed the slight softening of his look.

'I admit I am a trial to you, Barny. I do not know why you bother with me.'

'Because you are a good friend, and you can be excellent company when you wish to be.'

'But I so dislike occasions such as these. The false smiles and simpering looks – the matrons determined to catch a husband for some fusby-faced daughter.'

Mr Norwell gave a crack of laughter.

'The matrons gave up trying to catch you years ago, Marius. And you may as well try to enjoy yourself. Mama is bringing Margaret to town next week and you know very well she will be calling upon you as an escort.'

'I shall tell her I am otherwise engaged.'

'Oh no you will not,' retorted Mr Norwell hotly. 'If you think I'll go gallivanting around town with m'sister on my own you are wrong. As our cousin it is your duty to attend us! So you must brush up your social skills, my friend.'

Lord Alresford did not reply, his attention caught by a group just entering the ballroom and he laid a hand on his friend's arm.

'Well then, I had best make a start. Will you introduce me to a lady, Barnabus?'

Mr Norwell's eyes gleamed hopefully.

'A lady? A *young* lady, Marius?'

'Yes, Lady Wyckenham's companion. But do not jump to conclusions, sir. I merely wish to be civil.'

'Well, I know Lady Wyckenham, so let us begin there.'

CHAPTER SIX

'Dear ma'am, I have been away for so long it is like coming to town for the first time.' Clarissa paused as they entered the

ball-room, momentarily stunned by the noise and bustle and light. 'Everything and everyone is new to me.'

Lady Wyckenham smiled up at her.

'Believe me no one looking at you would think you apprehensive. I have little doubt that I shall be besieged by your admirers tonight.'

'Mama-Nell!'

'It is true – and here come the first two now. Good evening, Mr Norwell.'

Lady Wyckenham turned her wide smile upon the young man, who bowed over her gloved fingers.

'Your servant, ma'am.'

'And where is your lovely wife this evening, Mr Norwell? I made sure to see her here.'

'Oh Julia is here, ma'am, dancing, I think. But never mind that: I have brought with me a friend, who is most anxious to meet you. Pray allow me to present the Earl of Alresford to you, ma'am.'

Lady Wyckenham's shrewd gaze flickered over the young men, noting their surreptitious glances at Clarissa, who was standing a little behind her. My lady smiled: it was not at all surprising. Clarissa had always been a spirited little thing, but now, dressed in a deceptively simple cream muslin, a slight blush suffusing her cheek and the candlelight glinting on her luxuriant dark hair, Lady Wyckenham felt a glow of pride for her stepdaughter, as she presented the gentlemen to her. They had not been in the ballroom five minutes and already the child was a hit!

Mr Norwell laid a hand on his friend's shoulder.

'Well well, Alresford, this is fortunate! Since Miss Wyckenham is so new to Town she has no dances reserved and you will be able to take advantage of her state and lead her out – what say you, sir?'

Lord Alresford's naturally sombre look deepened to a frown.

'Barnabus you are too forward.'

'No, no – you ain't promised for this dance are you, Miss Wyckenham?'

'Indeed she is not,' put in Lady Wyckenham, avoiding her stepdaughter's furious look.

Mr Norwell grinned. 'There you are then, Marius. Go to it, man, they are forming up now!'

Lord Alresford held out his arm.

'It seems we are besieged on all sides, Miss Wyckenham. Will you do me the honour of standing up with me?'

Clarissa laid her fingers on his sleeve and with a final, darkling look at Lady Wyckenham she walked off with him to join the dancers. She risked a glance up at him as he led her on to the floor.

'Between your friend and my stepmama there was no escape,' she said lightly. 'They seem determined we should dance.'

'I am sorry for it, Miss Wyckenham. I asked for the introduction because I felt I had not thanked you properly for your assistance on the road to town the other day.'

'Then I am sorry if your attempt at civility has resulted in this unpleasant experience, sir.'

'That is not what I meant, I would never—'

Her eyes twinkled.

'I know it, but the temptation to tease you was too great for me. Your solemn look made it irresistible.'

His brow darkened even further.

'Do you treat everything with such levity, Miss Wyckenham?'

'Yes sir, when I meet with pomposity.' She bit her lip. 'Now *I* am being uncivil. Forgive me, my lord.'

He inclined his head and said no more. The dance separated them, they came back together, but still there was silence. When they parted again Clarissa made up her mind that she would converse with him, whatever the cost. As the dance brought them back together she raised her eyes to his face.

'Who is Elizabeth?'

She observed the start of surprise in his eyes, a shadow of

annoyance, and thought at first he would not answer her, but at last he spoke in a low voice.

'We were betrothed.'

'Were?'

'She died.'

'Oh I am so sorry.' She looked again at his dark frock-coat, the lack of fobs and seals dangling across the front of his champagne-coloured waistcoat. 'It was very recent, I think?'

'Six years ago. You look surprised, Miss Wyckenham.'

'I am. I thought from your demeanour—' She broke off, at a loss how to continue. A recent bereavement would explain his sober appearance and stern looks, but six years! Clarissa thought his affections must have been very deep to produce such a period of mourning. They remained silent until the dance ended, and they were making their way off the floor before the earl spoke again.

'You may have found me a little lacking in grace, when we met in the wood at Tottenham, Miss Wyckenham.'

'Naturally I put that down to your fall, sir. I trust you are fully recovered?'

'I was a little bruised, no more.' They had come up to Lady Wyckenham. Lord Alresford raised Clarissa's fingers to his lips. 'I was very grateful for your assistance that day, ma'am. I am in your debt.'

Clarissa shook her head.

'No, no,' she said, with her delightful smile. 'I would not have you under an obligation to me, sir. Consider the debt paid off with the dance.'

Lady Wyckenham, who had listened to the exchange in growing wonder, watched him walk away.

'Well, what is this, my dear? What was the obligation?'

Briefly Clarissa explained their encounter in the wood, and at the end of it her stepmama tapped her arm in exasperation.

'And you did not think to tell me of it?'

'You will recall, Mama-Nell, the inopportune timing of my

arrival in Charlotte Street. Events there quite pushed it from my mind.'

'Well, to have Alresford in your debt is a coup, my love,' returned Lady Wyckenham, 'although I have to say he is not to my taste. He never smiles. His face is so sharp you could cut yourself upon it, and one would take him for a radical, his hair is so short!'

'And worse you can say of no one ma'am. But I agree he is an oddity. When we met I thought him taciturn, but put it down to the circumstances. Having danced with him, I see it is his natural way.'

My lady patted her hand.

'Then let us forget him, for I see Julia Norwell sitting over there, by the window, and I must introduce you.'

Lady Wyckenham led her towards a fair-haired young woman in orange silk, sitting alone on a sofa in one corner of the room. A stout gentleman in mulberry satin stood at her side, bending to address some remark, but Clarissa did not miss the look of unease on the young woman's face, or the way she shrank away from the speaker. They were now too close for Clarissa to enquire who the gentleman might be, and as they came up to Julia, he turned and sauntered off, the blue string fastenings of his knee breeches bouncing around his legs. Lady Wyckenham made the introductions but almost immediately her attention was claimed by a group of friends and she turned away, leaving Clarissa and Mrs Norwell smiling shyly at one another.

'Won't you sit down beside me, Miss Wyckenham?' Mrs Norwell patted the sofa. 'I understand you have been living with your sister?'

'Yes, I have been her companion for the past few years while her husband has been away with the army. However he is now returned, and my presence is no longer necessary – they are as inseparable as a pair of newlyweds!'

'Your sister is fortunate to have such a husband.' Mrs Norwell sounded a little wistful, but observing Clarissa's puzzled look she smiled brightly. 'Tell me what you mean to do in town. Is Lady Helen – Lady Wyckenham I mean – to present you at Court?'

'Goodness, no. She was kind enough to present me years ago, but that visit was cut short by the death of my father. I am here now merely to enjoy a little society with my stepmama. She has promised to take me to Paris with her next year. You know that Mama-Nell can never be in one place for very long.'

Mrs Norwell smiled.

'She has a great deal of energy. But I will not hear a word against her: she is a very good friend to me, and if she does go abroad I shall miss her sorely.'

A young gentleman approached and shyly reminded Mrs Norwell that the next dance was promised to him. Clarissa watched her new friend go off to dance and hoped that she might find at least one more partner before the evening was over. Hardly was the thought formed than she saw Mama-Nell bringing another gentleman over to meet her, and after that she did not sit down at the side of the room again.

It seemed to Clarissa that her dance with Alresford was her entrée into Society. Her hand was solicited for every remaining dance. Several turbaned matrons smiled and nodded at her as she passed, but she did not recognize them and could only surmise that they were members of the Belles Dames Club. Thoroughly enjoying herself, Clarissa was alive to the bustle and movement of the room. She noticed Mrs Norwell dancing once with her husband, her flower-like countenance glowing with happiness, a look which had quite disappeared the next time Clarissa saw her, for she was dancing with the gentleman in the mulberry coat. Upon enquiry, Clarissa's partner informed her that the gentleman was Sir Howard Besthorpe. The name meant nothing to Clarissa, but she was aware of a moment's anxiety for Julia. However, her partner

was speaking, and Clarissa gave him her attention, resolving to seek out Julia later in the evening.

CHAPTER SEVEN

Lady Wyckenham watched her stepdaughter's progress with growing approbation. How right she had been to bring the girl.

'So that's Wyckenham's daughter.'

The quiet voice at her side made her turn quickly, a wide smile lighting her face. She held out her hands.

'Robert! Robert – is it really you? Oh my dear friend, I thought you were still at sea. I did not expect you for another two weeks at least.'

Sir Robert Ingleton laughed as he lifted first one hand then the other to his lips.

'We had a fair wind and favourable tides. Besides, I could stay away no longer, madam, and you do not disappoint: you are every bit as bewitching as when I left these shores four years ago.'

Her fingers fluttered in his grasp, but she frowned and shook her head at him.

'Pray do not attempt to flirt with me, Robert, we have known each other far too long for that. Tell me instead when you arrived in London, and why you did not call to tell me you are safe ashore.'

His dark eyes laughed down at her.

'We docked at noon, ma'am, and upon learning from your admirable Simmons that you had gone out, I came to find you.'

Lady Wyckenham eyed him cautiously. It was too absurd to believe he had come to Orpington House expressly to find her,

but it was a pleasant thought.

'Dear me, then you must be very weary, sir.'

'Not too weary to dance with you, my lady, an you will.'

She graciously inclined her head and allowed him to lead her out to join the set that was forming. Only three couples separated her from her stepdaughter, and she was aware of Clarissa regarding her with lively curiosity, but chose to ignore it, hoping that she was not blushing.

'Did you receive my letters?'

'Thank you, yes. You have been a conscientious correspondent.'

The corners of his mouth lifted at her polite reply.

'As one of the main sponsors of my expedition, you were entitled to regular reports of my progress.'

'My late husband was eager to promote the scientific study of nature. I merely carry on as he would wish.'

'Have you no interest of your own in my progress?'

She looked up, met his eyes and was obliged to look away again, feeling the warmth spreading over her cheeks.

'Of course. Your letters were most informative. I long to see the new plants you have collected. The Royal Society must be delighted with you.'

'I am promised to meet with Sir Joseph Banks tomorrow, to take my plants to him and set a date for my lecture.'

'You must tell me when that will be and I will come to hear you speak.'

'I would much rather tell you privately, ma'am.' His grip on her hand tightened. 'Nell—'

She felt a fluttering of panic rising within her and something of it must have shown in her eyes, for Sir Robert gave a wry smile.

'Very well, nothing more. For now.'

Lady Helen breathed a sigh of relief, but at the same time she felt vaguely disappointed. Her partner behaved with perfect politeness for the remainder of the dance, but, as he

escorted her from the floor, he begged her permission to call upon her. Lady Helen hesitated.

'When you left England, Robert, Wyckenham was still alive.'

'I am well aware of that, my dear. But you have been a widow these three years and more. Now there can be no harm in my calling – unless you are going to tell me you have formed another alliance?'

'No, no. But, I have made a life for myself.'

'And it does not include me?' He guided her to a sheltered alcove and sat down beside her on a vacant sofa. Helen risked another glance at him. If only he would not look at her in that way, with such a wicked glint in his eye, and that faint smile playing about his lips. She opened her fan, then shut it again, her thumb tracing over the intricate carving of the ivory sticks.

'You have been away a long time, Robert.'

He grinned.

'It was not unexpected, the oceans are very large.'

'Four years, sir. I have changed – *you* have changed.'

'I do not think I am so very much altered.' He took the fan from her restless fingers and gripped her hands briefly in one of his own. 'I understand you, Helen. I have come upon you unawares and you are afraid I will hurry you into saying all the things we could not say while Wyckenham was alive.' He leaned closer. 'I loved you then, I love you now, but I can wait until you are sure of your own mind. For now I ask nothing more than friendship from you.'

She managed a tremulous smile. 'I should be very glad to give you that.'

'Good.' He leaned back and closed his eyes, stifling a yawn. 'Now, I must leave you if I am not to commit the unforgivable crime of falling asleep on Lady Orpington's sofa. I will visit you as soon as may be possible, but tomorrow we will be bringing the plants ashore, and I must see them despatched to their new homes. I shall be taking some myself to my old friend Gilbert White in Selborne. We have been corresponding, you see, and I

promised him I would bring his specimens personally.'

'Then we shall see you when you have completed your duties, Robert.'

He rose, and with his back to the crowded room he lifted the closed fan to his lips before handing it back to her. 'Goodnight, Lady Wyckenham. Please make my apologies to your delightful stepdaughter; I shall call upon you shortly to make her acquaintance.'

On the dance-floor Clarissa had watched her stepmother dancing with the broad-shouldered, distinguished-looking man. Her partner was not sure, but rather thought he was Sir Robert Ingleton, the notable scientist and explorer. Intrigued by her stepmama's reaction to the gentleman, Clarissa studied him more carefully. Beneath his frock-coat of cut-velvet he had a splendid physique, no sign of portliness strained the buttons of his white waistcoat and the satin knee-breeches fitted snugly over powerful thighs. He wore his own hair brushed into the latest style, and his open, friendly countenance bore the look of a man used to the outdoors. She watched him laughing down at Lady Wyckenham, and thought mischievously that his shoulder was at a most convenient height for the lady to rest her head. Upbraiding herself for being a shameless matchmaker, Clarissa turned back to her own partner, impatient for an interval in the dancing so that she could seek out her stepmama and find out a little more about the mysterious Sir Robert.

Never had a dance seemed so prolonged to Clarissa, but at length the orchestra stopped playing and she was free to go in search of her quarry. She found Lady Wyckenham standing by one of the open windows, fanning herself vigorously. There was no sign of Sir Robert. Instead, a tall gentleman in a claret-coloured coat was beside her, talking earnestly. As Clarissa approached he broke off.

'Ah, your daughter, I believe, ma'am.' He made an elegant bow, affording Clarissa an excellent view of his dark hair, flecked with silver and held at the nape of his neck with a diamond clasp. 'Won't you introduce me?'

Lady Wyckenham inclined her head.

'Certainly. Clarissa, my dear, allow me to present the Marquis of Ullenwood to you.'

Lord Ullenwood reached for Clarissa's hand and pressed a kiss upon her fingers, then he raised his eyes to look at her. They were very dark, she noticed, almost black, but they held a cold, calculating look that she could not like. 'Charming, charming. I understand that you have come to live with your mama, Miss Wyckenham. Is it to be a prolonged visit?'

'That I hardly know, my lord.' She smiled at Lady Wyckenham. 'I hope it will be so.'

'My stepdaughter has been away too long.' Lady Wyckenham drew Clarissa towards her and took her arm. 'I have planned a great many treats for us to enjoy together. I shall be glad of her company.'

'Indeed?' The marquis smiled, although it seemed to Clarissa that it never reached his eyes. 'Then I wish you a pleasant sojourn in town, Miss Wyckenham.' He bowed again. 'My lady.'

'I cannot like him!' Clarissa murmured, watching Lord Ullenwood walk away. 'I'm sorry, I should not speak so of your friends.'

'No longer a friend of mine.' My lady shuddered. 'Let us go down to supper. There are several ladies anxious to meet you.'

'Oh? Members of the—'

Lady Wyckenham shut her fan with a snap and interrupted her.

'Pray learn some discretion, child. It is a necessary requirement for members of our little group.'

Clarissa's eyes lit up.

'Then I am a member?'

Lady Wyckenham gave an exasperated sigh.

'It would seem I have no choice!'

In the supper-room, Lady Wyckenham and Clarissa joined a group of ladies gathered in one corner, many of whom Clarissa recognized as the matrons who had been nodding to her during the evening. Lady Gaunt was the most striking, dressed in a gown of bronze silk with a matching turban and with a bored, disdainful look upon her face. She waved to a servant to bring more chairs.

'You come at an opportune time,' she drawled. 'Alicia is at this moment fetching Julia Norwell. Poor girl has been frightened out of her wits by Howard Besthorpe. The old roué keeps making advances towards her.'

'Ah, the poor child!' exclaimed Lady Wyckenham. 'Only let me hear him and I'll set him to rights!'

'Barnabus should be doing that,' retorted a lady in purple satin. 'Why doesn't someone tell him?'

Lady Gaunt sighed.

'I would have done so, Letty, but he's gone off with his cronies and Julia, little fool, told him he might do so and with her blessing!' She looked up as Julia Norwell approached, leaning on the arm of a large woman dressed in green brocaded silk.

'So you found her, Alicia. Come and sit down, child, and let us decide what is to be done.'

Mrs Norwell sank limply on to a chair.

'What *can* be done?' she said in a sad little voice. 'We have already agreed; I must be resolute.'

Looking at the sad little figure drooping in her chair, Clarissa thought she had never seen anyone less resolute in her life. She turned her clear gaze towards Lady Gaunt.

'I am sorry if I appear very stupid tonight, but who is this Sir Howard, and what does he want?'

'Sir Howard Besthorpe is a rich philanderer who preys upon young women,' explained Lady Wyckenham. 'He wheedles and cajoles, always careful never to be so blatant that a husband

can call him to book, but he chips away at a poor woman's defences until she is too weary to fight him any longer.'

'Well, it is clear,' declared Lady Gaunt. 'He needs to be taught a lesson.'

'Yes, but how, Dorothea?' sighed Mrs Letitia Leighton-Kettering, the lady in purple satin.

Lady Gaunt smiled thinly. 'I am not sure you really wish to know, yet, what I have in mind, but if Julia will not go to Barnabus—'

'Oh no, I couldn't!' exclaimed Julia, shrinking into her chair. 'He – he would think I have been encouraging Sir Howard, and *indeed* I have not.'

'Well then, we shall lay a trap for Besthorpe,' said Lady Gaunt, sitting up very straight. 'Oh don't look so worried, Julia. All you have to do is to carry on as you are. Just allow me time to plan everything.'

Dorothea Gaunt could not be persuaded to say more and the group broke up soon after, with a meeting of the Belles Dames Club arranged at Charlotte Street in two days' time.

CHAPTER EIGHT

After the quiet existence she had led with her sister in Royston, Clarissa found herself pitched headlong into a social whirl which left her little time for reflection. Following the Orpington ball there were any number of invitations to be answered, visits to the mantua-maker and milliner and such drapers and emporia as could be guaranteed to furnish any young lady of fashion with the fabrics, gloves, fans and dancing slippers required for her stay in town. On the day

assigned to the next meeting of the Belles Dames Club,
Clarissa was engaged to drive out with Lady Sarah and she
was therefore unaware of the unusual activity in Charlotte
Street. Lady Wyckenham held several prolonged meetings
with her steward; delivery men toiled up the stairs to the
drawing-room with additional pieces of furniture, while the
servants gasped and giggled and shook their heads at the
ways of the Quality when they were instructed to put themselves at the disposal of a heavily veiled female who arrived
on the doorstep at noon.

Clarissa returned to the house with only enough time to change
for a quiet dinner with her stepmama. During the meal Lady
Wyckenham made a half-hearted attempt to persuade Clarissa
that she would not wish to join the meeting that evening, and
when that failed, she bowed to the inevitable and led the way
to the drawing-room.

'Oh heavens!'

Clarissa clapped her hands to her mouth as she looked
around the room. The heavy curtains had been drawn across
the windows and the room was warm with candlelight. The
sofas had been replaced by numerous chairs arranged in
groups around small card tables, while in the centre of the
room stood a round, green-baize table. Nearby was a long bench
bearing a highly polished wheel, its centre divided into sections
of red and black.

'Mama-Nell, what is all this?'

Lady Wyckenham's blue eyes twinkled with mischief.

'I thought it would be amusing to learn a little about the
gaming hells that the gentlemen enjoy so much.' She beckoned to a tall female in a sacque-backed gown of mustard
yellow to come forward. 'My dear, let me present to you Mrs
Nugent.' Lady Wyckenham's voice trembled a little. 'Also
known as Fleet-fingered Poll. She is to be our guide for the
evening.'

35

Mrs Nugent dipped a curtsy as Clarissa took in her heavily powdered hair and whitened face. The eyes that stared back at her were intelligent and held such a gleam of amusement that Clarissa warmed to her immediately.

'You must be wondering what her ladyship is doing invitin' me here.' She spoke in a voice that reminded Clarissa of the scrunch of gravel underfoot, so deep it was.

'Well, yes.'

The carmined lips parted to display a chequer-board of yellow and black teeth. 'I'm to teach you the finer points of the gaming tables, and my lady couldn't have found a better teacher, even if I do say so myself. I've been working at the tables since I was a slip of a girl. I can tell a Greek just by lookin' at him, and I've rubbed shoulders with all manner of great gentlemen, some of 'em who blew their brains out after a bad night's losses.'

'R-really?' Clarissa regarded her with a fascinated eye, but before she could question her more the door opened to admit the first arrivals, sisters Georgiana Flooke and Emily Sowerby, followed shortly after by Lady Maramond, who had taken up Alicia Greynard in her carriage. Lady Sarah Matlock and Julia Norwell came in with Lady Gaunt, with Mrs Leighton-Kettering following closely behind.

As the members of the Belles Dames Club arrived, Clarissa was amused to observe their reactions. They were very much as her own had been and it was some time before the general exclamations died down, wine had been served and the ladies were ready to hear what was in store for them.

Mrs Nugent moved towards the round table at the centre of the room.

'Gather round, ladies, for tonight I am going to teach you some of the secrets of the gaming table.'

'Oh goodness,' giggled Lady Sarah. 'I have never played anything more serious than whist or silver loo.'

Mrs Nugent nodded at her.

'And nor should you, my lady, if you knows what's good for you. But Lady Wyckenham here thought it might be interestin' for you to know just what your menfolk gets up to when they're out at all hours. For you ladies, though, I'd advise that you keep to the dance floor at Almacks, where a single rouleau would cost you fifty guineas.'

As she spoke she pulled on a pair of linen cuffs and arranged them to cover her fine lace ruffles. 'I've been working with elbow shakers since I was a slip of a girl, and I've learned to spot a Captain Sharp, the cheating bullies who prey on the unwary; I know every rig and row used by the Greeks who think they can cheat their way to a fortune. M'lady has asked me to come along tonight and teach you a few tricks so that you don't become pigeons, dupes who lose everything and end up in the hands of the gull-gropers – money-lenders,' she explained, seeing their blank looks. She picked up a small leather box. 'So let's start now with St Hugh's bones – the dice, my dears. Let us begin with hazard.'

Julia Norwell gasped.

'I have heard Barnabus speak of it as the Devil's own game.'

'Aye, my dear, so it is: it's called hazard because it can make a man or undo him in the twinkling of an eye.'

Fascinated, Clarissa and the other ladies watched and listened as Fleet-fingered Poll explained the mysteries of the game. She told them the best numbers to call as a main or a chance, and how to calculate the chances of winning. She spoke of Fulhams, up-hills and down-hills, which they were to understand were loaded dice, and how to spot the diversionary tactics of those who would cheat them.

'What happens if the dice roll on to the floor?' asked Clarissa.

'It would be a no throw,' replied Mrs Nugent. She fingered the bevelled rim of the table. 'That's why the edge is raised. 'Tis the same if a die should hit something on the table, an elbow, perhaps, or a fan.' She looked towards Julia, who quickly

snatched her fan from the green baize. 'Thank you. So, shall we play?'

Lady Wyckenham put out her hand.

'Just a moment: we all know that one can lose thousands on a throw: I'll have no one leaving my house a sous the poorer tonight.'

Lady Gaunt tutted.

'Shame on you, Helen: where will be the fun if we cannot bet?'

'Indulge me, Dorothea. I know full well that you like deep play, but some of us are quite new to this. We shall write out our vowels and they will all be burned afterwards.'

Mrs Norwell and Lady Alicia exchanged looks of relief, but Lady Sarah cried out against such poor-spirited behaviour.

'Well, at the end of the evening we shall have a reckoning, and whoever has lost the most shall be asked to pay a forfeit,' declared Lady Wyckenham.

Lady Maramond's sharp eyes narrowed.

'What sort of forfeit?'

Lady Wyckenham waved her fan.

'Oh, I have not thought of it yet, Augusta, but you may be sure something will come to me. I know – we shall ask whoever has won the most to set the task.'

Clarissa looked at the dice lying on the table.

'Is it true, Mrs Nugent, that men can become addicted to these games?' she asked.

'Aye, miss. I've known young men drop a thousand pounds at a sitting and vow they will never return, but they are back the following night. Now, I'll pass the box to the lady on my left. . . .'

CHAPTER NINE

A noisy hour was spent at the hazard table, where the ladies played with much spirit but very little calculation, then Mrs Nugent led them on to the card tables.

'Of course if we was in a real club there would be a new pack of cards called for at every deal,' she said. 'The old ones are thrown upon the floor until by the end of the night you would not be able to see the floor.

'Now, for the card games. Whist you will all be familiar with: piquet calls for skill and a calculating mind, but at all costs avoid "put", my dears, if you wish to keep your fortune, for 'tis the game of the sharpers. We'll begin with faro.'

By the time the party broke up for supper, Clarissa's head was reeling with talk of punters and bankers, the *carte anglaise*, how to spot someone fuzzing the cards or reversing the cut.

'I am sure I shall not remember the half of it,' declared Sally Matlock, taking Clarissa's arm as they went downstairs for a light supper.

'For my part I think it is most instructive,' remarked Mrs Leighton-Kettering who was following behind with Lady Alicia at her side. 'I am eager to play at roulette after supper.'

'I am not at all sure that this is legal,' murmured her companion.

'I am very sure that it is not,' laughed Clarissa. 'I must hope that my stepmama will have the evidence removed first thing in the morning, if we are not to be locked up for keeping a gaming house.'

The candles were burning low in their sockets by the time the party broke up. The ladies gathered together and counted the

pieces of paper each had won during the evening.

'And who has fared least well?' asked Georgiana. 'Who must pay the forfeit?'

'It should be me,' sighed Julia. 'I am a very poor card player.'

'No, it is Clarissa,' announced Lady Wyckenham. 'Dorothea seems to have fared best, but even she has not amassed a fortune.'

Mrs Nugent gave a hearty laugh.

'It's few enough fortunes is won at the gaming tables, my lady: far more is lost to the sharps and Greeks.'

'A very useful lesson, then,' remarked Mrs Leighton-Kettering. 'And what is to be Clarissa's penalty?'

The room fell silent. Lady Gaunt tapped her fan against her cheek, her eyes narrowed.

'Dorothea, you will not suggest anything outrageous,' Lady Wyckenham warned her.

'No, no, of course not. I *did* consider suggesting a promenade along St James's Street. . . .'

'Dorothea, you could not!' gasped Julia Norwell. 'Only . . . only. . . .'

Lady Gaunt finished the sentence for her in her forthright style.

'Only Cyprians and light-skirts are seen there. Yes, I realize that. But a forfeit needs to be something challenging—'

'But respectable.' Lady Wyckenham was adamant. 'I will not allow Clarissa to go beyond the bounds of propriety.'

'Very well,' said Lady Gaunt. 'She shall collect trade cards from the silk mercers – nothing improper in that.'

'That is very acceptable,' said Clarissa with a smile. 'I am sure I can do that.'

'Very well, tomorrow you shall collect ten – no, twelve – trade cards from different mercers in town, each one signed and dated to prove you were there.'

Clarissa nodded.

'Very well. Mama-Nell, is that respectable enough for you?'

Lady Sarah clapped her hands.

'How delightful, I adore visiting silk warehouses.'

'Perhaps you would like to help me?' suggested Clarissa.

'No, that would not be allowed,' said Lady Gaunt. 'And you will not have all day for your task, Clarissa, that would be too easy for you. We will meet up with you at, say noon, tomorrow. Now, where shall we meet . . . somewhere out of town . . . Julia, may we agree to meet at Norwell House?'

'Of course. Come and take tea with me.'

'Then it is agreed.'

Lady Gaunt signalled to her page to bring her more wine.

'When the viscount returns to town I think I shall ask him to have a roulette table installed: a most entertaining game.'

'I admit I quite enjoyed playing,' offered Mrs Norwell in her soft voice. 'However, I do not think I should like to risk my money on a card, or the throw of the dice.'

'That is where we differ,' said Lady Gaunt, taking a pinch of snuff. 'I find the whole thing quite, quite dull without the risk of losing a fortune.'

'That is because you are a wicked woman,' smiled Lady Wyckenham. 'Besides, Gaunt is as rich as Croesus. If you lost a fortune you would merely apply to him for another.'

'Well, Emily and I have no fortunes to lose, so we are quite safe,' laughed Georgiana from the other side of the room.'

'Now that's where you are wrong, ma'am,' said Mrs Nugent. 'Handsome young women like yourselves have other assets that men will take instead of money.'

'Oh heavens!' murmured Mrs Greynard. 'I never thought of that.'

'Don't be a goose, Alicia!' snapped Lady Maramond. 'You and I are well past the age of worrying over our virtue: it would be a very odd man to want *that* from us!'

'I know it will seem very tame after this evening, but I do hope you are all coming to my supper party next week?' Mrs Leighton-Kettering looked about her hopefully.

'Your soirées, Letitia, have the distinction of bringing together many people of strong intellect and decided opinions,' declared Lady Maramond. 'I am heartily sorry that I cannot be there, but I have a long-standing engagement that cannot be gainsaid.'

'Oh, you will be missed, Augusta. I have such a treat for you all. Oswald has persuaded Sir Joseph Banks to loan to us the paintings and sketches that have just arrived from the Society's latest voyage. Sir Robert Ingleton has agreed to release them to my care for the evening and we have high hopes of finding more sponsors for the Royal Society. I depend upon you all being there to support me.'

Clarissa looked at Lady Wyckenham to see how she reacted to the mention of Sir Robert, but the lady appeared to be deep in discussion with Mrs Nugent. She turned and smiled at Letitia.

'Well, Augusta might not be able to attend, but I assure you Mama-Nell and I will be there. Julia, what about you?'

'I should dearly love to be there, but Lady Norwell and Barnabus's sister are arriving and it will not do for me to be away from the house.'

'Well, I am coming, and I believe Matlock is accompanying me,' said Lady Sarah.

Letitia Leighton-Kettering nodded. 'So most of the Belles Dames will be there to support me – thank you. And pray be early, my dears, for I fear it could be a dreadful crush!'

'Ooh, miss, I don't like the look o' this weather, to be sure I don't.'

Clarissa sipped her hot chocolate and looked towards the window.

'Is it raining, Becky?'

'Aye, miss. The road is awash, so it is.'

'Then you had best put away the apricot muslin and find my blue walking dress. And boots. I think we shall need them.'

Becky stopped and looked at her.

'We?'

Clarissa tried not to laugh at the look of horror on the abigail's face.

'Yes, Becky. We are going shopping today. It is a pity about the rain, but it cannot be helped.'

Lady Wyckenham's carriage rolled into New Bond Street at an unfashionably early hour, Clarissa hoping to avoid the crowds. Unfortunately, although the ton was not yet abroad, the street was packed with drapers' carts and wagons delivering goods, and the carriage was soon snarled up in the traffic. Clarissa descended to the flagway, followed by her reluctant maid, and instructed John Coachman to meet her at that spot again at half-past eleven.

'Thank goodness we have an umbrella,' she said. 'I had hoped we might be able to take the carriage from one shop to another, but I see that will not work. We will be obliged to walk.' She laughed as Becky pointedly stepped around a puddle. 'Come along. The sooner we collect these trade cards the sooner we can get dry again.'

The task proved much harder than Clarissa had imagined. Although New Bond Street had its share of milliners and modistes, jewellers and hatters, there were few silk mercers, and by the time she had walked the length of the street and back again on the other side, she had only four cards to her collection. A helpful assistant in the last shop directed her to a silk mercer in Piccadilly and Clarissa set off there on foot, ignoring Becky's mutterings that they should not walk so far in the rain. From there it was but a step to King Street in Covent Garden, where Clarissa was relieved to find an abundance of silk merchants all eager for her business.

'We should have come here first,' she said, counting up her trade cards. 'I knew of King's, of course, and Hinchcliffe and Croft, but I never dreamed there were so many other silk

43

merchants to call upon.'

'No, miss, and you shouldn't be calling on them, neither,' retorted her maid, trying to hold up an umbrella over both of them. 'They should be calling on you.'

'Oh, Becky, don't show me that Friday face. Admit it, this has been amusing.'

'Amusing! Getting soaked to the skin and wearing out good boot-leather, all for a silly wager.'

Clarissa realized that her maid was seriously displeased. She resolved to make it up to her, and was trying to decide on a suitable present when she heard the church clock chiming the half-hour. She stopped.

'Heavens! We should be in Bond Street to meet John Coachman by now! We shall never reach Knight's Bridge by noon.'

'And what did I tell you?' muttered Becky with gloomy satisfaction. 'Never heard of such silly goings-on.'

Clarissa ignored her.

'We must find a hackney carriage, or—' She stopped.

To Becky's amazement her mistress suddenly left the shelter of the umbrella, picked up her skirts and dashed across the road, not waiting for the crossing sweeper to make a way through the dirt.

Clarissa reached the flagway before looking up at the driver of an elegant town chaise drawn up at the side of the road.

'Is your master with you?'

The rain poured from the broad brim of his hat as the coachman looked down at her. 'Aye, madam. He's here now.'

Clarissa turned to see Lord Alresford coming out of the watchmakers. His head was bent against the rain and she was obliged to step in front of him before he saw her.

'Miss Wyckenham!'

'Good morning, my lord, I wonder if I might beg a favour of you.' Clarissa ignored the mutterings of her abigail, who had by this time caught up with her and hoisted the umbrella once more over her head.

'Of course, madam, I am at your service.'

His prompt response was very encouraging. She gave him her sunniest smile.

'My lord, I am desperate to get to Norwell House by twelve o'clock, but my carriage is at the far end of New Bond Street.'

'Then let me escort you. It will be as quick if I take you there myself, rather than try to get you back to your carriage with all this traffic.'

'Thank you, sir, you are very good.' She looked round. 'You may go and find our coach, Becky, and tell the driver to come on to Norwell House for me. Oh, and you had best keep the umbrella.'

'It is very good of you to take me out of your way, my lord.' Clarissa settled herself in the chaise and untied the ribbons of her chip hat, which had gone sadly limp in the rain.

'It is no trouble, ma'am, I had finished my business. Your urgency – I hope Mrs Norwell is not ill?'

'Oh no, nothing like that.' Clarissa turned her head to look at him, reading the concern in his face. She said lightly, 'I have an appointment with her, and I do not wish to be late.'

She noted a very slight softening of his look, as though he approved of her diligence. She wondered what he would say if she told him the truth. She removed her bonnet and regarded the wet chip straw with a rueful smile.

'I fear my poor hat will not recover from its soaking.'

'You seem to have been out in the rain for some time.'

'Yes. We started in Bond Street very early this morning. My maid was not at all pleased, but it had to be done.'

'You mentioned that your carriage was in New Bond Street – so how did you come to be in King Street, Miss Wyckenham? Surely it is a long way to walk in the rain.'

'We had several calls to make on the way . . . I have been collecting trade cards from the silk mercers, you see.'

'Trade cards!'

'Yes, the small cards they give out to advertise their wares.'

Something like a growl escaped him.

'I know very well what they are, ma'am. I am amazed that you did not wait for a better day.'

'Oh no, that was impossible. It is for a wager, you see.' The words were out before she realized she had said them: Clarissa risked a glance at his face and saw that the harsh look had returned. She tried to look contrite. 'You will think that a trumpery reason for importuning you, my lord.'

'Not at all, madam. It is, perhaps, a trumpery reason for being out in such weather.'

That made her smile.

'I shall not melt from a little rain, sir. Besides, gentlemen will go to much greater lengths for their wagers . . . or so I understand.'

'I believe they do, Miss Wyckenham.'

The humour in his voice surprised her, and she turned again to look at him, and noticed the reassuring twinkle in his hard eyes. She realized she was smiling up at him in the most idiotic way, and felt the blush stealing into her cheeks. She looked away, for the first time aware of the dangers of riding alone in a closed carriage with a gentleman. To her relief the coach turned off the road and into the drive of Norwell House. Lord Alresford took out his watch.

'It still wants ten minutes to the hour. You are within your allotted time, Miss Wyckenham.'

The carriage drew up; the earl jumped down and turned to hand her out while a footman in Norwell livery held up a sheltering umbrella.

'Thank you for conveying me here, my lord.' She paused. 'I really should not have imposed upon our slight acquaintance.' Her fingers were gripping his and she quickly withdrew her hand: he would think she was flirting with him! He gave a stiff bow.

'It is always a pleasure to be of service to you, Miss Wyckenham.'

Clarissa turned and hurried into Norwell House, keeping her head high, but she was keenly aware of his disapproval. It did no good to tell herself she cared little for his good opinion: the pleasure in achieving her goal was diminished.

CHAPTER TEN

Recalling Leititia Leighton-Kettering's warning, Clarissa insisted that Lady Wyckenham order her carriage early for the soirée. The ladies set off after an early dinner, the mild May evening allowing them to enjoy the delights of an open carriage to carry them to Portman Square. Lady Wyckenham had been encouraged by the warm weather to put on a high-waisted gown of the palest green silk, and glancing at her own jonquil muslin, Clarissa felt her spirits lift as they always did when spring was giving way to summer. The entrance hall was already packed with guests and their hostess had time only to wave to them before her attention was claimed by Sir Joseph Banks and his party. Clarissa and her stepmama followed the crowds to the book-room. This grand apartment had been commandeered by the Royal Society for the evening and the paintings had been placed on special stands in front of the book-lined walls, while smaller drawings and sketch-books had been spread out on a large mahogany desk.

Clarissa saw Sir Robert Ingleton talking to a party of gentlemen, but as they entered he moved across the room to join them.

'Lady Wyckenham – Miss Wyckenham. I hoped you would be able to come,' he said, smiling and holding out his hand to Lady

Wyckenham. 'I have only today returned from Selborne.'

'And are all your plants safely stored now, sir?'

'Aye, we lost one or two during the long sea voyage, but the rest are even now being cared for in hot-houses and gardens across the country.'

Clarissa looked about her.

'There seems to be a great deal of interest in your expedition, Sir Robert.'

He nodded. 'Sir Joseph is very optimistic that we will find more sponsors here tonight, which means I cannot spend the evening with you, as I should like to do, but must earn my keep doing the pretty to our prospective patrons. Damnation, Sir Joseph is already summoning me. I must go – Helen, I promise I shall return later and give you a personal tour of all the paintings.'

'So we are at liberty to browse as we please,' remarked Clarissa, as Sir Robert hurried off.

'You may do so,' declared Lady Wyckenham, 'I have seen Alicia Greynard on her own and she is looking so forlorn I must go and speak to her. No, no, Clarissa, there is no need for you to come too. Stay and look at the pictures.'

Left to herself, Clarissa strolled about the room. There were any number of well-executed paintings; birds, animals and plants depicted in glowing colours, but she particularly liked the hastily drawn sketches of the islands with natives in strange, exotic dress. They gave a tantalizing glimpse of the life lived in the grass huts, fishermen on palm-lined beaches with rugged mountain ranges in the background. She longed to learn more, and determined to accompany Mama-Nell when Sir Robert gave her the promised tour. She smiled to herself: she had no doubt Sir Robert would think her positively *de trop*.

As she turned from the contemplation of a particularly colourful bird, she found herself confronted by a group of people dressed all in dark colours, and she had the sudden impression of regarding a colony of rooks. She was aware of the laughter

bubbling within her even before she realized that one of the group was Lord Alresford. On his arm was a young woman of slender build, dressed with puritanical severity in a dark gown relieved only by a scattering of lace at her neck and wrists.

'Miss Wyckenham.' Lord Alresford's deep voice recalled her attention. She dropped a curtsy.

'I am so sorry, I am blocking your way. Such a crowd – I had not thought so many people would be interested in Sir Robert's expedition.'

'Indeed.' The earl looked down as the young woman beside him twitched his sleeve. 'May I present Miss Florence Medway to you? And Sir Gordon and Lady Medway, of course.'

Clarissa gave them her ready smile and tried to banish the thoughts of rooks and crows that threatened to overset her gravity. Sir Gordon wore an old-fashioned bag-wig and dark frock-coat with a grey silk waistcoat stretched across his portly frame. His lady was robed in a high-waisted gown of the darkest blue brocade, relieved only by the cream lace fichu draped about her shoulders. It filled the deep, rounded neckline of her gown, the whole effect reminding Clarissa very much of a plump pigeon. She gave herself a mental slap: she must stop comparing them all with birds.

Lady Medway turned her faded blue eyes upon Clarissa and scrutinized her from the top of her luxuriant black curls to her gold satin slippers. Miss Wyckenham raised her brows, not at all sure she liked such an inspection, then she glanced up at Lord Alresford and was surprised at the disdainful look upon his face. When their eyes met briefly she thought she detected an apology there.

'You are related to the Leighton-Ketterings, perhaps?' asked Lady Medway.

'No ma'am. My stepmama, Lady Wyckenham was one of the sponsors for Sir Robert's expedition.'

There was a sudden gleam of interest in the lady's eyes.

'Indeed? Lady Wyckenham, you say. A sponsor – how enter-

prising.' Lady Medway's plump face creased into a smile. 'Perhaps, Miss Wyckenham, you would give us the pleasure of your company as we go round the room and study these charming pictures.'

'A most worthy cause,' remarked Sir Gordon in a loud, carrying voice. 'The advancement of science – very good thing.'

'When it is for the benefit of mankind, Papa,' put in Miss Medway. 'We should all do what we can to give comfort to those less fortunate than ourselves.' She bent her earnest gaze upon Clarissa. 'Do you know just how Sir Robert's expedition will be advantageous to us all?'

'I have no idea,' Clarissa responded cheerfully, and earned a scornful glance from Miss Medway.

'For my own part, I think there is more than enough to do here, ministering to the poor and sick. Would it not be better if Sir Robert's energies were turned towards remedying the ills of his fellow countrymen?'

The smile deepened in Clarissa's eyes.

'I think Sir Robert's enterprise is as much for the adventure as the science. Who is to say that if he did not travel the world his *energies*, as you call them would not be wasted in the clubs and gaming hells of London?'

'Not all men are given over so totally to amusement,' put in Lord Alresford.

'Indeed not,' she agreed. 'Some are not given to any amusement at all.'

Lady Medway gave a little laugh.

'Come, Miss Wyckenham. Surely you do not sneer at any gentleman who devotes himself to good works.'

'Certainly not, but I would question the wisdom of not allowing oneself any time for pleasure.'

'Lady Medway looks perplexed, but that remark was aimed at me, I think.' murmured Lord Alresford. 'Miss Wyckenham would like us all to be as frivolous and carefree as she is.'

Clarissa met his frowning gaze steadily.

'Your opinion of me is formed upon short acquaintance. You see only my social face. One is expected to be – what were your words? – frivolous and carefree in company.'

'Come, come, Alresford, I think you are too harsh upon the lady,' boomed Sir Gordon. 'I am sure Miss Wyckenham can be serious when occasion calls for it.'

Clarissa read the disbelief in Lord Alresford's face and realized with a jolt just how angry his contempt had made her. With a heroic effort she swallowed the rebuke hovering on her lips and instead forced herself to keep smiling.

'My lord, let us agree that our acquaintance is too brief to allow a correct character reading, on either side.'

She was rewarded with the stiffest of bows.

'I believe many people improve upon acquaintance, Miss Wyckenham. It will be my pleasure to confirm it in this case.'

CHAPTER ELEVEN

'. . . And all the while Alresford was wishing our paths had never crossed!' declared Clarissa later, when she recounted the conversation to Lady Wyckenham over supper.

Her stepmama's elegant brows raised in surprise.

'You are piqued because a man thinks you frivolous? But, my dear, I thought that was exactly the impression you wanted to portray.'

'No! Yes . . . that is—'

Lady Wyckenham interrupted her.

'Since you were betrayed by James Marlow you have been at pains to show the world that you care not a whit. You are charming, polite and considerate but you will allow no one

inside the defensive wall you have built around yourself. Not even me.'

Clarissa stared at her. After a small silence, she said quietly, 'Is that how I seem to you, Mama-Nell?'

'It is.'

'You must think me very selfish.'

'No, my darling, but I think it time to change. You have shut yourself away inside that shell for far too long.'

'But I don't know how to change.'

Lady Wyckenham laughed gently, and reached up to flick Clarissa's pale cheek with one finger.

'The fact that Lord Alresford's comments have upset you shows that you are changing, my love.'

'And what has his lordship been saying to you?' demanded Lady Gaunt, coming up in time to overhear her words. Lady Wyckenham looked up and said with a slight tremor in her voice. 'He had the effrontery to call Clarissa frivolous.'

'Looked down his well-bred nose at you, did he?' drawled the viscountess.

'I *did* offer him provocation,' admitted Clarissa. 'I wish he were not so severe.'

'He was not always so,' said Lady Gaunt, sitting down at the table. 'He changed after Elizabeth Medway died.'

Clarissa looked up. 'Oh?'

'She was his fiancée – the niece of Sir Gordon Medway, who is here tonight with his wife and daughter Florence.'

'Yes, I met them.' Clarissa gave a rueful smile. 'I fear it was my responses to Miss Medway's opinions that drew Lord Alresford's disapproval. Now it all makes sense.' Lady Gaunt took out her snuff box and helped herself to a pinch.

'Very religious family,' she said. 'Well connected, of course: live in Mount Street, but never seen at anything as pleasurable as a ball or rout. It is our host's connection with the Royal Society that has tempted them here tonight.'

'And no doubt Sir Toby will make Sally invite them to their

soirée on Monday se'ennight,' added Lady Wyckenham. 'Sally told me that her husband is well acquainted with the family. Clarissa and I are already engaged to attend: will you go, Dorothea?'

'Where, my dear?'

'To Sally Matlock's supper party next week: poetry and play-readings.'

'I suppose I must, if only to support dear Sarah.' Lady Gaunt cast a roguish glance towards Miss Wyckenham. 'Such evenings are a favourite pastime for Sir Toby, and he is so obliging in all other ways that Sally arranges a literary evening for him occasionally.'

Clarissa gave a vague smile, her thoughts otherwise engaged.

'How did she die, Lady Gaunt?'

'Who, my dear?'

'Elizabeth – Alresford's future bride.'

'Scarlet fever, contracted while working with the poorer families in Spitalfields.'

'Ah, how sad. It is no wonder, then, that he thinks so little of me.'

'It is widely rumoured that his lordship has transferred his affections to Florence. It would not be an unequal match: Florence is quite an heiress, and their combined estates would be considerable.'

'Well, I hope he will not delay in marrying her,' declared Clarissa. 'Then they may be earnest and worthy together, and leave lesser mortals to enjoy themselves!'

'Talking of enjoyment,' said Lady Wyckenham, 'We are set for Vauxhall next week. I have reserved a supper-box and I think we shall all wear dominos, that we may wander through the gardens without being recognized.'

'Helen, my dear, surely you do not expect us to eat our supper clothed from head to toe in a silk domino?' murmured Lady Gaunt.

'No, Dorothea, but I think it will be more exciting to go about the gardens in disguise,' Lady Wyckenham's mischievous smile appeared. 'We can venture into the Dark Walk: I wager some of us have never been there.'

'An excellent notion!' cried Lady Sarah. 'I have just had a new domino delivered, beautiful emerald green – to match my eyes.'

'Sarah you are incorrigible,' laughed Lady Wyckenham. 'Clarissa, have you a domino – no? Then we shall have to purchase one—'

'No need,' put in Lady Gaunt. 'I have a spare one – scarlet silk, perfect for such a *frivolous* lady.'

They all laughed, and Lady Gaunt sat back in her chair, holding out her hand to a gentleman who was approaching. 'Well, Sir Robert. Have you escaped from your many admirers?'

He bowed over her fingers with careless grace.

'I have, ma'am, and I have come to take my patroness upstairs to view the paintings.' His lazy glance travelled to the orange and cream jelly set before Lady Wyckenham. 'But I see you have not yet finished your supper, and I know how much you love flummery, so I will not ask you to leave it. . . .'

Lady Wyckenham put her hand on Clarissa's arm.

'My stepdaughter, however, *has* finished and would be delighted to accompany you.'

Clarissa felt the colour warm her cheeks, but she met Sir Robert's enquiring glance with her own smiling eyes.

'I would indeed be honoured if you would explain some of the sketches to me.'

'Come along then.'

He led her back to the book-room and proceeded to guide her around the pictures, describing the islands where they had found the various plants and trying to explain the long latin names they had been given.

'A valuable record for the Royal Society, Sir Robert. My step-mother will be fascinated: she is a very good artist, you know.'

'I do know. I have been fortunate enough to see some of her work. In fact,' he added, 'I am going to give her a couple of specimens that have flowered since they were first captured. I want her to paint them for me.'

'Indeed? That is a great compliment to her talent, sir.'

'I know she can do it.'

Clarissa stopped to examine the painting of a brightly coloured flower.

'Have you known Lady Wyckenham a long time, Sir Robert?'

'Oh, for many years.'

'You were never at Wyckenham Hall, I think, when my father was alive. And I cannot recall seeing you in London when I made my come-out three years ago.'

'While you were making your curtsy at Court, Miss Wyckenham, I was sailing to the West Indies.'

'You seem to have spent little time in England, sir, and yet you told me you have a property in Cheshire?'

'Yes, Newfield Hall. I have an excellent gardener who keeps all in order for me.'

'A gardener! That is all very well, Sir Robert, but what of the house – who keeps that in order?'

'My steward, of course.'

'And will you live there now, or do you have another voyage planned?'

'I have not yet decided.' He bent a quizzical smile upon her. 'Has this interrogation anything to do with your stepmama?'

Clarissa chuckled.

'Perhaps I should ask you if your intentions are honourable.'

'And how would you respond if I said they were not?' he countered.

A dimple peeped. Clarissa said demurely, 'I should be sorry for you. Mama-Nell has already told me she will not take a lover.'

Sir Robert put back his head and laughed aloud, causing several of the other guests to look up. Clarissa threw him an

enquiring glance and he shook his head at her, grinning.

'I do not know which shocks me more, Miss Wyckenham. That you should repeat such a thing, or that Lady Wyckenham should discuss it with you.'

'Shocking, is it not?'

'No – refreshing and delightful!'

'Pray do not encourage me to be outrageous, Sir Robert.' Clarissa was ready to continue her tour, but as she stepped back and turned she collided with a solid body behind her. 'Oh, I am so sorry – oh . . . Lord Alresford!'

'Your pardon, Miss Wyckenham, the fault is mine, of course.'

'No, no, how could it be? You could not see me behind you.' She gave him her ready smile, but could see no softening of the hard features as Lord Alresford bowed and walked away. Stifling a sigh, she cast a rueful look at Sir Robert. 'You see, sir, my levity is not to everyone's taste.'

'I met Lord Alresford for the first time this evening, and admit I find it odd that such a sober gentleman should be great friends with Barnabus Norwell, who is such a lively spirit. I am told Alresford suffered a tragedy some years ago and has never recovered.'

'Evidently.'

'You sound disapproving, Miss Wyckenham.'

'I am sorry, I should not be, especially when I know the gentleman disapproves of *me*, but . . .' Clarissa paused, and when Sir Robert remained silent she continued with some difficulty, 'I have no doubt that we have all suffered some tragedy in our lives, but we do not wear our heart on our sleeve. Indeed, what right have we to inflict such gloom upon our fellows? There is enough sadness and suffering in the world, we should not add to it without good reason.' She looked up, feeling a little self-conscious. 'Goodness, how dreadfully pompous that sounds! Pray, Sir Robert, let us move on before I infect us both with a fit of the dismals. Tell me what you know about this creature: it looks like a perfectly ordinary little beetle. . . .'

CHAPTER TWELVE

The press of guests had thinned a little when Lady Wyckenham found Sir Robert Ingleton at her side.

'So, sir, you have shown my stepdaughter all your fine drawings? Sir Joseph Banks himself was kind enough to take me round, so I have been well entertained.'

'Good. I am sorry I could not get back to you earlier. Your stepdaughter is very charming, Helen. She was certainly most appreciative of the illustrations from the voyage. She tells me she is come to live with you?'

My lady sighed and plied her fan.

'Ah, so this attention is a ploy: you are smitten with Clarissa.'

He grinned. 'The devil I am! I have only just met the chit. But now you come to mention it, she is a beauty.'

The fan snapped shut and landed smartly across his knuckles. He laughed at her.

'Jealous, Nell?'

'Not in the least,' she replied with great dignity. 'Merely, I will not have you speaking so lightly of my stepdaughter.'

'Then tell me how it comes about that she has been out for three years and has not been in Town before now?'

'She was presented shortly before Wyckenham's death. Her season was cut short and since then she has been acting as companion to her sister.'

'Companion?' he raised his brows. 'Your daughter a *companion*, Nell?'

'It is true. Her sister Anne was newly married to an army man when their father died and then Anne's husband was sent off to America very soon afterwards. Clarissa chose to keep her company.'

'And she has been there for the past three years? I would

have thought you anxious to marry off the girl, not leave her wasting away as a companion.'

'She did not wish it.'

Sir Robert's eyes narrowed.

'You look ill-at-ease, Nell. Now what have I uncovered here? Some scandal in your family closet?'

'Nothing of the kind,' she replied quickly. 'I wish you would keep your sordid imagination in check.'

'Aha. So there is a mystery!'

Lady Wyckenham rose and shook out her skirts.

'Nothing of the sort. Now if you will excuse me, it is late. I must find my daughter and take her home.'

She gave him her hand to kiss, which he did with great aplomb.

'Goodnight, dear lady. Shall I see you at Lady Matlock's soirée next week?'

'Yes, we shall be there, I think. Clarissa is minded to go.'

Sir Robert squeezed her fingers before releasing them. 'Until then, my lady. 'Tis a full week away, but I must bear it, for I have several pressing engagements that cannot be postoned.'

My lady knew a degree of relief: she found Sir Robert was beginning to disturb her peace of mind.

CHAPTER THIRTEEN

The ladies of the Belles Dames Club descended upon the Spring Gardens in Vauxhall like a flock of gaily coloured birds. There were only six of them present, for sisters Emily and Georgiana were engaged to attend a family party, Lady Maramond had cried off with a headache and Julia Norwell

was promised to join her mama-in-law at whatever party of pleasure had been designed for her entertainment.

They travelled by coach to arrive at the entrance on Kennington Road while it was still light and walked through the wide avenue to find their supper box. Unusually, Clarissa found herself to be one of the more sober members of the group. Lady Wyckenham was her usual assured self, and Lady Gaunt swept through the gardens with her little black page running at her heels, but it was as though the coverings of masks and dominos had released another side to the decorous Letitia Leighton-Kettering and Alicia Greynard, who were both giggling like schoolgirls with Lady Sarah. Clarissa glanced down at the scarlet domino Lady Gaunt had loaned her: the silk shimmered as she moved and, while she was in no doubt that it hid her identity, Clarissa was aware that the bright colour attracted a great many bold stares from the masked gentlemen roaming the gardens. She was glad they had two burly footmen in attendance: Lady Gaunt had brought them along, to add to their comfort. Clarissa stared at the taller of the two footmen, and it was a few moments before she realized why he looked so familiar. Then she gasped.

'Mama-Nell,' she whispered. 'Lady Gaunt's servant—'

Lady Wyckenham followed her glance. 'Yes, Clarissa. It is Grantham.'

'Is – is he not the wrestler. . . ?'

My lady chuckled.

'Yes. Lady Gaunt has hired him.'

They swooped upon the supper boxes which bordered the Grand Walk. The boxes were enclosed on three sides, but at the front only the raised floor separated them from the gravel path. Each box was set with a large table, covered in a snowy cloth and with enough chairs to seat half-a-dozen diners in comfort. Once they had located their box, the ladies divested themselves of their dominos and settled down to enjoy the music being played by the orchestra perched on the balcony of the ornate

Gothic rotunda. The supper boxes were arranged around a central promenade and the ladies were kept amused observing the people who moved in a constant stream across their view. Mrs Leighton-Kettering, sitting at one end of the supper table, was the first to spot a familiar face.

'Good heavens, it's Lady Norwell. Look, she is coming this way. Barnabus and Julia are with her – and who is the other lady . . . ah, Margaret Eastwood, her married daughter,' she explained to Clarissa. 'And – oh my, Barny has even prevailed upon Alresford to accompany them!'

Lady Sarah leaned closer to Clarissa and murmured, 'So there's a damper, even before the evening has begun. My goodness, just look at Lady Norwell's gown: the lace alone must have cost a king's ransom. And she is such a *round* woman; why does she insist on wearing hoops when the effect is to make her as wide as she is tall? And Margaret is the same. We were at school together, you know, and she was just such a fusby-faced girl then: she must know that those ostrich feathers do not suit her.'

By this time the party was upon them and Mrs Leighton-Kettering waved to catch their attention. Lady Norwell stopped in front of the box to exchange pleasantries. Mr Norwell stood smiling before them with his mama on one arm and his wife on the other, and coming up behind them Clarissa spotted Lord Alresford escorting an overdressed matron. It was not difficult to guess that this was Mrs Margaret Eastwood, for the likeness between mother and daughter was remarkable.

'Julia,' exclaimed Lady Sarah in mock horror. 'How could you!' she lifted her domino from the back of her chair. 'They are almost identical.' She saw Julia's look of anguish and went off into a peal of laughter. 'Oh I am jesting, you know I am! Pray don't look too worried, my love. I shall give my dressmaker a fine trimming tomorrow for daring to tell me I was the only customer to have this emerald green!'

Julia, recovering, gave a soft laugh.

'We must make sure we keep well apart in the walks tonight.'

Julia looked up at her husband as she spoke, and Clarissa thought she had never seen Mrs Norwell look so happy.

'My dears, such a squeeze!' declared Lady Norwell, in her good-natured way. 'We shall not stay too late, of course. I understand these affairs can get very rowdy after midnight.'

'Oh good,' murmured Lady Gaunt.

Lady Wyckenham leaned forward, saying hurriedly, 'Will we have the pleasure of seeing Sir Isaac in town, ma'am?'

'Oh dear me no. My husband cannot be prised away from the country.' Lady Norwell gave a gusty sigh. 'I vow I believe he would sell the house at Knight's Bridge if he could, but as it is, Barnabus and Julia make good use of it, and we are always happy to join them, are we not, Margaret?'

Margaret Eastwood nodded, setting the mustard yellow plumes on her head wobbling.

'Indeed we are, Mama. Of course, if would be better if Mr E could be here to share it with me, but he is needed on parish business you know, and Lord Alresford is being so gallant.' She simpered and smiled up at her escort. Lord Alresford's attempt at a smile nearly overset Clarissa, who could not resist saying, 'An uncommon treat for you, my lord, to be able to indulge yourself in an evening of unalloyed pleasure.'

'Uncommon indeed!' cried Barnabus, overhearing. 'Marius spends far too much time alone with his books and his business. Get yourself a good manager, I tell him. Leave the estates to him and come out and enjoy yourself.'

'Which is precisely what I have done,' my lord responded.

Barnabus snorted.

'Gammon. Don't tell me you would not prefer to be alone in your study with a book.'

Clarissa saw the glimmer of a smile in those harsh features.

'I would not be so impolite.'

'Barny, I will not let you roast poor Alresford,' cried Mrs Eastwood. 'He has been most charming. Why, I could not wish for a livelier companion.'

Clarissa laughed, and quickly turned it into a cough, but she knew Lord Alresford was not deceived. The rueful gleam was still in his eyes as he shook his head.

'Thank you, ma'am, but you know you are being too generous.'

Lady Norwell gave a fat chuckle.

'Perhaps she is, Marius, but we have known you since your cradle and are accustomed to your quiet ways.'

Lady Wyckenham gave both gentlemen her wide smile.

'You are fortunate in your escorts, Lady Norwell.'

'I know it, my lady, and mean to enjoy it while I may – Lord Alresford is escorting us all to Drury Lane tomorrow night, is that not good of him? Now, we are going to see the cascade. Come along, Barnabus . . . Julia, keep up, my love.'

The party moved off and the ladies settled down to their supper. Mrs Leighton-Kettering was about to help herself to a slice of the wafer-thin ham when a figure in the crowd caught her eye.

'Oh dear, Sir Howard Besthorpe. I do hope he will not approach.'

'I will give him the smallest of nods, like so, and turn my shoulder to him,' said Lady Alicia. 'That should give him the hint.'

'It has, Alicia. Clever you. He is walking on. What a figure of fun he looks, to be sure, with those long ribbons at his knee! Does he not know that the fashion is changing to buckles? Mr Leighton-K tells me the gentlemen call him Blue-bow Besthorpe in the clubs. I do hope he does not pester Julia this evening.'

'Oh I would not think that at all likely when she is escorted by her husband and his family,' said Lady Gaunt, making herself comfortable on a chair at the back of the box. A slight

gesture brought Grantham to her side to pour wine into her glass.

Only Clarissa, watching from the far side of the table, observed Dorothea slide her hand under the skirts of Grantham's frock-coat and run her fingers up his thigh. She raised her eyes to the wrestler's face and had to admire his composure. He gave no sign that Lady Gaunt was caressing his buttocks but continued to pour the wine. After a moment, however, he became aware of Clarissa's gaze and looked across at her, his own eyes so full of mischievous amusement that she was obliged to look away and hide a smile behind her fan.

As the wine flowed, the chattering increased and, when they had finished their supper, Lady Sarah declared that she wished to take a walk.

'We need not go far,' she said, 'but I would like to see the lamps and grottos, now that it is dark.'

Lady Wyckenham, Mrs Leighton-Kettering and Lady Alicia preferred to stay in the box, listening to the music, but Clarissa and Lady Gaunt agreed to go with Lady Sarah. Mrs Leighton-Kettering glanced at the two footmen.

'Will you not take an escort?'

Lady Gaunt gestured to her black page.

'Only Samuel. The others shall stay here to protect you, and to procure more wine for our return.' She picked up her burgundy domino and drew it around her.

'Come, ladies, let us brave the terrors of the Dark Walk!'

CHAPTER FOURTEEN

Clarissa was enjoying her first experience of Vauxhall. The paths were crowded with couples promenading through the gardens, many heavily disguised in dominos or elaborate costumes. A fresh breeze rustled through the trees and bushes. It set the coloured lamps swaying and the shifting shadows added to the sense of magic. At various points there were small grottoes adorned with imitation Greek statues. There were no lamps in these areas, and Clarissa guessed that they were extremely popular with trysting couples.

'Let us take this path,' said Lady Gaunt, leading the way and at a pace that had her small page running to keep up. 'As I recall there is a particularly fine figure of Paris in one of these arbours . . . ah, here we are.'

The path curved about a high hedge and Clarissa followed Lady Gaunt as she slipped through the archway and into a shadowed grotto. Lady Sarah followed them a few moments later, saying, 'I am sorry, I did not see you turn, and had to come back. What is it you wanted us to see, Dorothea?'

Clarissa went closer to the statue.

'Is it meant to be Paris?' she asked. 'The light is too poor here for me to see.'

'Oh I can assure you it is a very fine specimen,' purred Lady Gaunt, running her hand over the cold stone. 'I am reminded very much of Grantham.'

'Your wrestler?' Clarissa laughed. 'Then one would suppose the statue to be very handsome.'

'Oh yes,' replied Lady Gaunt. 'And so very . . . athletic.'

Lady Sarah reached out to touch the statue.

'Athletic perhaps, but cold, not a bit like my dear Toby.' She giggled, then stopped as Clarissa laid a hand on her arm.

'Hush, Sally. Someone's coming.'

There was a rustling of the bushes around the arbour, a scrunch of feet on the gravel path and a hoarse whisper.

'Mrs Norwell – Julia!'

'It's Sir Howard,' hissed Sarah. She put up her hand to stifle a giggle. 'He must have seen me enter and mistaken my domino for hers!'

'Julia, dearest. My little flower.'

Lady Gaunt motioned to the others to be quiet and said, in a high, breathless voice, 'Oh sir, pray do not come in! I am too shy to face you directly. Stay where you are and I will talk to you.'

Sir Howard gave a gusty sigh.

'Oh my little angel! You – you are alone?'

'Of course, sir.'

'Then let me come in and keep you company – I have waited very patiently, my dear, but—'

'Oh no, no!' gasped Lady Gaunt, still in that breathless voice. Clarissa and Sarah stood behind her, doubled up in silent laughter. 'I am expecting my husband to join me here at any moment.'

'Then tell me quickly where we can meet . . . my little dove.'

Lady Gaunt gave a dramatic sigh and leaned closer to the hedge.

'Oh, my dear, dear sir.'

'Tell me where I may come to you.' Sir Howard's voice was quivering with excitement. 'Anywhere, any time – I am yours!'

'At home – tomorrow night, at ten o'clock. My husband and his family are going out. We shall be quite, quite alone.'

Clarissa stared at Lady Gaunt, her laughter giving way to surprise. There was a pause, then Sir Howard spoke again, his thin voice even higher.

'T-ten o'clock, at Norwell House?'

'Yes. You cannot miss it – it is the first big house past the Knight's Bridge toll-gate. Do not fail me, my dear one.'

There was another shuddering sigh from the far side of the hedge.

'My angel, my dove! I shall be there. At last, I shall be able to show you how much I adore—'

'Yes, yes, but someone comes, sir. You must away, or we are undone!'

'Until tomorrow night then . . . Julia.'

'Until tomorrow . . . Howard.'

The three ladies stood in silence until they heard Sir Howard's heavy tread moving away. Lady Sarah was the first to break the silence.

'Dorothea,' she said in an awed voice, 'what are you about, you wicked woman?'

Lady Gaunt pressed her handkerchief to her lips in an effort to quell her own laughter.

'Oh what a wonderful jest! I vow I could not have planned it better!'

'Planned what?' demanded Clarissa.

'Why, Sir Howard is about to learn his lesson. He will come to Norwell House tomorrow night and we will give him a night he will never forget.'

'We will?'

'Yes, Sally, for I know you will both want to be with me in this! We will need Julia, too, of course. You heard Lady Norwell say they were off to the theatre tomorrow – Julia must persuade them to go without her. It will be perfect.'

'Dorothea I cannot bear this another moment!' cried Lady Sarah, trying to sound severe. 'Just what are you planning?'

'Join me at Norwell House at half an hour before ten tomorrow night and you will know everything,' Lady Gaunt promised her. 'Howard Besthorpe has made many a poor girl's life a misery with his unwanted attentions. Perhaps after this he will be a little more careful in his assignations. Come, we must get back, and we must find Lady Norwell's party and tell Julia of our little scheme. Sally, you must go back to Lady Wyckenham – it would not do for Besthorpe to see you and Julia together, and wearing the same colour – I do not rate his intelligence

very highly, but he might guess something is afoot.'

They were soon back within the Grand Walk, where Clarissa and Lady Gaunt made their way around the promenade until they found Lady Norwell's party enjoying supper in one of the boxes situated behind the orchestra. Lady Gaunt sailed up to the box and engaged Lady Norwell in conversation, while Clarissa, following her instructions, tried to catch Julia's eye. Barnabus and his sister were giving Dorothea their attention, but Lord Alresford had risen upon their approach and was now standing against the painted back-wall of the box, idly surveying them all. As she moved towards Mrs Norwell she was acutely aware that he was watching her.

'I have never been to Vauxhall before,' she remarked. 'I was quite entranced by the gardens. The musicians are very good, are they not, Mrs Norwell?'

Julia looked a little bemused.

'Yes, although I am not very musical—'

Clarissa hurried on.

'I see you have finished your meal, pray give me your company to take a closer look at the orchestra. I would dearly love to study the gothic architecture.'

Julia hesitated, and Clarissa was forced to risk a pleading glance. With relief she saw Julia take up her fan and prepare to come with her. Immediately Lord Alresford stepped forward and picked up Julia's emerald domino.

'Perhaps it might be best if I accompany you, Mrs Norwell,' he murmured, throwing the cloak around her shoulders.

Clarissa put up her hand.

'No, no, there is no need, my lord. We do not go far, and I promise we shall not move out of sight of the box.'

The look with which he met her rather hurried assurances gave her a jolt of surprise. Surely that could not be a gleam of malicious humour in those dark eyes?

With a faint shrug the gentleman nodded and stepped back to allow them to leave the box. Clarissa took Julia's arm, but as

they walked away she felt as if his eyes were fixed upon her, and she had to steel herself not to look back.

'You wanted to speak privately with me, I think.'

Mrs Norwell's soft voice brought Clarissa back to her mission.

'Yes. You have seen Sir Howard Besthorpe is here tonight?' Julia shivered.

'I did see him, but thankfully he has not approached me.'

'He mistook Sally Matlock's green cloak for your own and followed her.'

'Oh heavens!'

'Dorothea Gaunt and I were with her, so there was no danger. He spoke through a hedge, thinking he was addressing you.'

Julia giggled.

'Like Pyramus and Thisbe.'

'I beg your pardon?'

'Shakespeare.'

Clarissa gave a gurgle of laughter.

'Of course – speaking through a chink in the wall! Why did I not think of that? Well, Dorothea answered, pretending to be you, Julia, and she told Sir Howard to be at Norwell House at ten o'clock tomorrow night.' She saw Julia's startled look and patted her arm. 'Dorothea has a plan to stop Sir Howard's attentions to you once and for all.'

'Oh if only she could.'

'Well, Lady Gaunt is a very forceful character, but she says she needs you there, if it is to work. It will be necessary for you to cry off from the theatre tomorrow night. You must insist that everyone else should go and you will remain behind.' Clarissa drew a breath. 'Dorothea also says it would be best if you were alone. Can you send the servants away?'

'The servants? How can I do that?'

Since Clarissa had no answer she remained silent, but after a moment Julia said slowly, 'What is Lady Gaunt's plan?'

'That I cannot tell you – in truth, I do not know,' admitted

Clarissa. 'Can I tell her you agree?'

'I-I am not sure . . . Barnabus has arranged the box at the theatre especially for me. . . . You say it will rid me of Sir Howard for good?'

'Dorothea says so.'

Clarissa felt Julia's hand tighten on her arm.

'Very well, I will do it!' whispered Julia, looking straight ahead of her. 'I will do it.'

'Good.' Clarissa realized she had been holding her breath and laughed softly. 'Who would have thought joining the Belles Dames Club would involve so much intrigue?'

'It is very good of you all to help me,' responded Julia. 'Shall we go back now? You can tell Lady Gaunt her plan can go ahead.'

'By all means, but first, since it was the reason I gave for stealing you away, I think we really must admire the orchestra.'

CHAPTER FIFTEEN

As the ladies of the Belles Dames Club made their way back to their carriages, they tried unsuccessfully to learn Lady Gaunt's plans for the following night but she would tell them nothing, promising to reveal all only when they reached Norwell House.

'But that is no good to me!' cried Mrs Leighton-Kettering. 'You know I am holding a dinner tomorrow night, so I cannot join you.'

'Nor I,' added Alicia Greynard. 'Really, Dorothea, it is too bad of you to arrange these things before asking the rest of us.'

Lady Gaunt waved one languid hand.

'Well, it could not be helped, the opportunity was too good to miss.'

Lady Wyckenham tapped her arm with her closed fan.

'Come, Dorothea, surely you can give us some hint of what you mean to do?'

But Lady Gaunt was not to be moved and the ladies went their separate ways, still grumbling at their friend's secretive nature.

Lady Wyckenham's frustration was still simmering when they at last reached Charlotte Street.

'It is just too bad of Dorothea!' she complained. 'I would very much like to know just what she expects to do. I cannot say that I like this. Dorothea can be so impetuous, and is apt to be a little wild at times. Good evening, Simmons, how good of you to wait up for us.'

'Good evening, my lady. I thought I should, seeing as there's a letter for you.' He indicated a sleepy-looking footman standing behind him.

'A letter?' Lady Wyckenham held out her hand for it, tore open the seal and unfolded the crackling sheet as she walked across to the console table at one side of the hall, where a cluster of candles gleamed in a silver holder. Clarissa removed her domino and handed it to the butler, all the time keeping her eyes upon her stepmama. Lady Wyckenham read the note, her face impassive, then folded the sheet. She turned to the footman.

'Thank you,' she said. 'There is no reply.'

The servant bowed and Simmons opened the front door to let him out. Clarissa frowned.

'What is it, Mama-Nell? What was that letter?'

'Nothing to worry you, my dear.' Lady Wyckenham set off up the stairs.

Clarissa followed her.

'But it has worried *you*, madam.'

Lady Wyckenham laughed.

'Mama-Nell, was it from a man – is he, is he importuning you?'

My lady's steps faltered but only for a moment.

'Yes.'

'Like Sir Howard Besthorpe and Julia?'

'Not quite like that, my dear.'

She hurried up the stairs to her room, but at the door Clarissa stopped her.

'Mama-Nell, will you not tell me? Perhaps I may help you.'

'Bless you, child. It is nothing, a mere inconvenience that I must resolve.'

'But Mama-Nell—'

Lady Wyckenham flashed her a brief, mischievous smile.

'Do you know, I find I can be quite as secretive as Dorothea Gaunt? Go to bed, Clarissa, and do not worry yourself over me.'

CHAPTER SIXTEEN

It had been arranged that Lady Gaunt would collect Clarissa and Lady Wyckenham in her carriage the following evening, and shortly before the appointed hour Clarissa walked into Mama-Nell's dressing-room.

'Lady Gaunt said to wear something dark, so I thought this riding habit would suit, since it is midnight-blue. What do you think?' She stopped, blinking in surprise to find her stepmother still seated at her dressing table. 'Madam? You are not ready, you have not changed.'

'Oh, Clarissa, my love – you must give my apologies to Dorothea. I am not able to come with you tonight.' My lady did

not turn from her mirror, but her voice sounded unnaturally bright.

Clarissa crossed the room and stood behind Lady Wyckenham, staring at her reflection in the mirror.

'Mama-Nell, what is this, what is wrong?'

Lady Wyckenham did not meet her eyes.

'Why, nothing, my love. My, how suspicious you are grown! No, I-I have an appointment that I had overlooked and I cannot break it, so you will have to go without me. I am sure you will manage splendidly, whatever Dorothea has arranged, and you must tell me all about it when you return.'

Clarissa frowned.

'This has something to do with the letter you received last night, does is not?'

Lady Wyckenham stood up.

'I will not lie to you, Clarissa. Yes, it has. But as I told you last night, it is a mere inconvenience. I shall soon resolve it.'

'Then let me help you!'

'No; you are pledged to Julia Norwell this evening. Now, I hear someone at the door, most likely it is Dorothea Gaunt, so off you go now and do not keep her waiting.' She smiled and came forward to give Clarissa a swift hug. 'Go, Clarissa.'

Lady Wyckenham stayed only until she heard Lady Gaunt's carriage drawing away from the house before she sent for her own coach. When it pulled up at the door some twenty minutes later, she was ready, attired in a mannish riding outfit of dark brown camlet with a matching beaver hat set on top of her gleaming curls, and a heavy veil hiding her face. She directed her coachman to a house off Piccadilly and when it pulled up she alighted, saying, 'Wait for me here, Jacob. I shall not be long.'

A liveried footman bowed her into the house.

'If madam would be pleased to wait in the drawing-room, his lordship will be with you directly.'

With her hands tucked inside her swansdown muff, Lady Wyckenham followed the servant into a brightly lit apartment, richly decorated in red and gold. A good fire blazed in the hearth but although she felt a little faint, she did not unbutton her tight-fitting jacket, nor did she put up her veil. She wandered restlessly about the room, looking up at the dark portraits that seemed to stare down haughtily at her from the walls.

'You are admiring my ancestors.'

She jumped.

'I did not hear you come in.' She fought down her nerves as she turned to greet the Marquis of Ullenwood. 'My lord.'

He bowed, the light glistening on the silver streaks in his dark hair.

'My lady. I did not expect such a prompt response to my letter.'

She shrugged.

'You wished to talk to me. I am here.'

'Will you not sit down?'

'No.' The word was out before she knew it, and Lady Wyckenham cursed her nerves. 'Ah.' Lord Ullenwood smiled. Or, she temporized, his lips curled but there was no warmth in those dark eyes, no hint of gentleness. He continued, 'Very well, madam, let us get to the point. I would trade with you.'

She gave him a scornful glance.

'There is nothing to trade.'

'Oh but there is,' he said softly. 'We both know that I have certain . . . letters, written in your own fair hand.'

She paled.

'I thought you had destroyed them.'

The marquis spread his hands.

'You asked it of me, I know, but I could not bring myself to do so. They were such touching letters, you see.'

'I was very unhappy at the time.'

'I am aware – you sought solace in my arms, did you not?'

'Elliot, I trusted you. I thought you were my friend.'

'Friendship is such a fragile thing, Helen. When you spurned me—'

'I found I could not love you and I told you so: it was not meant cruelly.'

'Your passion cooled,' he said. 'Mine has never died.'

'Then I am sorry for it, but there is nothing I can do.'

'Oh but there is.'

She shook her head.

'Elliot, it is over. When Wyckenham died I was distraught; I turned to you for comfort, but that was a mistake.'

'I cannot allow that.'

'So what would you have me do?'

'Come back to me, Helen.'

'I cannot. I do not love you.' She tilted her head to one side. 'Surely that would make me a wretched mistress?'

The marquis walked towards her.

'I would have you on any terms. Helen—'

As he reached for her, she retreated behind a chair.

'Stay away, my lord. I have told you I am not for you.'

'You might change your mind.'

'Because of the letters?'

'Yes.'

'I think not.' She pulled one hand free from her muff, her fingers gripping a small silver pistol. 'You will give me the letters. Do not laugh at me: I will not allow you to coerce me.'

He looked down at the pistol in her hand.

'What do you propose to do?'

'I will shoot you if you do not give me the letters. I am quite serious, my lord.'

'Then we have reached an impasse, for I do not have them.'

'You lie!'

He spread his hands.

'I mean they are not in this house. They are safely locked in a bank vault, my dear.' Again that hateful smile. 'So, shoot me

if you must, Helen, but it will not get you the letters. Are you sure you will not sit down?'

Helen was not listening.

'You must have them. I could shoot you and search the house.'

Lord Ullenwood looked apologetic.

'Ah – there is the little matter of my servants. I do not think they would allow you to do that.'

Her shoulders drooped: she gave a sigh and replaced the pistol inside her muff.

'Oh do what you will! I was a widow when I wrote to you: it may cause a scandal for a week, but I have endured worse.'

She went to the door.

'And what of the children?' She stopped. 'Your stepchildren, madam. How do you think they will like having the family name bandied about the clubs? Your letters were very detailed, my love. And these young people, they are not so broad-minded as we were in our day, eh?'

She turned towards him, the colour draining from her cheeks.

'You would not.'

He stared at her, and she felt as if his eyes bored right through the heavy veil.

'Oh, I would,' he said softly.

'To publish those letters would be the actions of a scoundrel.'

'No, no, you wrong me: it would be the actions of a man very much in love.'

'Fustian! This is no way to gain my regard.'

'Perhaps not, but if it is the only way I can have you—'

Lady Wyckenham regarded him for a moment. She said quietly, 'Very well. What must I do to have you return my letters?'

In the darkness of Lady's Gaunt's carriage, Clarissa wondered if she should tell Dorothea of her worries. Mama-Nell had told

her it was nothing: perhaps she should believe her. Clarissa decided to keep her own counsel, at least for the present.

They collected Lady Sarah from Dover Street and arrived at Norwell House some thirty minutes before ten o'clock. A nervous lady's maid admitted them to the house and Julia informed them that she had sent the other servants to the servants wing.

'I let it be known I have the headache and need silence – they have all retired for the present: Barnabus and his mama and sister will not be returning until midnight.'

'Well we shall be done by then, my dear, so you need not look so anxious.' Lady Gaunt put down the large portmanteau she had brought in and took off her cloak. 'Send your maid away, Julia, and let us prepare.'

The clock in the stable tower struck ten and the ladies were gathered in one of the upstairs rooms at the front of the house. As the last chime died away there could be heard the clip-clop of hoofs on the drive. Lady Gaunt nodded.

'Show yourself, Julia. We must make sure Sir Howard knows you are here.'

Obediently Julia picked up a branched candlestick and moved towards the window.

'It is he,' she gasped, her voice scarcely above a whisper.

'Good,' said Lady Gaunt. 'Can you manage a smile, and perhaps a wave?'

Julia leaned forward, then jumped back with a little cry.

'Oh – he has seen me!'

Clarissa heard Dorothea suppress a sigh of irritation.

'Well, that is just what we want, my dear. You may relax now, Julia. You have done your part. Now I must play *my* role as your maid.'

CHAPTER SEVENTEEN

Dismounting on the drive of Norwell House, Sir Howard looked about him in some surprise. By the light of the flaring torches burning on either side of the door he could see the grounds were deserted. He looked up as the door was opened by a lanky serving woman.

'Ah – your mistress is expecting me,' he said. 'Is there someone to look to my horse?'

The woman bobbed a curtsy.

'Madam thought it best to send the servants off for the night, sir.' Sir Howard felt his excitement rising. The maid waved vaguely towards a hedge. 'If your lordship will tie the reins to that bush he'll be safe enough. Then if you'd be good enough to follow me.'

Sir Howard almost skipped up the steps. The door was shut firmly behind him and he found himself in a large, echoing hall.

'Where is your mistress?'

Silently the servant picked up a single candle and led the way up the stairs. Sir Howard followed, his eyes dwelling on the shadowy figure. She was too thin for his taste – in general he preferred plump, rosy-cheeked maids – but the woman walked with a certain sway to her hips that was definitely alluring: he smiled to himself. Perhaps when he had finished with the mistress he would give her a tumble, it might be amusing.

There were no lights burning on the half-landing, and by the time they reached the first floor the only illumination came from the maid's single candle She led Sir Howard through a series of passages, twisting and turning, then down another set of stairs until he was quite bewildered.

'How much further?'

'We're here now, sir. Madam was not wishful that you should be shown into her husband's chamber, her being a very modest lady, you understand.'

'No, no, of course not.' Sir Howard licked his lips at the thought of the treat before him. He adored modest ladies, and enjoyed discovering the charms previously reserved for their husbands.

The maid opened a side door and led him into a small bedchamber.

'Now, sir, if you please. Mrs Norwell wishes me to undress you.'

'Undr – oh, aye, aye.'

'She is wishful to come to you as any bride would do,' muttered the servant, helping him out of his coat.

'A b-bride?' breathed Sir Howard, and felt almost giddy at the thought. Bless the little angel! He struggled out of his waistcoat and gave a yelp when he felt the maid's hands at the waist of his breeches.

'Everything is to come off, sir. Madam was very particular.'

'Yes, yes, I will do it.'

His fingers trembled as he fumbled with the buttons of his breeches while the maid unfastened the ribbons at his knees and began to roll down his stockings. Then he was standing on the cold boards, naked except for his fine lawn shirt. He shifted from one foot to the other, his eagerness barely concealed.

'Well, tell your mistress I am ready for her.'

The maid scooped up the discarded clothes and tucked them under one arm.

'Aye, I'll tell her.'

She picked up the candle and whisked herself out of the room.

Sir Howard stood very still. The room was dark and his eyes did not seem to adjust to the gloom. He realized that the shutters had been closed, allowing only a faint grey line to show the outline of the window. It was impossible to see across the room.

He gave a little cough.

'Mistress?' He called tentatively. 'Mrs Norwell, my little bird? Are you there?'

He heard her voice. It was very faint, and seemed to be coming from the far side of the room. Bless her, she sounded nervous.

'Oh sir . . . I am here, in the next room . . . can you find the door?'

Sir Howard stepped forward, cursing as his shin collided with a small stool and sent it skittering across the floor. He stopped, then began to move forward again, his hands stretched before him as he felt his way across the room. He found he was shaking with excitement, picturing the lovely Julia: would she be *en negligée*, as he had seen her at the window when he arrived, or was she already undressed? He felt himself growing hard at the mere thought of it. She must be such a romantic little puss to go to so much trouble. Here was a pleasure he had not anticipated.

'Oh hurry, sir, where are you?'

Again the breathless voice sounded from the next room, and the soft scurrying sound of movement. Two more steps brought him to the wall, a little fumbling found the door and he grasped the handle. It turned easily and opened on to more darkness. He frowned.

'Madam? Are you there?'

'Yes, yes, at the end of the passage – hurry, dear sir!'

A passage! Despite his excitement he felt his patience growing a little thin.

'My dear madam, is this really necessary? Pray bring a candle out to me.'

'Oh I dare not risk any of the servants seeing you. Perhaps I should not have given in to the temptation. . . .'

'No, no, my love, wait there – I shall be with you directly.'

Sir Howard reached out his hands to each side. Yes, he could feel the wall on his right and, yes, if he reached a little to the

left he could touch the wall there. He moved a few steps forward, his bare feet padding on the wooden boards. He began to move with more confidence. Ahead of him was a dim bar of light beneath a door. At last. His outstretched hands touched the solid wood and he hurriedly felt around for the handle. Moments later he was pulling the door open. He blinked.

'What is this, madam – are you outside?' He stepped out of the door and found himself in a paved yard at the back of the house. 'Madam I—'

The door slammed shut behind him. As he swung round he heard the bolts scrape into position.

'Julia? What is this – enough of this jest, madam, let me in.'

' 'Tis no jest, Sir Howard.'

He frowned. It was a woman's voice, but not Julia's sweet tones. This was a much stronger voice, and full of laughter.

'Let it be a lesson to you not to prey on young women who do not wish for your attentions.'

'What is this – what game are you playing? Let me in, I say, and give me my clothes.'

'No, sir – you will get nothing here tonight. You had best go home.'

'I cannot ride without my breeches!'

Sounds of smothered laughter came from the house and Sir Howard realized there was more than one voice behind the door. He cursed roundly and stamped his foot, stubbing his toe as he did so.

'God damn you – I will not leave without my clothes.'

'Your horse is where you left him.' The reply was curt, indifferent. 'Go now before Mr Norwell and his party return. You might find it difficult to explain why you are wandering around his house half-naked.'

Sir Howard stared at the door. His earlier excitement had gone, replaced with a growing sense of desperation. The door looked too solid to give way, and the windows were all shuttered. There was no way he could get back into the house.

Cursing, he began to make his way round to the front drive. The gravel was sharp beneath his feet, making him gasp, and the cool night air seemed to taunt him as it fluttered his shirt. He had just reached his horse when he heard the sound of a carriage approaching. Turning, he saw the bobbing lights of the link boys running down the drive ahead of the horses. He pulled at the reins, but instead of coming free they tightened themselves into a knot. In desperation he tugged again, harder this time, snapping the branch so that the reins came away, still knotted around a leafy stick.

The carriage had come to a halt by now and Sir Howard heard a smothered exclamation as Barnabus Norwell jumped down on to the drive. Sir Howard wished the link boys would move away with their flaring torches, but they stood their ground, grinning. They seemed intent on illuminating him as fully as possible.

'What the devil is going on here? Marius – your pistol. We have an intruder. Ladies, please wait in the coach.'

Sir Howard abandoned his attempts to mount his horse and turned.

'Norwell, d-don't shoot – I am not a robber!'

His voice came out in a squeak. The wind decided at that moment to blow a little stronger and Sir Howard had to give his attention to catching the edge of his shirt and holding it down.

'Besthorpe?' Barnabus's jaw dropped. 'What the deuce are you playing at?' he demanded, trying not to laugh.

Sir Howard's anger boiled over. He pointed accusingly towards the house.

'They tricked me!' he cried shrilly. 'They took my clothes, exposing me to ridicule – it is not to be borne!'

Mr Norwell looked bemused.

'Who tricked you?'

'Your wife sir! Your wife and her friends!'

'You have been here trying to seduce my wife?'

81

There was no trace of humour in Mr Norwell's face now.

Sir Howard eyed his clenched fists with trepidation, but he could not prevent himself from screeching, 'She tricked me! The little vixen told me to come at ten o'clock, because you would be from home, and she has led me a merry dance through the house, stealing my clothes, the doxy—'

He got no further. With a roar Barnabus launched himself forward and Sir Howard felt two strong hands around his throat, squeezing until the blood thrummed in his ears. He felt a hot searing pain behind his eyes, his hands scrabbled in vain to prise the fingers from his neck, then the next instant he was released and he fell to his knees, coughing and spluttering. Through his watering eyes he saw Lord Alresford gripping Norwell's arms.

'Enough, Barny, it would not do to kill him.'

'You are right, Marius, though at this moment I would dearly love to give him a thrashing. If you have harmed my wife, sir—'

Sir Howard struggled to his feet.

'No, no, I didn't touch her – never saw her, save through a window.'

Lord Alresford stepped between them.

'I suggest, Besthorpe, that you go home. I'd wager you have been up to mischief here and if you have been bested then all the better.'

'Aye,' growled Mr Norwell, 'Get off my land, before I put a bullet through your sorry hide.'

With a whimper Sir Howard scrambled up into the saddle. He heard muted giggling coming from the interior of the carriage, and hurriedly tucked his shirt about him before setting his horse at a canter along the drive, his exit spurred on by the sounds of laughter carried on the night air.

CHAPTER EIGHTEEN

'Sally – I hear them on the stairs, come and sit down.'

Reluctantly Lady Sarah came away from the window.

'You need not worry, Dorothea. No one saw me. I opened the shutter the merest crack, and besides, they were all too intent upon Sir Howard.'

'Did Barnabus really set upon him?' asked Julia, her eyes shining.

'Truly,' replied Lady Sarah. 'Besthorpe was shouting so loud that you all heard him, and when he mentioned you, Julia, Barnabus leapt upon him like a tiger. Alresford had to pull him off.'

'Oh dear, and has Sir Howard gone now?'

Lady Sarah came up behind Mrs Norwell and gave her a hug.

'Yes, yes he has gone, my dear. Riding bare-behind all the way to London town.' Lady Gaunt, who had been distributing cards around the table, looked up, smiling. 'With his shirt billowing around him and his legs all dangling down-oh?'

'Exactly!'

Clarissa waved a hand.

'Hush, they are here. Quickly now, Sally, come and sit down before they come in.' Lady Sarah slipped on to her chair and had just picked up her cards when the door opened and Lady Norwell sailed into the room. When she saw the ladies sitting around the card table she stopped, blinking.

'Well, bless my soul!'

Julia looked up at her.

'You are back early, ma'am. Was the play not to your liking?'

'No, 'twas very poor stuff, my love, and Barnabus was fretting over you, so we did not wait for the entertainment, and

since Lord Alresford had kindly agreed to take us in his carriage, he was obliged to leave early too.'

Clarissa was frowning at her cards, pretending to study her hand, but she was aware of Mrs Eastwood hurrying in behind her mama and Mr Norwell almost pushing past them to come up to his wife.

'Julia, what the devil is going on here?' he demanded. 'When I left you were prostrate with the headache.'

'And so she will be again if you continue to shout,' remarked Lady Gaunt. 'You can see she is still a little pale, Barnabus.'

From the corner of her eye Clarissa watched Lord Alresford come in and close the door behind him.

Mr Norwell's jaw tightened at Lady Gaunt's words but he said as calmly as he could, 'If you will excuse me for saying so, ma'am, that does not explain your presence here.'

'We drove out to the tea rooms at Kensington today, and stopped to take pot luck with Julia on our way back. Of course, when we found she was so poorly we stayed to keep her company until your return. I think you will agree, Barnabus, that we have cheered her up considerably.'

Clarissa admired Lady Gaunt's masterly approach. Barnabus did not look convinced, but could hardly say so.

'And you have had no other visitors?' asked Lady Norwell.

'N-no.' Julia shook her head. 'I sent the servants away, because I did not want to be disturbed, so if anyone had come, they would have had to go away again. We have kept to this room all evening.'

Mrs Eastwood clapped her hands together.

'Well, you will never guess what we found when we arrived – such a thing, I vow I am so pleased we did not stay for the farce for this was so much better! A naked man outside the house!'

'N-naked?' squeaked Julia.

'Margaret, do not exaggerate.' Lady Norwell admonished her daughter. 'He was wearing a shirt.'

'It was Sir Howard Besthorpe,' added Margaret.

Barnabus stared at her.

'You recognized him?'

'Oh yes.' Mrs Eastwood grimaced. 'Horrid man. He was used to follow me everywhere when I was last in town, until I asked Edward to put an end to it.'

Smothering an oath, Barnabus turned to his wife.

'Has be been pestering you, Julia? Why did you not tell me?'

Julia's soft eyes filled with tears.

'I did not wish to trouble you. . . .'

He was at her side immediately, dropping to his knees beside her chair.

'You never trouble me, my dear. There, there. Don't cry. I have sent him to the right about now.' He took out his handkerchief and gently wiped the tears from her cheeks. 'In future, my love, I want you to come to me with any little problem. Promise me.'

'But I don't understand,' cried Lady Norwell. 'Why should the man be parading around the house? Did you not hear or see anything?'

Lady Sarah waved towards the shuttered window.

'We had no interest in the outside world tonight, ma'am.'

'I thought I heard a dog barking,' offered Clarissa.

'If there was any noise outside I am sure we dismissed it as the servants.' Lady Gaunt glanced across the table at Julia, deep in whispered conversation with her husband. She rose to her feet. 'I think it is time we took our leave. I think our presence here now is definitely *de trop*. Please send for my carriage, Barnabus, and we will be away. Julia says you will not be at Lady Sarah's little poetry evening, so I do not know when we shall meet again.'

Lord Alresford had so far remained silent, but now he moved forward.

'It was very good of you to stay and keep Mrs Norwell company. So fortunate that she should be able to admit you, when all the servants had been dismissed for the evening.'

'Oh, the – the footman was still in the hall at that time,' said Julia.

The earl inclined his head at her, then turned towards Clarissa.

'Where did you say you had been today?'

Clarissa froze, her mind a blank.

She heard Lady Gaunt replying casually, 'The tea rooms at Kensington, Alresford. So you see, we were passing the door. But we must trespass upon you no longer. Come ladies.'

'Such a deal of travelling you have done today, my lady. You must be exhausted,' remarked Lord Alresford, in his smooth, unemotional way. 'Allow me to be of assistance. *I* will escort Miss Wyckenham to Charlotte Street.'

Clarissa gasped.

'No, no, my lord, we will not trouble you—'

'No trouble at all,' he interrupted her. 'Lady Gaunt's destination is Grosvenor Square, is it not? Mine, on the other hand, is Bedford Square, so Charlotte Street is not at all out of my way.'

The earl was standing a little behind Lady Norwell and her daughter, and only Clarissa saw his hand reach into his pocket and pull forth a fine blue ribbon: just such a ribbon as adorned Sir Howard Besthorpe's knee-breeches. She swallowed.

'How – how kind of you, sir. I will be delighted to accept your offer and save my friends an added journey.' She was aware of the surprised looks this speech received, but there was no opportunity to explain. Lord Alresford was holding her cloak, goodbyes were said and she found herself sitting opposite the earl in his luxurious town coach before Lady Gaunt's carriage had even pulled on to the drive. Clarissa clasped her hands nervously before her.

'It – it was very good of you to take me up, my lord.'

'Good be damned. You know why you are here.'

She felt her pulse racing at his words. Was he planning to ravish her? Clarissa was shocked to find the idea quite exciting. Resolutely she pushed the thought away. She said, trying to

keep her tone cool, 'No, sir. I have no idea why I am here, if it is not to be taken home.'

'I want you to tell me just what occurred tonight.' He held the ribbon up to the window, so that she could see it in the pale moonlight. 'This I found on the stairs.'

'Oh.'

'It is the ribbon from a man's knee-breeches.' Clarissa remained silent. 'Did you lure Besthorpe into the house?'

Clarissa considered her situation. The earl was no fool and it was clear he had already formed quite an accurate idea of what had happened.

'You will be aware,' she said slowly, 'that Sir Howard has been pursuing Mrs Norwell for some time.'

'I was *not* aware of it – and neither was Norwell, judging by his reaction tonight.'

'Well, it is true: Besthorpe has harassed her until the poor child is at her wits' end.'

'Nonsense. If she was indeed being importuned she should have told Barnabus.'

'You are a close friend of Mr Norwell: did he tell you that when he brought Julia to town it was on the understanding that they should not live in each other's pockets?'

'Yes, but—'

'Poor Julia was afraid that if she complained to her husband, he would think her a nuisance and pack her off to the country.'

'Nonsense!'

'Is it, my lord? From the little I have seen of Mr Norwell, he seems to behave very much as a single man. I have only once seen him accompany his wife to a ball, and even then he left her to make her own way home.'

There was a long silence.

'Absurd,' said the earl at last. 'Silly chit cannot have thought Barnabus would want her to fall into the clutches of a man like Besthorpe.'

'Perhaps not, but she certainly thought Mr Norwell would

expect her to extricate herself.'

'And you decided to assist her.'

'Since there was no help for it, yes.'

'So you concocted a scheme to ridicule Besthorpe.'

'In truth, I cannot claim that I had very much to do with the planning.'

'I would wager it was Lady Gaunt's idea.' When Clarissa did not reply he continued, 'Do you realize what a dangerous game you have been playing?'

'There was no risk. After all, there were four of us to stand together. I have no doubt that if Sir Howard had turned ugly—'

'But what of the servants, the gossip, madam? Such behaviour has laid you open to the sort of speculation a single lady should wish to avoid. Of all the thoughtless, hare-brained starts!'

She winced under the lash of his tongue, but retorted with spirit.

'Nonsense. There were no servants in the house at the time.'

'Oh weren't there? I have never known a household yet where the servants didn't know every intrigue that was afoot. And what about the link-boys, not to mention my own coachman – do you think he will hold his tongue when he is sharing a glass of blue ruin with his cronies tomorrow night?'

'Well then, you must insist upon his silence!'

'Never doubt it, but if this story isn't all over town by tomorrow I shall be amazed.'

'If Sir Howard is the subject of ridicule then it is no more than natural justice,' she retorted, thoroughly incensed. 'We acted to protect a friend, since she did not believe her husband would do so.'

'Nevertheless, it would have been more sensible to take your concerns to him.'

'Sensible! Aye, my lord, I would expect nothing less than good sense from you!' she flung at him.

'And why not? Anyone with an ounce of intelligence would

have done so but no, you and your friends were bent on making mischief. Bad enough that Lady Gaunt and Sally Matlock should be involved in this madness but you are a single woman, risking your name and your honour for a reckless scrape.'

'And if I am, what concern is it of yours, my lord? What is it to you?'

Silence. The darkness suddenly seemed charged with tension. Clarissa waited, sitting very straight and trying to control her breathing, which had become very irregular. She waited for him to speak again, but instead the coach stopped and the footman opened the door, saying in a colourless voice, 'Charlotte Street, my lord.'

Lord Alresford started to rise but Clarissa waved him back in his seat.

'Please,' she said icily, 'you owe me no particular attention. I can get down perfectly well without you. Remain in your carriage, Lord Alresford, and do not bother yourself about me ever again!'

CHAPTER NINETEEN

When Clarissa made her way to the breakfast-room she was ready for her stepmama to question her closely on the previous night's adventure, but she found Lady Wyckenham pondering some knotty problem of her own. Clarissa dismissed the servants and went to the table.

'Good morning, Mama-Nell.' She bent to kiss Lady Wyckenham's scented cheek. 'You look very pensive, my love: I thought you would be ringing a peal over me for not coming to

see you last night, to tell you all that had happed at Norwell House.'

'What? Oh – yes, my love. I am sorry, I was thinking. . . .'

Clarissa took a seat across the table and poured herself a cup of coffee.

'My dear ma'am, you are surely distracted this morning.' She put down her cup. 'It must be that man.'

'What man, my love?'

'The one who is importuning you.'

My lady's laugh sounded a little wild.

'What nonsense!'

'No it isn't. You told me last night that you had a little problem to solve.'

'I did?'

'Yes, you did. But judging from your behaviour this morning, the problem has not gone away, am I right?'

Lady Wyckenham pursed her lips, as if deliberating how much to disclose. Clarissa reached across the table and caught her hand.

'Please tell me, Mama-Nell. Even if I cannot help you, I want to know.'

My lady sighed.

'Very well. I went out last night, to try to recover some letters from a man I thought of once as a good friend. They were . . . intimate letters that I wrote to him a long time ago, but he is threatening now to make them public unless . . . well, I must get them back.'

'And who is this man?'

'The Marquis of Ullenwood.'

Clarissa frowned and sipped her coffee.

'I have met him, I think. A dark-haired gentleman?'

'Yes, although I would no longer use the term gentleman to describe him.'

'But you were friends once?'

'For a time I thought – but I was wrong. When I realized I

had mistaken my feelings for him I asked him to destroy my letters, and until recently I thought he had done so.'

'When were they written?' Clarissa hesitated, 'Was it – was my father alive?'

'Oh no, nothing like that. It was after Wyckenham had died. You know I shut myself away for a year, then I went to Europe. I met Lord Ullenwood in Venice. He was very kind to me and I thought . . . well, it came to nothing and I forgot the letters, until now.'

Clarissa refilled her coffee cup.

'Then it is simple,' she said. 'Let him publish the letters, Mama-Nell. He will show himself in his true light.'

'Oh no – as your stepmama it would reflect so badly upon you all, and just when William is trying so hard to make his way into government. I must get them back.'

'But what does he want for these letters?'

Lady Wyckenham blushed.

'He wants me to elope with him.'

'Dear heaven!' Clarissa's cup clattered into its saucer. 'And what have you told him – what answer have you given him?'

'None – how could I? I have asked him for a little time . . . to think.'

They sat in silence for some moments, then Clarissa looked up.

'Are they so very bad, these letters?'

A flush stole into Lady Wyckenham's cheeks.

'They are quite – explicit.'

Clarissa was about to declare that for herself she did not care if the letters were published, but the image of Lord Alresford rose before her. She remembered their argument in the carriage the night before and she held her peace.

'Well,' she said at last, 'we must get them back for you. I am sure the members of the Belles Dames Club will have some ideas.'

For the first time that morning she saw a gleam of amusement in Mama-Nell's eyes.

'Do you think we should ask our little group to help with such a delicate matter?'

'I am sure of it,' Clarissa replied stoutly. 'Especially after our success last night.'

She recounted the events at Norwell House and was relieved when Lady Wyckenham laughed at the description of Sir Howard's retreat from the scene. She was encouraged to describe her carriage ride with the earl.

'I have to confess to you that we nearly came to blows,' she said, tracing a pattern on the table with one finger. 'He was so out of reason cross with me! After all, what is it to him if I choose to help my friends? If Julia had not been so afraid to talk to her husband there would have been no need for us to treat Sir Howard in such a fashion. I am not ashamed of what we did.'

'Then put it from your mind, love.'

Clarissa sighed.

'But I can't, Mama-Nell. For years I have been used to doing as I pleased. Oh, never going outside the bounds of propriety, but I have never allowed anyone except yourself or Papa to censure my conduct, and to have that man saying such things to me – he had no right!'

'None at all my love.'

Clarissa glanced up.

'You are laughing at me.'

'No, no, but I wonder at the earl's ability to upset you – it is not the first time. Perhaps you are beginning to care for his good opinion?'

'Not at all!' retorted Clarissa, flushing. 'It is nothing to do with the man, it – it is the language he used – I would be as cross if anyone had said the same to me.'

'Well, I cannot be sorry that you are disturbed by his lordship's comments.' It was Lady Wyckenham's turn to reach across the table and catch at Clarissa's restless fingers. 'I have hinted at it before, my love, but now let us be plain: when

James Marlow died you built a wall around yourself, a defence
that kept the world at bay—'

'That was quite natural, when you consider what he did to
me!' Clarissa interrupted her.

'Let me finish, my love. To be jilted is a terrible thing for any
young woman, but to discover that your fiancé had run off with
your childhood friend was almost too much for you to bear, I
think, especially coming so soon after the death of your dear
father.'

Clarissa gave a brittle laugh.

'But that was so fortunate, for me. Papa's death meant we
had retired to Wyckenham Hall, and James's little escapade
was more easily hushed up. Imagine the furore if I had still
been in Town when he decided to run away. What manna for
the quidnuncs – it would have been gossiped over for months!'

Lady Wyckenham squeezed her hand.

'Perhaps it would have been better for you if it *had* been
known: perhaps then you would not have buried your grief and
anger quite so deep.'

'And if I did so, can you blame me? It was bad enough to
learn that James had broken his neck when his carriage overturned. To find out that he was on his way to Gretna, and with
my best friend at his side – I would not have the world know
how much that hurt me!' She broke off, feeling the anger that
she had suppressed for years coming to the fore. 'Perhaps I
could have forgiven her more easily if she had died too, but to
walk away without a scratch . . . and now, three years later, she
is happily married to the parson, and looks set to give him a
houseful of children. Do you want me to advertise my pain,
Mama-Nell? To spread my grief and my bitterness through
town? Because I promise you I have more than enough hurt
inside me to last a lifetime!'

'Stop it, Clarissa. You know that is not what I want. But it is
equally bad for you to shut out the world. Oh my darling girl, I
blame myself for letting you hide yourself away with Anne. If I

had not been so caught up in my own grief I could have helped you.'

'Mama-Nell you must not blame yourself for my troubles.' Clarissa took out her handkerchief and wiped her eyes. 'You see how Lord Alresford has overset me! I have never allowed myself to talk in this vein before.'

'Then he has my gratitude,' said Lady Wyckenham. 'Yes, you may stare, Clarissa, but if you are upset it is because you are recovering at last: oh I have loved the smiling, cheerful creature you are now but there is so much *more* to living, Clarissa: to live is to experience love, and fear, and sorrow. Without those how can we know true happiness?' She blinked and laughed softly. 'Goodness, I begin to sound like these new, revolutionary poets! Enough of this: we will go and order some new gowns – *that* will restore our spirits!'

CHAPTER TWENTY

Your sea of troubles you have passed
And found the peaceful shore
I, tempest-tossed and wrecked at last
Come home to port no more.

Polite applause followed and Lady Sarah cried, 'Well done, Mr Henderson, you bring the poet's work to life for us.'

The actor bowed and sat down.

Clarissa leaned closer to Lady Wyckenham, sitting beside her.

'Mr Cowper's words may have been written for someone returning from Ramsgate, but they could as easily apply to

others.' She raised her eyes to the gentleman standing behind their sofa. 'Do you not agree, Sir Robert, that those words could have been written for you?'

He grinned.

'I am very conscious of the fact that in all my wandering I have not yet been shipwrecked: pity, when I have taken the trouble to learn to swim.'

Lady Wyckenham shuddered.

'I pray you will not talk of it, even in jest, sir.'

'If it relieves your mind, Helen, I think this expedition will be my last. I am growing too old for such excitement and will let the younger men take over.'

Lady Wyckenham smiled up at him.

'Well that is good news, but what will you do? I do not see you as a man of leisure, Robert.'

'I have my gardens at Newfield Hall to tend, and my work with plants. I plan to catalogue all my discoveries, with pictures of each new plant – perhaps you would like to work with me, as my resident artist?'

'What a capital idea,' cried Clarissa. 'You draw like an angel, Mama-Nell.'

My lady plied her fan to cool her burning cheeks.

'Nonsense, I am not nearly good enough.'

'You know you are as good as any artist I have ever taken on a voyage,' returned Sir Robert. 'I know I would enjoy having you working with me on this project.'

Clarissa looked at her stepmother, but under her enquiring gaze Lady Wyckenham looked away.

'Perhaps, Sir Robert, you should discuss this again with my stepmama at some later date, when she has had time to consider it properly,' suggested Clarissa, earning for herself a grateful look from the gentleman.

'Nonsense, he is merely funning,' said Lady Wyckenham. 'Now who, I wonder, is to speak next – Sir Robert, you have prepared something?'

'Why yes, I have prepared a few lines by my good friend Gilbert White about the calm days of winter.'

'Oh, the weather.'

'It is a fascinating subject, Helen. At Newfield I have a small sun-house built in the grounds and when I am there I record each day's weather.' He leaned towards her. 'When you visit me I will show you. It is quite secluded.'

Clarissa hid her smile as she heard these words and noted the tell-tale flush mounting to her stepmother's cheek.

'Hush now,' she murmured, 'I think we have another reader. Goodness, I think our host is going to read to us.'

Sir Toby Matlock stepped up, resplendent in a powdered bag-wig and a gold and green frock-coat.

'Oh good,' said Lady Wyckenham. 'He usually provides something very entertaining.'

A hush descended over the room and Sir Toby took a deep breath and began to sing in a rich baritone.

'*Here's to a maiden of bashful fifteen, Here's to the widow of fifty. . . .*'

Lady Wyckenham nodded.

'Sheridan,' she whispered to Clarissa. 'He can always be relied upon to make us laugh.'

A movement by the door caught Clarissa's attention and she looked up to see Lady Gaunt entering, Mrs Sowerby and Mrs Flooke, the dashing sisters, at her side and her little black page holding up the train of her gown. They remained by the door until Sir Toby had finished, then made their way towards Lady Wyckenham. Lady Sarah came over to them, saying with mock severity, 'You are very late, Dorothea.'

Lady Gaunt raised one languid hand.

'Sally, my abject apologies. Emily and Georgiana were dining with me and dear Gaunt decided to join us.'

Lady Wyckenham looked up.

'I did not know your husband was in town, Dorothea.'

'*En passant*, my dear. He is on his way to Tonbridge, but

plans to join me here next week. Then he is off to Derbyshire for the summer.'

'And will you go with him?' asked Clarissa.

'My dear of course she will go!' cried Georgiana, dropping on to a nearby chair. 'Under her languid exterior Dorothea is passionately fond of her husband.'

Lady Gaunt looked pained.

'Georgy, you make me sound like a provincial,' she complained, gently descending on to the settee beside Clarissa.

'But you are fond of him?'

'Oh lord, yes, Clarissa. He lets me have my own way and live in town for a few months each year, but when I am bored, I run back to my darling Gaunt. Now who is to read next?'

Miss Wyckenham looked about her expectantly. Her eyes widened when a slim figure in grey satin made her way to the centre of the room.

'Miss Medway!' she exclaimed.

Lady Gaunt looked up and murmured, 'Then we are unlikely to hear comic verse.'

Looking through the crowd Clarissa saw Lady Medway seated in a far alcove, Lord Alresford at her side.

'I had not seen their party,' she confessed. 'I did not think Sarah was acquainted with them.'

'Most likely it is Sir Toby's doing,' said Emily, sitting close by. 'These little soirées are much more in his line and Sarah consults him on those to invite. I see Alresford is still dancing attendance. They say it is a match between him and little Florence Medway.'

Clarissa could not resist.

'He was engaged to her cousin, I think?'

'Yes: his poor bride died only days before the wedding.'

'Did you know her?'

'Elizabeth Medway? No.' She giggled. 'We were never introduced: she was far too virtuous for our company.'

Lady Gaunt raised her hand to indicate that the reading was

about to start. Miss Medway opened a large, leather-bound volume.

'I shall read to you from Mr Thomas Day's poem, *The Dying Negro*,' she began in a soft, well-modulated voice. 'As some of you will know, the poem was conceived some years ago, when Mr Day learned of a slave who killed himself rather than be sent back to the plantation.'

'Definitely *not* comic verse.' muttered Lady Gaunt, settling back in her seat.

Miss Medway read well and Clarissa listened, enthralled by the unravelling story of the Negro's abduction from Africa, the horrors of the plantation and his tranquil life in England, which was shattered when he was taken by slavers again. It was only when the reading came to an end that she realized the whole room had lapsed into a silence that continued for some moments after Miss Medway had closed her book. Then there was a burst of applause.

'Oh that was so affecting,' declared Lady Sarah, who had been standing close by during the recital. 'One wishes there was something to be done.'

'Give up sugar, to begin with,' said Sir Robert. 'If a protest interferes with trade, the government will take notice.'

Lady Sarah looked aghast, but her duties as hostess claimed her attention and she went off to encourage the next reader to take to the floor. He was a thin young man who shifted uncomfortably from one foot to the other while he ran a finger around his snowy neck-cloth.

'It is strange that Miss Medway should read that work because I, too, have chosen the same subject. If I may read to you a few lines from Mr James Grainger.'

'Even older than the previous poem,' murmured Lady Wyckenham.

The young man began his reading hesitantly but Miss Medway's impassioned rendition had prepared the way and his audience gave him their full attention, rewarding his efforts

with enthusiastic applause. Clarissa glanced at Lady Gaunt, sitting upright beside her. She was staring into space, one hand on the shoulder of her little page, who was kneeling at her feet. As one in a trance she repeated the lines from the poem, '. . . knock off the chains of heart-debasing slavery.' Her eyes dropped to the page's black curly hair. 'Yes, knock off the chains.'

Clarissa was about to ask her what she meant when Lady Wyckenham claimed her attention.

'My love, Sir Robert is escorting me into the supper-room, do you wish to come with us?'

'Thank you, Mama-Nell, I will sit here, if you do not object?'

As Lady Wyckenham went off on Sir Robert's arm, Emily Sowerby unfurled her fan.

'I do not see Sir Howard here this evening. How I wish we could have been with you at Norwell House, Clarissa, when you tricked him so finely. Dorothea told us all about it. Do you think he has left town, ma'am?'

She had to repeat the question before she gained Lady Gaunt's attention and even then that lady could only shrug.

'I have not seen him. Sally told me Sir Toby had invited him tonight.'

'Well, I do hope he is gone,' said Clarissa. 'So much more comfortable for Julia if he has retired to the country.'

Georgiana shuddered. 'Such an odious little man, and the Norwells have been transformed since your little trick, Dorothea. I saw Julia and her husband in Bond Street today. Barnabus was being most attentive.'

'Yes,' nodded Emily, 'And Julia was looking radiant. She positively *dotes* on Barnabus.'

'So it would seem we have done some good,' remarked Clarissa, relieved. 'I am so glad they are happy. Let us hope it deters Sir Howard from playing his little tricks on other poor women.'

'It may, for a while,' replied Lady Gaunt, 'but I doubt it will

be a permanent change.' She rose. 'Excuse me, I see Lady Martingale beckoning. . . .'

Emily and Georgiana moved away soon after and Clarissa was left alone. The crowd was thinning as the guests made their way to the supper-room and Clarissa decided she would go in search of Lady Wyckenham. She realized her fan had slipped from her lap and she was obliged to reach down to recover it from the floor. Her fingers had just clasped the fan when she became aware that a gentleman was standing in front of her. She noted the white silk stockings and buckled shoes and, as she straightened in her seat, her eyes travelled up over the biscuit-coloured knee-breeches to the midnight-blue coat, embroidered waistcoat and blindingly white neck-cloth. She continued to raise her eyes until she was looking at Lord Alresford's impassive countenance.

CHAPTER TWENTY-ONE

With the earl towering over her, memories of their last stormy meeting flooded through Clarissa, heating her cheeks.

'Miss Wyckenham.'

'Good evening, my lord.'

'You are alone, madam. May I escort you to supper?'

'No – I – that is, thank you, my lord, but I am not hungry.'

'If I may?'

Taking her silence as acquiescence he sat down beside her on the sofa. Clarissa found herself with nothing to say and after a few moments the earl broke the silence.

'You are enjoying the readings, Miss Wyckenham?'

'Yes, my lord. I was much struck by Miss Medway's recital.'

'Yes. She reads well, but I believe the subject matter made some of the audience uncomfortable.'

'As it should,' she replied. 'Slavery is surely an abhorrence to any free man or woman.'

'You think it should be abolished?'

'I do, yet I am at a loss to know how it is to be achieved: if slavery were to vanish overnight there would be such a void to fill: it is bound up with a great deal of our commerce, I think. There would be great opposition.'

The earl regarded her more closely.

'You have clearly given the matter some thought, ma'am.'

'Not as much as it deserves, but—' she broke off as Lady Medway and her daughter approached, and felt a pang of regret that her tête-à-tête with Lord Alresford had been interrupted.

The earl rose as the ladies approached, Lady Medway fluttering her fan towards him by way of a greeting.

'There you are, my lord. Florence was just wondering what had become of you. Miss Wyckenham, good evening to you.'

'How are you enjoying the evening, Miss Wyckenham?' asked Miss Medway with a sweet, false smile. 'No doubt the Sheridan was to your taste?'

Clarissa responded with a wide smile of her own.

'Of course, I always enjoy his work. May I congratulate you on your own performance, Miss Medway?'

The young lady lowered her eyes and gently smoothed her hands over her gown.

'Thank you, Miss Wyckenham. Mama was concerned it might be a little too . . . advanced for this evening: it is well known that Lady Sarah and her friends are more inclined to levity than serious discussion.'

Clarissa continued to smile, but her eyes glittered dangerously.

'Each has its place, Miss Medway. An unvaried diet of serious topics cannot be healthy: so ageing, do you not agree?'

The earl hurried into the breach.

'I believe Miss Wyckenham shares your sentiments on slavery, Miss Medway.'

Florence acknowledged this with no more than a lift of an eyebrow.

'Oh? Is that the fashionable view now? I had thought it a little too complicated for most ladies to comprehend fully.'

'Oh, what is complicated?' asked Lady Wyckenham coming up at that moment.

The earl bowed to her.

'We were speaking of abolitionism, ma'am.'

My lady nodded sagely.

'Ah, yes. You are right, then. A very weighty subject.'

'But not one ladies of any rank should ignore,' added Miss Medway. 'Yet I daresay there will be precious few at Mr Sharp's next meeting.'

'One has to be advised of an event before one can attend,' responded Lady Wyckenham, a gentle rebuke in her tone. 'Where was it announced?'

'Oh I am sure there was some report of it in the newspapers.' Lady Medway waved her hand in a vague way.

'It takes place on the fifteenth, above the Golden Lion in Eagle Street,' said Miss Medway. 'Holborn: not a venue to appeal to the fashionable.' She laid her hand on the earl's arm. 'Forgive me, my lord: we came to find you to go down to supper and I have been rattling on, quite forgetting my hunger, or mama's. Shall we go?'

Lord Alresford inclined his head and with a nod towards Clarissa he led his party away.

'Well!' Lady Wyckenham opened her fan with a snap. 'Such a display of self-righteousness.'

'Indeed, Mama-Nell, I fear Miss Medway thinks us very frippery creatures.'

'She is mistaken,' declared my lady. She beckoned to Lady Gaunt who was crossing the room with Emily and Georgiana.

102

'My dears, I hope you are free next week, on Thursday evening?'

The ladies looked at one another.

'There is a masked ball at the Pantheon,' said Georgiana, 'but we need not go.'

'And I had thought I would look in at Lady Somerton's rout,' added Lady Gaunt. 'But if you have something more interesting to offer, Helen. . . .'

'Something of a much more improving nature,' declared Lady Wyckenham, a martial light in her eye. 'On Thursday night the ladies of the Belles Dames Club will be attending Mr Sharp's meeting in Eagle Street.'

'Grenville Sharp, the reformer?' asked Emily.

'The very same,' affirmed my lady. 'We will be supporting his call to abolish slavery.'

There was a stunned silence, the ladies looked at each other, then Lady Gaunt laughed.

'Why not?' she said. 'It might be amusing. We must tell Sally.'

'But what should one wear?' cried Emily.

Clarissa gave a gurgle of laughter.

'Something incredibly dull, I think!'

CHAPTER TWENTY-TWO

'An abolitionist meeting, in Holborn?' Lady Sarah laughed. 'And I thought you could not possibly get up to any mischief tonight!'

'It is not mischief,' objected Lady Wyckenham. 'We are to attend a serious lecture.'

'Then, of course, I shall come with you!' was the prompt reply. 'I was afraid you would find my little evening very poor fare. The Belles Dames Club has been so adventurous recently that

I wanted Toby to go to Newgate and find me a notorious high-wayman to read for us tonight, but he would not hear of it.'

'Fie on you, Sally, to think we cannot enjoy a quiet evening of refinement.'

'Well, that's why I invited Mr Henderson to come and read for us – he has made Mr Cowper's comic poem *John Gilpin* all the rage you know, and has promised to perform it for us at the end of the evening. But it was Sir Toby who insisted on inviting the Medways, to lend a little gravitas to the event. Which they do: their dowdy colours make me feel positively gaudy, and I made such *efforts* to look serious tonight!'

Clarissa looked at Lady Sarah's olive-green gown and the snowy fichu around her shoulders. On any other lady the plain muslin with its long sleeves and white ruffles would have looked eminently sensible, but it merely enhanced Sarah's flaming hair and sparkling eyes. It was easy to understand why staid Sir Toby doted upon his lovely wife.

The guests seemed in no hurry to settle down for more poetry and Clarissa accompanied Lady Wyckenham around the room, meeting acquaintances and wondering idly if Lord Alresford was enjoying his supper when Mama-Nell's voice suddenly caught her attention.

'Clarissa, my love, here is Lord Ullenwood come to speak to us.'

Her head snapped round. The marquis held out his long white fingers and she gave him her hand, which he raised to his lips with practised ease. Clarissa studied more closely this man who was persecuting Mama-Nell. On their first meeting she had thought him much older, but now realized that despite the silver threads lacing through his thick, dark hair he was not yet above forty. His lean, handsome face was definitely attractive but she imagined that the mobile mouth could twist into a sneer as easily as a smile. There was a world-weariness about him, a languid manner that she felt sure was assumed.

'Lord Ullenwood.' Her tone was cool, for she was prepared to

dislike him and it came as something of a shock to realize the man's charm when he wished to use it; she was drawn to his deep, deep brown eyes.

'Delighted to meet you again, Miss Wyckenham.'

She put up her chin.

'I have learned a great deal about you since our last meeting, my lord.'

'Indeed?' Those dark eyes gleamed with amusement. 'Nothing too infamous, I hope.'

'Merely the truth, sir.'

Lady Wyckenham gave an audible gasp and rushed into speech.

'I-I did not think you a lover of poetry, Lord Ullenwood. You have missed the majority of the readings.'

He turned towards her.

'Yes, I did not realize it was so late. But no matter. I came here solely to see you, madam.'

Lady Wyckenham fanned herself vigorously.

'You flatter me, sir.'

'No, I merely wanted to remind you that we have a little matter of – ah – unfinished business to discuss.'

'My, my, Lord Ullenwood, how mysterious you make it sound,' remarked Clarissa.

He looked at her.

'And what do you know of the matter, Miss Wyckenham?'

Clarissa returned his gaze steadily, her own dark eyes challenging.

'I know enough to tell you that my stepmama is not one to be bullied, sir.'

'Cl-Clarissa you mistake,' muttered Lady Wyckenham.

'Indeed you do, Miss Wyckenham. I have no intention of – ah – bullying anyone. Merely I am anxious to resolve our differences.' The marquis smiled. 'As Lady Wyckenham observed, I do not often attend these soirées, but upon occasion I have even been known to read something of my own. When the spirit

moves me, I can be persuaded. My own inclination runs towards the sonnets, or . . . love letters.'

Lady Wyckenham paled. She gripped Clarissa's arm.

'You would not!'

Clarissa felt the breath catch in her throat as she looked from her stepmother to the marquis. Their eyes were locked: Mama-Nell's imploring, Lord Ullenwood's implacable.

'No,' he said at last. 'I would not . . . tonight.' He bowed. 'Come, ma'am. Let us not quarrel. I am here to tell you that I am planning to leave town shortly. We will need to resolve our . . . little problem before then.'

With a smile and a bow he walked away and Lady Wyckenham gave a shuddering sigh.

'You heard him, Clarissa. He wants an answer.'

'And that answer must be no, Mama-Nell. We shall wrest the letters from him!'

'But how?'

'I don't know: I must consult Lady Gaunt. After all she found a solution to Julia Norwell's problem.'

'But Lord Ullenwood is no Sir Howard. He is a much more dangerous adversary.'

'Then we must be much more clever,' retorted Clarissa. She patted the small hand still gripping her arm. 'You must not worry, Mama-Nell. We shall come about, you'll see.'

CHAPTER TWENTY-THREE

Having decided to admit the members of the Belles Dames Club into her confidence, Lady Wyckenham was anxious to call a meeting, but it was a full week before they could convene. In

the meantime she showed no sign of her anxiety as she went about her daily business. She drove out with Sir Robert, went to the theatre with Clarissa and spent a few hours each day in her attic studio, working on the two plant specimens Sir Robert had given her to paint. At such times she found she could forget for a while the threat hanging over her.

She saw Lord Ullenwood only once, at a masquerade. The variety of costumes and disguises prevented her from recognizing the Marquis until she was going down the line with him in a country dance.

'I know you,' he said, following the accepted mode of address. 'You look enchanting tonight, my lady. What are you – Queen Mab?' His eyes raked over her green silk with its overdress of gossamer gauze.

'Titania,' she answered, recovering from the shock of recognition. The marquis was dressed as a pirate, complete with a full-bottomed wig and a leather eye-patch. Very appropriate, she thought bitterly, but as the dance separated them at that moment she had no opportunity to tell him so. He came to find her shortly after, and insisted on escorting her down to supper.

Clarissa watched her stepmother leaving the room and did not doubt the identity of her piratical companion. Lord Ullenwood's behaviour roused her indignation but she admitted to herself that there was little to be done until the letters had been retrieved. A voice at her side recalled her attention.

'Do I know you, madam?'

She looked round to find Sir Robert Ingleton at her side, easily recognizable despite his disguise.

'Well, sir, do you know me?' she asked, watching him through the slits in her own golden mask.

He gave her his charming, crooked grin.

'Indeed I do, Miss Wyckenham, but what is this? You are dressed as a goddess, yet your countenance suggests you are

about to demand a human sacrifice.'

She chuckled.

'Was I frowning so direfully, Sir Robert? My thoughts were many miles away. And I am one of the Muses, you see.' She pointed to the golden lyres embroidered on the skirts of her robe. She cast an admiring glance at his costume. 'And what are you – Sir Frances Drake? How appropriate.'

'I thought so. But you are evading my question: will you not tell me what caused such a frown to crease your brow?'

Despite her stepmama's outright refusal to involve him, Clarissa was tempted to tell him of Lady Wyckenham's letters – but only for a moment. Instead, she said, 'I wish it was you taking Mama-Nell down to supper! She has gone off on the arm of Lord Ullenwood.'

Sir Robert spread his hands.

'Alas, my lady refused me. Having danced twice together she did not want to attract attention.'

'Oh I am sorry: yet I know she likes you above all others.'

'Thank you. I wish I could believe that.'

She put out her hand.

'It is true. Perhaps she is a little unsure of her own heart, but no one seeing you together could doubt that she adores you.'

'Do you really think so?'

'Yes, truly.' She sighed. 'I think you should ride up one day and whisk her away.'

'Much as I would like to do so, I fear such behaviour would be frowned upon in our civilized times.' He glanced over his shoulder. 'Ah, I see I am about to be ousted by an eastern caliph!'

Clarissa saw Lord Alresford approaching, dressed in an exotic eastern costume. He bowed stiffly.

'Excuse me. I came, Miss Wyckenham, to beg the honour of the next dance with you, if you are not engaged?'

'And I am very much in the way, am I not?' said Sir Robert. 'I shall away to sail the seven seas!' With a wicked grin and a wink at Clarissa he sauntered off.

Lord Alresford stood looking down at her, and Clarissa sought for something to break the uncomfortable silence.

'I did not expect to see you here, my lord.'

'Lady Norwell persuaded me to come – Barnabus is here too, with his wife,' he added, before she could ask him the question. 'They are dancing together at this moment.'

'I am glad.' She glanced at his costume. 'An eastern potentate, my lord?'

'It was Lady Norwell's idea. She refused to let me wear a domino.' He smiled at her and for one heart-stopping moment Clarissa remembered their meeting in the wood, when he had opened his eyes and looked at her. She found herself smiling back, quite forgetting everything else until he held out his arm.

'The next dance is about to start, Miss Wyckenham. Shall we?'

The spell was broken. She was back in the ballroom.

'Of course, my lord. Though I fear we shall make an odd couple.'

The earl took his place opposite her, bowing as the music began.

'Are we really so far apart, Miss Wyckenham?'

They circled, bowed, turned, passed, clasped hands, came together and moved apart. Clarissa had never experienced such a dance. Perhaps it was the exotic costumes, but each touch of the earl's ungloved fingers sent a tingle running through her skin. Her senses were heightened: she was vividly aware of every note played, every step danced. The garish colours of her partner's dress dazzled her: she heard the laughter around her but she found herself speechless, and danced in silence with her partner. Never had a country dance seemed so long, yet when the music stopped she felt it was too soon.

'Have you eaten, Miss Wyckenham, may I escort you to supper?'

She nodded, wanting to prolong these new sensations for as long as she could.

'I – um,' she swallowed and tried again. 'Will you be joining Lady Norwell's party next week, my lord? I believe – that is, Julia told me – she is engaged to attend Lady Maramond's rout on Tuesday.'

She had to repeat her question, for the earl seemed distracted.

'Lady Maramond? I-I am not sure – yes, I think . . . will you be there?'

'Lady Wyckenham intends to go, sir, and I shall accompany her.'

'Then, yes, I shall be there.' He looked round. 'Barnabus is calling, they want us to join them – do you object?'

As he led her over to Lady Norwell's table Clarissa did not know whether to be glad or sorry: she felt bewildered by the emotions raging within her. However, the necessity of making polite conversation with Julia and Lady Norwell proved calming and when Lord Alresford returned her to the ballroom she had regained much of her serene manner, and her fingers trembled only a little as his lips brushed across them.

A grey dawn was breaking when Lady Wyckenham's carriage made its way back to Charlotte Street and, as they rattled over the cobbles, Mama-Nell apologized to Clarissa for leaving her alone for most of the evening. Clarissa was quick to respond.

'Pray do not make yourself uneasy, ma'am,' she said 'There were so many friends and acquaintances present that I was never lonely, I assure you.'

'I know, my love, but much as I adore masquerades I am well aware that many use it as an excuse to behave with impropriety.'

Thinking of her dance with Lord Alresford, Clarissa realized how easily she could have been led into impropriety herself, had the gentleman been willing. She found herself sighing.

'I was never subjected to anything of that nature, Mama-Nell.'

'It was not what I had planned,' continued my lady fretfully, 'but Lord Ullenwood monopolized me for so much of the evening.'

'I saw him take you down to supper.'

Lady Wyckenham shuddered.

'I did not wish it; indeed, I would have refused him, but—'

'I know, Mama-Nell. The letters.' Clarissa hesitated, then said slowly, 'I talked with Sir Robert Ingleton this evening: I wanted so much to tell him about the marquis.'

'Clarissa, you did not!'

'No, Mama-Nell, but I feel sure if he knew—'

'If he knew he would despise me!' cried Lady Wyckenham. 'I could not bear that.'

'Then you *do* care for him.'

For several moments there was silence.

'Yes, I do,' whispered Lady Wyckenham at last. 'But until those letters are destroyed I will not tell him so.'

'But he might be able to help you.'

'Really, Clarissa. I am no blushing maiden, begging to be rescued from every little predicament.'

'This is hardly a *little predicament*, Mama-Nell.'

'All the more reason not to involve Sir Robert,' retorted my lady. 'I am a grown woman, and will extricate myself from this mess – with the help of my friends, of course.'

CHAPTER TWENTY-FOUR

When the ladies of the Belles Dames Club met again it was at Lady Gaunt's house in Grosvenor Square, the Viscountess declaring that she was far too fatigued to put on a mask again

that week and that everyone should come to her.

Lady Wyckenham and Clarissa duly arrived at the Gaunt mansion, suitably enveloped from head to toe in their dominos. They were shown into the drawing-room by Grantham, and Clarissa immediately noticed that their hostess's little black page was missing. When she enquired, Lady Gaunt merely smiled.

'Samuel? I have sent him up to bed. The novelty wears off, you see, as with anything.' She directed a lively glance at Clarissa. 'Besides, young Grantham is so much more useful, don't you think? He has adapted very well to his – ah – duties. Of course, I do not let him clean the silver. It makes the hands so terribly rough, I understand.'

Clarissa laughed.

'Dorothea, you are incorrigible. What will the Viscount say when he finds out?'

'Oh when he returns to town I shall send Grantham off to make his way in the world: just now he is accumulating a nice little sum towards his – ah – retirement.' She broke off as more members of the club arrived and as soon as they were all assembled, she dismissed the servants and the ladies divested themselves of their masks with a collective sigh of relief.

Clarissa lost no time in explaining the reason for the meeting. As she had expected, the ladies were all eager to help Lady Wyckenham, but not one of them could offer a way to recover the letters. Lady Gaunt's heavy lids drooped as she pondered the problem.

'Ullenwood is not unattractive,' she mused. 'Perhaps I should seduce him.'

Julia stared at her with wide-eyed innocence.

'Would he give you the letters?'

Lady Gaunt shrugged her white shoulders and said wickedly, 'I have no idea.'

The ladies laughed, but Alicia Greynard's little hand formed itself into a fist and she banged on the arm of her chair.

'The man is wholly unprincipled,' she said fiercely. 'He should be punished for putting poor Helen through this torment. If I had my way I'd – I'd rip out his tongue!'

'That is hardly the way to make him tell you where the letters are,' retorted Letitia Leighton-Kettering 'Come, ladies, let us be sensible. He told Helen his letters were in a bank vault: do we know his bankers?'

Lady Wyckenham blinked at her.

'Heavens, Letitia, do you mean to break in and steal my letters?'

'Of course not, my dear, but between us we might know someone within the bank, a nephew, perhaps, or a relative of one of our servants?'

Sally Matlock nodded.

'That is very good, Letitia. We must discover which bank he uses.'

'And how do we do that?' demanded Lady Wyckenham. 'Surely you do not expect me to ask him?'

'No, no, Helen,' said Letitia. 'I think that we should ask our menfolk. No need to tell them why we want to know.'

'I will ask Barnabus,' said Julia, 'but he is not of Lord Ullenwood's set.'

'Neither is Toby,' said Lady Sarah, 'but perhaps if I am very nice to him he would ask his friends – discreetly, of course.'

Lady Gaunt nodded.

'Very well. We will try to discover his bank.'

Mrs Flooke had been pondering the problem, and now she said, 'Even if we could find his vault, I do not see how we could get into it, not without breaking the law.'

A despondent silence filled the room.

'Well,' said Lady Gaunt at last, 'first let us see what we can discover. After all, it is the only plan we have at the moment.'

'There is another way,' said Lady Wyckenham unhappily. 'I could agree to his terms.'

This brought such a vehement chorus of disagreement that

my lady threw up her hands. 'But I do not have much time: I have to give him an answer before the end of the month!'

Lady Gaunt nodded. 'We must move quickly. We will all be at Augusta's rout on Tuesday: we will meet there to report our progress.'

The meeting broke up early, the ladies promising to make what enquiries they could concerning Lord Ullenwood. They all left Grosvenor Square in reflective mood but Clarissa at least refused to be downhearted.

'We will come about, Mama-Nell, you will see,' she said stoutly. 'The ladies of the Belles Dames Club will not allow one man to defeat them.'

Across the darkened carriage she heard her stepmama's tinkling laugh and hoped that she had raised her spirits at least a little.

They did not speak again until the carriage pulled up in Charlotte Street, but when they walked into the hall, Lady Wyckenham looked about her in bewilderment at the unaccustomed activity. Two footmen were heaving a large trunk up the stairs and the butler was giving instructions to a third for the disposal of the various small bags and boxes that littered the hall.

'Simmons, what on earth is happening?'

'Lord Wyckenham has arrived, ma'am.'

'William, here?' squeaked my lady.

Simmons allowed himself a rare, fatherly smile.

'Indeed, ma'am. He arrived not five minutes since. He is in the drawing-room, madam.'

Lady Wyckenham stared at Clarissa.

'Now what on earth can have brought your brother to town?'

'I have no idea, Mama-Nell, but I will go to him immediately.'

'Yes, do,' said my lady, accompanying her up the stairs. 'I shall speak to Mrs Simmons, to make sure the best bedcham-

ber is prepared for him. Make my excuses, Clarissa, and tell William I shall join you both directly.'

CHAPTER TWENTY-FIVE

'William, my dear. This is such a surprise!' Clarissa hurried forward, hands outstretched towards her brother. 'But it is too bad of you, why did you not send word that you were coming, and we would have been here to meet you?'

Lord Wyckenham bent to place a chaste kiss upon her expectant cheek. He was a tall, spare gentleman, some ten years older than Clarissa. His dark colouring was the sum total of the likeness between brother and sister. His demeanour was serious and he had developed a manner that he liked to call statesmanlike, but which his sister thought pompous. However, she was fond of her brother and she embraced him in an impetuous fashion that made him wince.

'Good evening, Clarissa. I hope I do not need to wait for an invitation to visit my own house?'

'Of course not, but we would not have gone out, had we known you were coming, and Mama-Nell would have given orders for your rooms to be prepared. As it is, she is gone now to speak to Mrs Simmons and will join us after. While we wait, William, will you not sit down, or perhaps you would like me to order you supper?'

'Thank you but no, on both counts. I have been travelling since dawn and stopped to dine on the road.' He exhaled and said repressively, 'I have come directly from Bath.'

Clarissa's eyes twinkled.

'That is as I would expect, Brother, since you wrote to tell us

you were going there a week ago. Is your business complete now?'

'No, but I was obliged to postpone it following the alarming reports I have received.'

'My dear William, is Mr Pitt's government about to fall? Does that mean you will not be assured of a place in the next cabinet?'

'Clarissa, I do wish you would not treat everything with such levity, it is most unbecoming. The reports concern Lady Wyckenham.'

'Mama-Nell?' Clarissa's immediate thought was that Lord Ullenwood had published the damning letters, but common sense told her it could not be so.

'Yes. I have been most shocked by what I heard in Bath.'

She sat down and folded her hands in her lap, saying cautiously, 'And what have you heard, Brother?'

For a long moment he looked down at her, frowning, until Clarissa said with a touch of impatience, 'My dear William, I am three and twenty, I am no longer a child. If you are wondering whether your revelations will shock me, you may be easy.'

His frown deepened and he began to pace the carpet, his hands clasped behind his back.

'There are rumours,' he said, 'that our stepmother has started a club – a clandestine group – exclusively for females. *The Belles Dames Club.*' His mouth twisted in distaste.

'Indeed? And how comes it that you have heard of it, William, if it is so secret?'

'Things have a way of becoming known, Sister. If members of this club do not speak of it you may be sure their servants will talk. Of course, it is unlikely that you know anything of this matter, but you may have seen some of its members here – I understand Mrs Flooke and her sister attend regularly, as does Viscountess Gaunt and Lady Sarah Matlock. All married women. They have nothing in common with you, my dear.'

Clarissa felt her temper rising at his complaisant tone.

'It so happens that I *do* know of this, William. I am a member.'

He stopped pacing to stare at her, open-mouthed.

'Do you mean to tell me that – that our stepmother has drawn you into her nefarious activities?'

'There is nothing nefarious about it: we meet for our own amusement, that's all.'

'Amusement!' Two spots of colour burned on his cheeks. 'It is all over Bath that Mama-in-law has turned her house into a gaming hell.'

'Oh, William, how like you to listen to tittle-tattle and give it credence! It is nothing of the sort. You refine too much upon it.'

'Oh do I? Well, Sis, do you know what they are calling this club? Not the Belles Dames Club, I can tell you! No, it's the Bedlam Club, which is not at all the same thing!'

'No, it is mere mischief-making. I assure you, William, it is all very innocent.' Clarissa crossed her fingers in the folds of her gown.

'Well, I cannot like it, Sister, and so I shall tell Mama-Nell. And if she persists in this nonsense then I shall send you off to live with your Aunt Fanny in Deal.'

Clarissa stared at him, horrified. Lady Wyckenham's musical voice broke the tense silence.

'William, my love, I am sorry I have been so long, but your trunks had been taken to the guest room, you know, and I have had everything moved to the Blue room. After all, it was your father's bedchamber and yours now, by right.' She came forward as she spoke, holding out her hands to him. As he bent to kiss her fingers, the look she gave Clarissa over his head was brimful of merriment.

Lord Wyckenham straightened and said stiffly, 'Thank you, madam. I shall not be staying many nights.'

'But this is very sudden, my dear.' Lady Wyckenham sank down on to a sofa and disposed her skirts about her. 'From your

last letter I made sure you would be in Bath at least until June.'

'And I should be there now, madam, if I had not been so disturbed by the reports I have received.'

'Oh dear,' my lady was all sympathy. 'How tiresome for you.'

'It is indeed, ma'am, and worrying, too, since these reports concern you.'

She fixed him with her limpid blue eyes.

'Me? My dear William, what on earth have I to do with anything?'

As he fought to control his indignation, Clarissa said gently, 'William has heard of the Belles Dames Club, Mama-Nell.'

'Oh is that all?' exclaimed Lady Wyckenham, her brow clearing.

'No, ma'am, that is not all,' snapped William. 'The tales that reached me have been of a most shocking nature.'

'You have been listening to gossip, William. Never advisable, and Bath is the very worst place for it. I think it is because there are so many sick people there, with nothing better to do.'

Lord Wyckenham strode up to the sofa and stood, towering over his stepmother.

'Do you deny, madam, that you have formed this – this club?'

'No, William, of course not.'

'And that your members meet here, in secret?'

She smiled up at him.

'Well, we did wish to be discreet, but it can hardly be a secret, my love, if you learned of it in Bath.'

He drew a breath and made a visible effort to speak calmly.

'Mama-Nell, it will not do! This club is the *on-dit* of the moment – the most scandalous stories abound, and now Clarissa tells me that you have made her a party to it all.'

'She is a grown woman, and I could not very well exclude her, but I do not see the need for you to post all the way from Bath, my love, on the strength of these rumours. If you had written to me I should have been happy to enlighten you.'

'I do not wish to be enlightened, madam. I came here to tell you that these meetings must stop. I will not have the family name so – so *besmirched*.'

Lady Wyckenham laughed.

'William, I hardly think my little meetings will dishonour the family name. I am disappointed that you are so ready to believe everything you hear of me.'

'Very well, madam: explain to me about your club. What is your reason for it?'

'Education,' she replied promptly.

He regarded her suspiciously.

'And what of these rumours of the gambling hell you have set up in my house?'

Lady Wyckenham smiled.

'My dear boy, do you really think I would do such a thing? Search the house if you wish; better still, you shall come with us tomorrow night, and see just how scandalous the Belles Dames Club really is. We are off to Holborn.'

'Holborn!'

'Yes, to attend a lecture given by Mr Sharp on the abolition of slavery.'

'Sharp, you say? Granville Sharp? He is one of the Clapham Saints – Evangelical Anglicans,' he added, observing Clarissa's blank look.

'You know more of the speaker than we do, Brother.'

'Yes, well, I cannot see that there is anything reprehensible about such a lecture, apart from the location.'

'Which is why we shall be very glad of your escort, William.' My lady rose. 'Now, it is late and you must be wishing for your bed, so we will leave you. Come, Clarissa.'

She sailed from the room and Clarissa followed her. As they mounted the stairs my lady allowed a sigh to escape her.

'It was inevitable that the word would get about, but it is very unfortunate that William has learned of it so soon. Oh, why could he not stay snug at home in Devon? Bath has always

been a hot-bed for scandal and rumour.'

'I fear he is very much shocked, Mama-Nell. He has threatened to send me off to Deal to live with my aunt.'

Lady Wyckenham chuckled at that.

'Poor William has never liked my influence on you, my love. We can only hope that the sobriety of tomorrow night's meeting will convince him that I am a worthy guardian for you.'

'Pho, madam, let him think what he will. I am of age, and free to make my own decisions.'

'Of course you are, Clarissa. Nevertheless, we must be more circumspect while your brother is in town.' She giggled. 'It could have been worse, however. Think of his shock if he had met Fleet-fingered Poll here!'

CHAPTER TWENTY-SIX

The Wyckenham carriage came to a halt in Eagle Street and Lord Wyckenham looked out dubiously at the Golden Lion Tavern.

'The meeting is above here?'

'Yes, I believe it is,' said Lady Wyckenham.

The footman let down the steps and they descended to the road. There was no crossing sweeper and they were obliged to pick their way through the rubbish to the entrance. As they reached the doorway a second carriage drew up. Lady Gaunt's footman, Grantham, jumped out and let down the steps then stood back, straightening his waistcoat and looking very smug: Clarissa tried not to think about what had been going on in that closed carriage.

Lady Wyckenham had spent the morning scribbling notes to

all the ladies, warning them of the addition to their party, so Lady Gaunt showed no surprise at finding Lord Wyckenham waiting for her.

With little ceremony they made their way upstairs to find the rest of the Belles Dames Club had already arrived. Lady Gaunt drew Clarissa away as the ladies took a moment to greet Lord Wyckenham.

'Well,' she mused, 'at least our sober dress must meet with his approval.'

Clarissa lifted her fan to hide her smile.

'It could not have been more fortuitous.'

She glanced around her. The room was a large one, and had once been a handsome apartment, but the paintwork was badly faded and there was a distinct smell of dust and stale beer. Wooden benches and chairs had been placed in rows across the floor while on a raised dais at one end of the room stood a table and several more chairs. Two scholarly-looking gentlemen were standing by the table: Clarissa guessed that one of them would be the speaker, Granville Sharp. The room was filling up and a sudden flurry of activity heralded the entrance of Sir Gordon Medway's party.

Clarissa watched them enter, Sir Gordon with his wife on his arm while his daughter was escorted by Lord Alresford. Sir Gordon made his way towards the dais, obviously well acquainted with the speaker. Lord Alresford looked about him as the pleasantries were exchanged. His eyes alighted on Clarissa, she smiled and was rewarded by a small bow in her direction. He did not smile, but she was well enough acquainted with him to note the softening of his countenance as he looked at her: she was sure he was glad to see her there and she was unaccountably warmed by the knowledge. Any social discourse had to wait, for one of the gentlemen was calling the meeting to order. Lord Wyckenham and the ladies of the Belles Dames Club chose seats at the back of the room, but there was no shortage of chairs and by the time the meeting started the

room was little more than half full. Most were soberly dressed and looked to be traders or clergymen. Apart from Lady Medway and her daughter, the Belles Dames Club were the only ladies present. Lady Gaunt's footman, Grantham, remained by the door, declining to sit in the presence of his mistress, even in such a liberal gathering.

Clarissa gave her attention to the speaker, Granville Sharp. He was a thin-faced man of about fifty years of age who spoke eloquently on the legal rights of the slaves, their iniquitous treatment on board the slave ships and the growing number of former slaves in London who had fought for the British during the American War. From a large trunk on the table he produced iron handcuffs, leg-shackles and thumb screws which were used to subdue the slaves during their journey across the Atlantic. Even from a distance Clarissa could not suppress a shudder at the images he conjured for his audience. Concluding his talk, he indicated the pile of pamphlets by the door, asking everyone to take one, read it, pass it on. He urged them to join his society for effecting the abolition of the African slave trade.

As the audience politely applauded him at the end of the speech, Clarissa leaned closer to her brother.

'This is a cause worthy of your support, William.'

'Perhaps, perhaps.'

People were leaving, filing out of the door and talking in subdued tones as they went. Lord Wyckenham left his party and made his way to the dais to talk to Granville Sharp. Clarissa followed the other ladies towards the door. Their progress was necessarily slow for the ladies were eager to discuss all they had heard. She saw Lord Alresford making his way towards her until they were separated by no more than a row of chairs.

'I hope you found the evening enlightening, Miss Wyckenham?'

'Yes, my lord, and disturbing. No one could listen to such a

speaker and fail to be moved. You are a supporter of the cause, sir?'

'Very much so. I was bringing papers from Cambridge to Mr Sharp when we first met.'

Clarissa looked up, surprised that he should mention an event that she considered so particularly their own. Miss Medway's appearance at his side seemed an unwelcome intrusion.

'Lord Alresford has been one of Mr Sharp's staunchest allies, has he not, Mama? Long before it became *fashionable* to support the cause of abolition.'

Clarissa let the barb pass. She saw her brother was looking at her and beckoned him to join her, a hint of mischief in her voice as she begged to be allowed to present him to Lady Medway.

'It was Miss Medway who encouraged us to come along this evening,' she added.

Lord Wyckenham bowed.

'Indeed? Then I am most grateful, Miss Medway. It was a most instructive evening: I don't know when I have heard a more engaging speaker on this subject. . . .'

Clarissa moved away to join her stepmother.

'My dear, what are you about to make William known to that woman and her daughter?' hissed Lady Wyckenham.

'I know, it was very bad of me, but I thought they deserved each other.' Clarissa glanced back to the little group where William was talking earnestly to Miss Medway while Sir Gordon, Lady Medway and Lord Alresford stood at a distance. 'I love my brother dearly, but I find his lecturing very tiresome and thought it a good idea that someone else should have their share: if Miss Medway isn't yawning behind her hand by now then I will admire her fortitude!'

'Clarissa, how can you be so cruel?' retorted Lady Wyckenham, trying not to laugh. Everyone else had gone, and they waited for William to finish his conversation. At last he

came over and made their way downstairs together. The landlord was waiting at the door for them. He tugged his forelock and addressed William.

'All the others are gone, my lord, savin' your own party and Sir Gordon's. You'd best wait in here until your carriage is at the door. There's a crowd outside that's got wind o' the meeting and they're ready for mischief. They won't come too close, but you'd be better to stay indoors.'

William looked alarmed, but Sir Gordon stepped forward.

'It's what we've come to expect,' he said. 'The ignorant and uneducated do not realize that we are working for the good.'

'I think it more likely they are incited by those who are not so ignorant,' remarked Lord Alresford. 'The slave-traders have no wish to see Mr Sharp's cause succeed.'

'You mean, they pay people to disrupt the meetings?' said Clarissa.

'Aye, Miss Wyckenham, frequently,' said Sir Gordon. 'You will not have noticed, but we had a couple of the landlord's lads keeping watch on the entrance this evening, to make sure no hecklers came in, but we cannot stop them gathering on the street.' He looked up. 'Ah, here's the carriage now. My dear . . . Florence, be ready.'

Sir Gordon's coachman brought the carriage as close as he could to the door. Lady Medway took her husband's arm and hurried out of the inn. Immediately the shouting and jeering increased. Lord Alresford took Miss Medway's arm, but, as they moved towards the inn door, William stepped forward.

'With your permission, madam, I will come with you to your carriage: you will feel safer with a gentleman on either side of you.'

'William, where are you going?' cried Lady Wyckenham.

Clarissa squeezed her arm. 'He is only seeing Miss Medway safely to her carriage, Mama-Nell.'

As they watched, Lord Alresford followed Miss Medway into the coach and William slammed the door shut. He ducked away

as a clod of earth flew past his head, but to Clarissa's relief no one came near enough to accost him.

'The landlord's men must be keeping them at a distance,' she muttered, as much to herself as to her stepmother.

William shouted to the coachman to drive on. Almost immediately the Wyckenham carriage took its place. The footman leapt down and opened the door and it was the work of a few moments for William and the landlord to escort the two ladies to the coach. William jumped in, slamming the door behind him and seconds later they heard the thud of something hitting the side of the carriage. Through the window they could see a small crowd of men and boys in the road, but although their jeers were menacing but they did not attempt to approach. Clarissa found herself holding her breath until the carriage was moving along Eagle Street at a smart pace.

'Thank goodness they are hurling nothing more damaging than earth,' said Lord Wyckenham, taking off his hat to examine it.

'Well,' remarked Lady Wyckenham, directing a quizzical gaze towards him, 'I hope you are satisfied, William: that was by far the most dangerous meeting yet of the Belles Dames Club!'

CHAPTER TWENTY-SEVEN

The Belles Dames Club was much affected by Mr Sharp's impassioned lecture and it was the subject of conversation for days afterwards. However, the ladies could not think how best to promote the cause of anti-slavery, and with the exception of Lady Gaunt, who declared that she was sending little Samuel away to school in preparation for making him a free man, the

cause was largely forgotten by the time the ladies convened at Lady Maramond's rout. They had slipped away into a small ante-chamber provided by their hostess to discuss the much more pressing problem of Lady Wyckenham's letters.

'I must not stay long,' said Augusta Maramond. 'I must attend to my guests, and my cousin, Neville Shirley has arrived most unexpectedly. He is a sea captain,' she added, with a touch of pride. 'We see him but rarely, since he sails out of Bristol, but occasionally he comes to town on business.'

'Very well,' said Lady Wyckenham, sinking down on to a sofa. 'Let us be as quick as we can. After all, we do not want to raise any more speculation than necessary.'

'So, what news do we have?' asked Lady Gaunt, looking around the room.

A depressing silence fell until Lady Maramond lifted her hand.

'I have discovered Lord Ullenwood's bankers,' she said. 'It was purely coincidence, for we were dropping our cousin at Coutts today and as we pulled up in the Strand, the marquis appeared at the door to the bank. He was being shown out by an important-looking gentleman and there was much bowing as he left.' Lady Maramond gave a little laugh. 'Neville said that Lord Ullenwood must be making a deposit, because he would not get such treatment, since he would be taking money *out*.'

Lady Gaunt nodded.

'Good. So we know he banks with Coutts. How can we gain access to his account do you think?'

'If Augusta's cousin is a client there perhaps he can help us,' suggested Lady Sarah.

'No, no, Neville is not a client, Sally. He merely had letters of introduction from one of his investors. Apparently they need a few days to verify the papers before they will hand over any money.'

'Are there any other ideas?' asked Lady Gaunt.

This time the silence was complete.

'Perhaps we could make more enquiries,' offered Letitia Leighton-Kettering.

'And just what do we do then?' demanded Lady Wyckenham, spreading her hands. 'Even if we found someone who worked for Coutts Bank we could not ask them to break open Lord Ullenwood's strongbox. It is hopeless.'

'There is another plan.'

All eyes turned to Lady Gaunt. She paused to take a pinch of snuff.

'We will make the marquis think that you agree to his terms, Helen. He will give you the letters and once you have destroyed them, you will be free.'

'No.' Lady Wyckenham shook her head sadly. 'Lord Ullenwood will not give me the letters until he is sure of me.'

'Then you must persuade him that you are in earnest. Once you have the letters safe we will ensure that you do not fall into his clutches.'

'And how will we do that, Dorothea?'

'With force, if necessary,' returned Lady Gaunt. 'We will kidnap you.'

Lady Sarah laughed, but Alicia Greynard gave a little moan.

'Oh do not worry, Alicia, there will be no danger,' said Lady Gaunt. 'It is quite simple: Helen will agree to elope with the marquis on the understanding that he hands over the letters at the start of the journey. As soon as the letters are destroyed we will strike. Which of you can ride astride? Georgiana, Emily? Good, I thought as much.'

'I can,' said Julia unexpectedly.

'Excellent. That will be four of us.'

'I have never done so,' murmured Lady Maramond, looking anxious. 'I do not think I could do so now.'

'It will not be necessary, Augusta. I think four will be suffi-cient for what I have in mind.'

'And just what is that, Dorothea?' demanded Lady Wycken-ham.

127

'We will dress as highwaymen and hold up the coach to rescue you.'

'Impossible!' declared Lady Wyckenham.

'Is it?' asked Lady Gaunt. 'If you play your part convincingly, Helen, we can trick the marquis finely.'

'But I would have to – to *lie* to him.'

Lady Gaunt's finely pencilled brows rose.

'Is that too high a price to pay for your freedom?'

'N-no, but . . . I am not happy about it.'

'Well I think it is a capital plan!' declared Lady Sarah and was noisily supported by Mrs Flooke and her sister, who declared themselves very ready to don men's clothing.

'I am afraid that I share Helen's doubts,' said Lady Maramond.

'And I,' said Mrs Leighton-Kettering. 'It is fraught with difficulties.'

Clarissa found Lady Gaunt's attention fixed upon her.

'What is your opinion, Clarissa, are you too squeamish for this adventure?'

'Oh, I have no qualms about using tricks upon this villain.' She sighed. 'What other choice do we have?'

'Then it is agreed: we will hold up the coach.'

'And what of the rest of us?' demanded Augusta. 'If you four are dressed as men, what shall *we* do?'

'You will be needed as look-outs: but you must stay out of sight.'

'There is no need for you all to be there,' said Lady Wyckenham.

There was a general outcry at this, and Clarissa was touched by the way the ladies wanted to support Mama-Nell, even those who had reservations.

'No, Dorothea, I cannot let you do this,' said Lady Wyckenham. 'There is too much risk.'

'But Mama-Nell,' said Clarissa, 'there is no other way.'

My lady looked helplessly at her stepdaughter. Lady

Maramond rose.

'Well, you know I do not like the plan, but if we can think of nothing better then we must attempt it. In fact, it will be quite exciting! Now, I must go. Let me know what you decide.' She slipped out of the room and the other ladies looked at one another.

'We must not delay too long,' said Mrs Leighton-Kettering. 'We should leave here one or two at a time, to avoid suspicion.'

'So are we agreed?' demanded Lady Gaunt.

There was a general murmur of assent and the ladies rose to leave. Only Lady Wyckenham looked unsure. Mrs Leighton-Kettering came forward and took her hand.

'Helen? It really is up to you, you know.'

'Oh Letitia, I know, but it is such a risk! What if you were caught?'

Lady Gaunt snapped open her fan.

'Even if Lord Ullenwood should suspect the truth, do you think he would let it be known that he was bested by a group of females?'

'Quite true,' Letitia nodded. 'From what I know of the marquis he is very proud – if he were to have the authorities pursue us then he may be sure we would make known his infamy. Come, ma'am, we want to help – you know you would do as much for any one of us.'

'Oh . . . very well.'

'I knew you would see sense in the end, Helen.' Lady Gaunt kissed her cheek. 'You must leave everything to me. We will meet tomorrow to decide upon a suitable spot for you to meet the marquis. Shall we call on you?'

'No, it is best perhaps if we meet somewhere else, while William is staying with me. I know he is rarely at home, but I would not have him discover our plans.'

'New Bond Street then,' suggested Lady Sarah. 'There can be nothing suspicious in a group of ladies meeting *there*.'

'So Lord Wyckenham is still with you,' said Georgiana, cast-

ing a pitying glance at Clarissa.

'Yes, although why I do not know,' said Lady Wyckenham bitterly. 'Unless it is to spy on me! He insists there will be no more meetings at Charlotte Street. Except of course, for my little party next Thursday; not even William can object to you all coming to that.'

'Well, Helen, it *is* his house,' Letitia Leighton-Kettering reminded her gently.

'Perhaps you should set up our own establishment, my dear,' suggested Lady Gaunt.

'If I decide to stay in town, Dorothea, I think I shall. However, I have a mind to go abroad again.' She threw a resentful look towards the viscountess. 'If we survive this escapade I may be *obliged* to leave the country.'

CHAPTER TWENTY-EIGHT

The ladies went back to the main reception rooms and Clarissa tried hard to be amused. The rooms were hot, crowded and noisy and apart from the members of the Belles Dames Club there were few people she knew well. She turned to Lady Wyckenham standing beside her.

'You are not in spirits, Mama-Nell.'

'Oh dear, is it so apparent?'

'Only to me, my love, because I know you so well. I wish Sir Robert were here to cheer you.' Her stepmama did not contradict her and she added gently, 'We need not remain: order your carriage as soon as you wish, Mama-Nell. I shall not object.'

'Thank you Clarissa, but I think we must stay a little longer.

I see Sir Howard Besthorpe is here: look how he glares at poor Julia.'

'At least he makes no effort to accost her. Come, Mama-Nell. Since we are here, let us find some entertainment.'

'Augusta's cousin is over there,' murmured Lady Wyckenham. 'We could join his admirers.'

Clarissa glanced across the room: a sandy-haired gentleman was holding forth at great length on the dangers of the sea.

'No, I thank you. I heard more than enough from Neville Shirley when we were introduced earlier. He is a man very much in love with his own voice, and a very loud one it is! Besides, I did not care for the way he held on to my hand and positively *leered* at me.'

'He could not have done so if William had been with you,' opined Lady Wyckenham. 'I am quite cross with William for crying off this evening. Since he is determined to stay in town, I feel the least he could do is to escort us to such an evening as this.'

'For my part I am glad he did not come,' declared Clarissa. 'It might have been difficult to explain to him why we should be closeted with our hostess for more than half an hour. It would have been sure to arouse his suspicions.'

'If he is so suspicious then he should be here with us,' retorted Lady Wyckenham. 'Oh, I am sorry, Clarissa, I do not mean to snap at you. If it were not for those tiresome letters I am sure I should find William's prosy ways amusing.'

'I know, my love and I see someone who will coax you into a better mood – good evening, Sir Robert – did you know I was just wishing you would be here?'

Sir Robert Ingleton was obliged to stop as Clarissa stepped in front of him, but he did not appear to object and turned to greet Lady Wyckenham with his lazy smile.

'I was looking for you earlier,' he said, taking her hand and raising it to his lips. 'Are you this minute arrived?'

'N-no, we were – ah – in the card-room.'

'Losing your fortune, ma'am?'

My lady gave him a roguish smile.

'I rarely lose at cards, Sir Robert.'

'Then perhaps you should try a fall with me – at cards,' he added as she raised her brows at him. He held out his arm. 'Well, madam?'

'Yes, do go, Mama-Nell,' Clarissa urged her. 'But beware sir; my stepmother has been learning some new tricks.'

'Has she now?' Sir Robert looked intrigued. 'Then I hope she will practise on me.'

Laughing, Clarissa stepped back and watched Lady Wyckenham go off happily with Sir Robert to the card-room. She did not doubt they would flirt shamelessly but neither did she doubt that it would lift Mama-Nell's spirits to be in such pleasant company, and if she should divulge her troubles to Sir Robert at the same time, so much the better, for Clarissa thought him eminently capable of dealing with any problem.

With Lady Wyckenham thus engaged, Clarissa was free to join the group around the pianoforte, including several members of the Belles Dames Club. Lady Sarah was seated at the instrument, accompanying Julia Norwell and her husband as they sang a duet. This was followed by one of the other young ladies playing a lively air and after this it seemed quite natural for the younger members of the party to call for dancing. Lady Maramond raised no objection, the carpet was rolled back and a country dance was soon under way. Clarissa preferred to watch the proceedings and retreated to stand before the series of long windows, where she could observe without being pressed to join in. She was so engrossed that she did not see the Marquis of Ullenwood approaching.

'All alone this evening, Miss Wyckenham? Where is your dear stepmother?'

His soft words made her jump and it was a moment before

she could command her voice to reply calmly.

'Lady Wyckenham is here, my lord. We did not think it necessary in such a gathering as this to be constantly together.'

Until now, she added silently. Lord Ullenwood's mocking eyes ran over her.

'You seem ill at ease, Miss Wyckenham. You are not afraid of me?'

He stepped closer. Clarissa fought off a desire to move away. She raised her chin.

'No, my lord. Should I be?'

He leaned towards her until she could feel his breath on her cheek.

'Oh no,' he said softly. 'I have only one woman in my sights, Miss Wyckenham.'

Indignation seared through Clarissa. Her eyes blazed.

'If you mean Lady Wyckenham—'

His straight black brows rose.

'Yes?'

She closed her lips. It cost her a great deal to bite down the retort that hovered on her tongue, but she knew that to oppose the marquis could jeopardize Lady Gaunt's plan. She was aware of someone approaching and turned her head to see Lord Alresford standing at her elbow. Lord Ullenwood looked up.

'Ah, Lord Alresford.'

'Ullenwood.' The earl's face was impassive but Clarissa felt rather than saw the suppressed anger in his rigid stance.

The marquis laughed gently.

'You wish me at the devil, eh, my lord? Very well, I am going. Miss Wyckenham: your servant.'

As Lord Ullenwood sauntered off, Clarissa realized she had been holding her breath. She let it go now in a long, soft sigh.

'I did not know you were here, my lord.'

'I have not long arrived.' The earl's lip curled as he glanced at the marquis's retreating form. 'You seem to delight in dubi-

ous company, Miss Wyckenham.'

She shook her head.

'You wrong me, my lord. I was never more glad to see you.' She spoke without thinking, only realizing what she had said when she saw the look of surprise on his sharp features. She felt a blush rising through her body and staining her cheeks.

'Would you – perhaps – like to dance, madam?'

It was said awkwardly and Clarissa, equally ill at ease, declined. She glanced up as a footman approached, bowing.

'Your pardon, madam. My lady has ordered that the windows should be opened. . . .' Clarissa stood aside to allow the servant to reach the casement. After a brief struggle with the catch he pushed open the long window to reveal the smooth paving of the terrace. Clarissa had expected the earl to walk away, but he remained at her side. She waved a nervous hand.

'The cool air is very pleasant: the room had grown warm.'

He looked out.

'There is a moon. Would you care to stroll in the gardens? It will be cooler.' His tone was matter-of-fact, even brusque.

There was no hint of the lover in his manner. Intrigued, Clarissa took his arm and allowed him to escort her out on to the terrace. After the overheated salon, the cool breeze on her skin was refreshing. She breathed deeply.

'How pleasant to be able to escape.'

'You dislike these parties, Miss Wyckenham?'

'In general, no, but tonight – there are too many people, too much noise. I do not care for it.'

'Most young ladies seem to revel in it.'

'Do they?' She wrinkled her nose. 'Did – did your fiancée enjoy such gaiety?' She noted his hesitation and rushed on, 'I am sorry, I should not have said—'

'It is no matter, it was a long time ago. No. Elizabeth had no time for such frivolous entertainment.'

She sighed and said, 'Recently my life seems to have been

nothing more than frivolous entertainment.' Clarissa glanced up at his profile, outlined against the night sky and she was emboldened to ask a question that had been troubling her. 'My lord, you called me Elizabeth that day – in the wood. Do we – are we . . . similar?'

'No,' he said shortly. 'Elizabeth was very beautiful.'

She blinked. He turned to her, and even in the dim light she could see his consternation.

'Forgive me, I did not mean—'

She laughed up at him.

'I believe you, my lord, but it is a just reward for my temerity. I should not have asked such a question of you.'

He continued to look at her, then he raised one hand and gently traced the line of her jaw.

'You have a different kind of beauty,' he said softly. 'It radiates from you, makes one happy just to be near you.'

Clarissa stood very still. His touch on her face had caused a riot of conflicting sensations within her: an urge to run away fought against paralysis. Paralysis won. She felt very light-headed, and as if someone had set free a sackful of moths within her stomach. She knew he was going to kiss her, and that she very much wanted him to do so. His dark head came slowly towards her until he was close enough for his lips to meet hers, his shadow blocking out what little moonlight there was. She was enveloped in darkness, and the lack of sight seemed to enhance her other senses.

The touch of his lips shocked Clarissa. Her knees grew weak and she was obliged to lean against him, or risk falling. His lips were gentle and Clarissa found herself responding to his first, tentative kiss: it was the most natural thing in the world to kiss him back. She was aware of the roughness of his skin, the faint smell of sandalwood that clung about him. He broke away, raising his head a fraction and she could feel his ragged breath fanning her cheek. With a little cry she reached up and pulled him back to her, kissing him with a fierce hunger that fright-

ened her. It had to end. He broke away, gently holding her away from him.

'I am sorry.' He stepped back a pace. 'I should not have done that. It was unforgivable.'

She gave a shaky laugh.

'Only if you do not mean to repeat it.'

Her eyes had grown accustomed to the gloom and she could see that he did not even smile at her jest.

He said, 'Forgive me – forgive me.'

Then, with a stiff bow, he turned on his heel and left her.

CHAPTER TWENTY-NINE

The dancing had finished and the rooms were beginning to empty when Lady Wyckenham came back into the salon to look for her stepdaughter. Sir Robert had wanted to escort her home. She had refused, of course, but it had been very tempting. In fact it was becoming ever more difficult to keep Robert at a distance, but the spectre of those irresponsible letters written to Lord Ullenwood hung over her: once she had destroyed them, perhaps then she could forget her foolishness and be the honest, faithful woman Robert believed her to be. So for tonight she had sent him away and now, when she felt thoroughly dispirited, she could not find Clarissa.

Lord Ullenwood was talking with a group of friends in one corner of the room and when he saw her he excused himself and came towards her. For an instant Lady Wyckenham considered running away, but common sense prevailed: she stood her ground and accorded him a cool greeting.

'Lady Wyckenham. You have proved very elusive this evening.'

She hunched an impatient white shoulder.

'I have been well entertained, my lord. That was the reason I came tonight.'

Lord Ullenwood's voice crackled with irritation as he replied.

'And I came here for no other reason than to find you, madam.'

'How disappointing for you. Now if you will excuse me—'

He caught her wrist.

'Not yet, Helen. You try my patience. Remember, I can ruin you.'

'You have threatened to do so, certainly,' came the swift, angry retort.

Their glances clashed, both in the grip of their anger. The Marquis recovered first. He released her.

'We have trifled long enough, madam. I leave for Bath next week. You will come with me, or face the consequences.'

She felt the heat drain from her face. Lord Ullenwood towered over her, a dark, menacing shadow.

'Well, what is your answer?'

She swallowed, and ran her tongue over her dry lips.

'I have no choice.'

'We all have choices, Helen.'

'If – if I go with you – you will give me my letters?'

'Once I am sure of you.'

'I want them . . . as soon as we set off. Surely you can promise me that much.'

She saw the triumph blaze in his eyes, but he answered gravely enough.

'Very well. You have my word. And I always play square, Helen. You should know that.'

'Very well. I will go with you.'

She watched him step back, his head raised. He looked victorious: she could almost imagine that he would throw back that

mane of black hair and howl his triumph to the skies. Instead he took her hand.

'You have made me the happiest of men, my lady.'

Her lip curled.

'Then you have very singular pleasures, sir.'

He laughed at that, and flicked her cheek with one long, white finger.

'You loved me once, Helen. I will make you do so again.'

'Mama-Nell – I am sorry, were you looking for me?'

Lady Wyckenham turned to find her stepdaughter standing at one of the open windows.

'I was on the terrace, Mama-Nell. You are ready to leave now?'

'Yes, my love. If you please.' She reached out and drew Clarissa towards her. 'My love, your hands are ice-cold! How long have you been outside? It is only May; you should not be venturing out without your wrap.'

'I am sorry, Mama-Nell, I did not notice.'

Lady Wyckenham looked closely at her.

'Are you feeling quite well, my love? You are very pale.'

'Quite – quite well, ma'am. Now, by all means let us go home.'

'Very well. I think we should tell Dorothea we are leaving.'

Clarissa hung back.

'Is that necessary, Mama-Nell? She is talking to Captain Shirley.'

'Yes, of course we must, my love. Come, it need not delay us many minutes. Goodness, what is Dorothea about, to be encouraging him so?'

As they approached they could hear Dorothea's voice, but instead of her usual dry tones, she sounded warm and inviting.

'. . . it is such a long way to Bristol, Captain. Do you tell me you make the journey alone – is it not dangerous?'

Lady Wyckenham bit her lip to stop herself laughing out

loud at Dorothea's look of admiration.

'Aye, well, it is, ma'am, and there's many a rogue hanging around the coaching houses watching for the unwary traveller. That's why I always sets off with no less than six outriders.'

'Six! My dear captain, you must be a rich man if you can afford such an entourage.'

The captain touched the side of his nose and winked at her.

'That's the clever part. Anyone watching thinks I travel well protected. They come with me as far as Colnebrook – past Hounslow Heath, you see, for that is the most dangerous stretch – then I pay 'em off.' He broke off as he realized that Lady Wyckenham and Clarissa were coming up to them, and my lady prettily begged pardon for interrupting. A glance at Lady Gaunt was rewarded with the most innocent of stares. They took their leave, the captain insisted on kissing the ladies' hands and Lady Wyckenham felt Clarissa shudder as they walked away.

'To think that odious man has the power of life and death over the poor slaves on his ship: it fills me with repugnance!' she muttered. 'I hope never to see his smug face again.'

They collected their wraps and as they waited in the vestibule for their carriage, Lord Ullenwood sauntered out with a party of gentlemen. As he passed he gave a little bow and kissed his fingers to them.

'Mama-Nell.' Clarissa was instantly suspicious. 'What has happened? Has he – has he spoken to you?'

Lady Wyckenham felt her spirits slump even further.

'Yes,' she said dully. 'It is all agreed.'

Lady Wyckenham would not say more during the short coach journey back to Charlotte Street and since they alighted at the same moment that William arrived at the front door, Clarissa could not press her further.

Lady Wyckenham greeted her stepson with delight.

'Why William, my dear boy, you are home very late. How was

your lecture?'

'Oh, very interesting, ma'am, thank you.' He stood back to allow the ladies to precede him into the house. 'How was Lady Maramond's? I am sorry I could not come with you, but when I heard of the lecture on the Plight of the Poor and Alternatives to the Workhouse—'

'You could not bear to miss it,' Clarissa finished for him. 'Really, William, I do not recall you were always so zealous about the plight of your fellow man. Have you been converted, Brother? Have you had your own road to Damascus?'

William looked uncomfortable.

'We must all do what we can to give comfort to those less fortunate than ourselves.'

Lady Wyckenham took his arm.

'For shame, Clarissa, do not tease your brother. Come, William. We will go into the drawing-room and you can tell me all about your evening.' As she walked off with William, Lady Wyckenham gave her stepdaughter such a saucy look that Clarissa could not help but smile. Her stepmama was determined to tell her nothing more that night. Clarissa declined the invitation to go into the drawing-room, and retired to her bedchamber. She allowed Becky to undress her, but once she had dismissed her maid and was lying between the warmed sheets, she could no longer ignore her own over-riding concern: Lord Alresford's behaviour on the terrace.

His kiss had shaken her. She had been kissed before, by James, her fiancé, by fumbling schoolboys and once by a man who considered himself a rake, but those kisses had not moved her and any attempt to embrace her she had repulsed. Anne had laughed when they had discussed this, and told her that when she was in love it would be different. Is that what it was, thought Clarissa, love? Alresford's touch had sent a wave of heat raging through her body and she had found herself pressing herself against him, willing him to keep his arms around her while she enjoyed the novel sensation of his mouth on

hers. But now, lying alone in the darkness she was confused: she was not at all sure that she even liked the earl. Certainly she did not think constantly about him, or sigh whenever he came into view, but when he was near everything seemed a little more . . . comfortable. She laughed to herself.

'That is not the feeling one should have about a lover,' she murmured, snuggling her hand against her cheek. 'That is the feeling one has for a favourite old gown!'

CHAPTER THIRTY

The next morning Clarissa rose early and spent the first hour dashing off notes to all the members of the Belles Dames Club. Then she went to Lady Wyckenham's bedroom and announced that she had invited everyone to pay a morning visit.

Lady Wyckenham, sipping at her hot chocolate, spluttered and was obliged to put down her cup.

'You have invited them all here? But William—'

'Dear ma'am, I know we said we should not meet here again, but your news last night is too urgent to discuss in a shop! Besides, how can William object to your having visitors?'

'I know it is unreasonable,' muttered Mama-Nell, nervously plucking at the bedcovers, 'but I am sure he will be suspicious.'

Clarissa did her best to reassure her, and when William looked into the drawing-room moments after the last of the ladies had arrived, she was prepared to deflect any awkward questions. However, William merely bowed to the assembled ladies and made his stately way across the room towards his stepmother.

Lady Gaunt, who had known William since he was a baby,

said playfully, 'My goodness, William, is that a new coat? Very smart, my dear. I vow you are looking positively modish.'

He afforded this sally no more than a faint smile and addressed himself to Lady Wyckenham.

'I am going out, ma'am, and wondered if you have any commissions for me?'

'Going out?' She smiled at him, inordinately relieved. 'I *had* thought to collect a parcel of muslin today from New Bond Street. . . .'

'Well, that is on my way, ma'am, if you would like me to call in for it.'

'Did you not tell me you were going to Whitehall today, to see William Grenville?' asked Clarissa. 'I thought that was why you were staying in town. Whitehall is in quite the opposite direction, surely.'

William flushed a little.

'Yes, well, I have another engagement today, in Mount Street. I have arranged to see Grenville tomorrow. Mama-Nell?'

'I thank you for your offer, William, but I do not think it would accord with your dignity to fetch anything as dull as muslin!' remarked Lady Wyckenham, twinkling. 'Simmons shall send a footman for it.'

Lord Wyckenham did not seem amused at such levity. With a hasty bow he left them, and as the door closed behind him his stepmother gave a very audible sigh of relief. Clarissa came over and kissed her cheek.

'You see, ma'am, he did not suspect a thing.'

'No he did not appear to mind at all, did he?' replied my lady, relaxing.

'Now he has gone,' said Lady Sarah, 'perhaps you will tell us why you have called us all here so urgently? I have had to cancel a visit to my mantua-maker.'

Clarissa hastily begged pardon.

'Mama-Nell has received the ultimatum from the marquis!'

Clarissa was well satisfied with the reaction to her news. A

murmur of anticipation rustled around the room. Lady Wyckenham shifted uncomfortably in her chair.

'Well, tell us, Helen,' commanded Lady Gaunt.

Clarissa dropped to her knees before her stepmama and grasped her hands.

'Yes, Mama-Nell. You would not tell me anything more last night, and you will agree that I have been very forbearing and not pressed you. Now, however, you must explain if we are to help you.'

Mrs Leighton-Kettering leaned forward.

'You must not be embarrassed, Helen my dear. We are all your friends, you know.'

'I know, Letitia, and indeed I am grateful.'

'So what have you agreed with him?' demanded Lady Sarah.

'He leaves for Bath next week, and I am to go with him. He has promised to give me the letters as soon as we set off.'

Lady Gaunt closed her fan and tapped it gently against the arm of her chair.

'Hmm. Bath. He will go across Hounslow Heath. That is where we will strike.'

'And what is your plan, ma'am?' asked Clarissa, a little sceptical. 'If we waylay him is it not possible that he will suspect a trap and snatch the letters back from Mama-Nell?'

'I will destroy them as soon as they are in my hands. I shall tear them up.'

Lady Gaunt regarded her pityingly.

'Helen, do you know how difficult it is to tear a letter so small it cannot be put back together? No, what you will do, my dear, is ask the marquis to stop the coach on the Heath. There is a pond, no more than a few yards beyond the gibbet at the crossroads. You must tell Lord Ullenwood to stop there, and you will drop the letters into the pond. The water will soon make the ink run, and they will be worthless.'

'That is an excellent idea, Dorothea,' remarked Mrs Greynard.

'Thank you, Alicia. We will be waiting, and as soon as the letters are gone we shall snatch Helen up and ride away with her.'

Georgiana and Emily applauded this, but the others looked doubtful.

'Do you think the marquis will let me go quite so easily?' asked Lady Wyckenham.

'We shall surprise him. He will not be expecting us. And if his guards show any resistance we will fire our pistols to show we are in earnest.'

'Pistols?' cried Letitia, looking shocked. 'You said nothing about pistols, Dorothea.'

'We can hardly masquerade as highwaymen without them! But be easy, ladies.' Lady Gaunt put up a hand as the murmuring grew louder. 'We shall only use the weapons if there is no other way.'

'Well, that is a very good thing,' declared Lady Sarah, 'because I cannot shoot.'

'Nor I,' said Julia. She glanced around the room, her big eyes begging for understanding.

Augusta Maramond was sitting beside her on the sofa and leaned forward to pat her hands.

'No one would expect it of you, my dear. I think, Dorothea, that perhaps you should be the one to wield the pistol. I have no doubt that you are an excellent shot.'

'I am, of course,' agreed Lady Gaunt.

Clarissa gave a little crow of laughter.

'You are a complete original, ma'am! But to be serious: can it work, do you think?'

'We could be hanged for what we are planning,' said Lady Wyckenham gloomily.

'Nonsense.' Lady Gaunt's tone was bracing. 'If you will play your part, Helen, I have no doubt that we can bring you off safe. The marquis and his henchmen will see only four highwaymen: they would never think to suspect a group of women of such a crime.'

It took some time to convince Lady Wyckenham, but at last she agreed that it was their best hope of retrieving the letters.

'Good, then it is settled.' Lady Gaunt rose. 'Now, I must be away. Helen, you are to confirm the arrangements with the Marquis.'

'He said he would send me word.'

'Very well, you must inform me as soon as you know when he plans to leave for Bath.' She stooped to press her rouged cheek against Lady Wyckenham's pale one. 'Be easy, Helen my dear. This will soon be over.'

'I hope so, Dorothea. I do hope so.'

'Well, William, what an honour to have you accompany us to church.'

Lord Wyckenham scowled across the carriage at his sister, but Lady Wyckenham intervened before he could retort.

'Now, Clarissa, that is unfair. We were not expecting your brother to join us in town.'

'No, but since he is here I could wish he would show us a little more attention, Mama-Nell.'

'I came to town for one purpose: to assure myself that the rumours of your involvement in some irregular club were untrue,' he replied in quelling accents.

'And are you reassured?' asked Clarissa, honey-sweet.

'I think the rumours were greatly exaggerated. You will recall that I walked into one of your meetings the other day: I saw nothing more dangerous than a group of bored, gossiping ladies.'

Although she was relieved at his words, Clarissa could not resist another attack.

'So you consider you no longer need to have a care for us.'

'Do not be absurd, Clarissa. Am I not coming to church with you? I have promised to be at home for Mama-Nell's party on Thursday evening, and I will be dining at home with you tonight.'

'*That* will be the first time in a week.'

'Leave him be, Clarissa.' Lady Wyckenham tapped her arm. 'As a man bent on a political career, I am sure he has many great people to petition: people with a connection to Mr Pitt. Am I right, William?'

'As a matter of fact, Mama-Nell, you are. At home in Devon I was very busy with county affairs, but London is where the real power lies, and when I saw Grenville yesterday he promised to consider me for a government post. Something small, to begin with, I suspect, but once I make my mark, who knows where it may lead?'

My lady smiled at him.

'Well that is very good news, William, and it reminds me: I hope you have no commitments for tomorrow, my love, because Letitia Leighton-Kettering has invited us to dine.'

His brightened immediately.

'The Leighton-Ketterings are very well connected, are they not?'

Clarissa saw the amusement flicker across her stepmama's face.

'I believe they are, William.'

'Then I will most certainly join you, Mama-Nell.'

'How splendid,' murmured Clarissa. 'Let us hope you are rewarded by there being at least two cabinet ministers in attendance!'

Upon their return from church, William went immediately to the library. Clarissa, removing her bonnet, saw Lady Wyckenham grow pale as Simmons handed her a letter.

'Such a long sermon, was it not, Mama-Nell?' She stepped forward and took her arm. 'Let us go upstairs; you shall rest while I read to you for an hour.'

Only when they were alone did Lady Wyckenham break the seal of her letter.

'Is it from the marquis?' asked Clarissa.

'Yes.' Lady Wyckenham sank down on to a sofa and opened the letter. She scanned the contents, refolded the paper and pushed it deep into the pocket of her gown.

'Well? What does he say, Mama-Nell? When does he want you to meet him?'

Lady Wyckenham did not answer immediately. Clarissa sat down beside her and took her hands.

'Dear ma'am, you must tell me,' she said gently. 'We need to know the details if we are to help you.'

Lady Wyckenham's stared at her, then shook her head.

'I have such good friends: they would risk so much for me.'

'Of course, Mama-Nell, we would risk everything for you, you know that. Now, tell me: when is it to be?'

Lady Wyckenham closed her eyes.

'Saturday,' she whispered. 'Saturday night, at eleven o'clock.'

CHAPTER THIRTY-ONE

Clarissa lost no time in passing the information to Lady Gaunt and when they met again at the Leighton-Ketterings' dinner the viscountess pressed her hand, her dark eyes gleaming with the light of adventure.

'So we have a day: have you told the others?'

'No. I did not want to risk too many notes. They should all be here tonight.' Clarissa moved on to join Lady Wyckenham, who was talking to their hostess. When Clarissa came up, Mrs Leighton-Kettering leaned forward to kiss her cheek.

'So it is Saturday,' she murmured. 'How thrilling.' She stepped back and resumed her normal society manner. 'Lord

Ullenwood is joining us later,' she said, at her most innocent. 'Oswald invited him to join us for supper: since he allowed *me* to choose so many of my own particular friends to sit down to dinner with us, I could hardly object.'

Looking around, Clarissa realized that most members of the Belles Dames Club were present: Alicia Greynard and her husband, Lady Sarah and Sir Toby were all talking to Mr Leighton-Kettering, and the Norwells had just arrived. She was about to turn back when she spotted the tall, black figure of Lord Alresford following Julia and Barnabus up the stairs.

Letitia observed her start of surprise and took advantage of William's talking to Lady Wyckenham to murmur, 'Oswald insisted on redressing the balance since I had invited so many ladies.' She raised her voice again. 'I did suggest Sir Robert Ingleton, but he has a prior engagement. However, he has promised to look in later.'

'Ingleton,' mused William. 'I have not seen him since he returned from his latest expedition.'

'That is because you have not come about with us,' murmured Clarissa.

William flushed.

'You know I have been busy!'

'Stop bickering, children,' commanded Lady Wyckenham. 'Oh look, Augusta has brought her obnoxious cousin, Captain Shirley.'

'No doubt Letitia felt obliged to invite him, since he is staying with the Maramonds.'

Out of the corner of her eye Clarissa saw Lord Alresford enter the room. She hoped he would not approach her but when he did not, her disappointment was as severe as it was irrational. She put up her chin and told herself she really did not care a button for the earl.

There were sixteen sitting down to dinner – the Leighton-Ketterings' idea of an intimate little meal. With so many

friends present, Clarissa's only anxiety was whether she would find herself sitting beside Lord Alresford, and since she could not make up her mind whether or not she wished for this, she found herself hanging back while the others took their seats. Lady Gaunt and Lady Wyckenham sat on either side of their host and with Lady Sarah and Sir Toby at that end of the table, Clarissa had no doubt that they would enjoy some lively conversation during their meal. She found herself sitting between William and Alicia Greynard's mouse-like husband, but since he was as kind as he was meek, she was perfectly content and felt more sorry for Julia Norwell sitting opposite, flanked by Captain Shirley and Lord Alresford.

Clarissa had formed no good opinion of the sea captain when they had met at Lady Maramond's rout and, as the dinner progressed, she saw nothing to change her mind. He had a commanding voice, and when he began explaining to Julia Norwell his shipping route, it was impossible for anyone at that end of the table not to hear him.

'. . . we call the section from Africa to the Americas the Middle Passage, you know, ma'am, and it can take anything from four weeks to three months. Very lucrative exercise it can be, too: we take goods to the African coast – brandy, firearms and the like and trade 'em for slaves. They are then taken to Barbados and when we have cleared the hold there we fill it with sugar or molasses. Of course, now the war is ended we will be able to call again in Virginia, to collect tobacco.'

'But is it not a very dangerous voyage, Captain?' asked Letitia Leighton-Kettering.

'Aye, ma'am. The Middle Passage is the worst, for with more than four hundred bodies on the slave deck, there is always the danger of disease breaking out, but the profits more than make up for the risk. This last voyage for example, when we reached

Barbados, we still had nearly three hundred slaves to sell.'

'Three hundred!' exclaimed Clarissa. 'But you said you had over four hundred on board.'

'Indeed I did, miss,' agreed the captain, puffing out his chest. 'And only lost a hundred of 'em on the journey. Now on the last leg, when we had collected—'

'Excuse me, Captain,' Clarissa, interrupted him. 'Is it not wrong to keep these poor people chained and imprisoned for weeks at a time? Does it not conflict with your Christian duty?'

Silence fell. Captain Shirley looked at first surprised and displeased by her interruption, then his face creased into a smile and he said, as if to a child, 'People? Madam, these are not people as we would know them. These are blacks. Savages. Heathens at best, but they have no more understanding of our civilized ways than animals. Less in fact, if you compare them to a good hunting dog!'

There was a little polite laughter and Clarissa felt her anger mounting.

'There are moves afoot to abolish slaving,' remarked Lord Alresford. 'What would happen then to your – ah – Middle Passage?'

'Why nothing, my lord, for it won't happen,' declared the captain. 'There are far too many Englishmen whose fortunes are built upon the fruits of the slave trade.' He looked about him. 'I doubt there is one family represented here that don't have some investment in the plantations.'

'But few are wholly dependent upon it,' replied the earl.

'Begging your pardon, my lord: you are forgetting that it is an Englishman's duty to help his country to prosper. Those who oppose the slave trade are traitors, sir, traitors!' He took another mouthful of beef and chewed vigorously. 'And another thing,' he said indistinctly, waving his fork at the earl, 'the slaves on their plantations ain't so very different from your own people here in England. Both are subject to the master's

whims, sir. If you choose to turn off a tenant farmer, where is he to go, how is he to live? He is as much at your mercy as any black.'

'True,' agreed Lord Alresford, 'although I have not transported him thousands of miles from his original home, against his will.'

Letitia gave a gentle laugh.

'My, my, we are getting very serious, gentlemen. Save this discussion for later, if you will, for I am sure it cannot be good for our digestion. Lady Maramond tells me this is your last night in town, Captain Shirley.'

'Yes, ma'am. I return to Bristol tomorrow. I—'

Letitia cut him off.

'Then I am sure we wish you a good journey, sir. Mr Norwell, how is your dear mother? Julia tells me she is unwell at the moment; what is it, a trifling cold? Oh, I am so glad it is nothing worse. Does she take lemonade and barley water? There is nothing better for a slight chill. . . .'

With the skill of a born hostess Mrs Leighton-Kettering turned the conversation and the captain, having lost his audience, gave his full attention to his plate.

Clarissa, however, found herself disturbed by the exchange. Her appetite had gone and she refused the syllabub and the marchpane. When the ladies withdrew she found herself describing the captain's conversation to Lady Gaunt.

'Yes, I heard most of it,' replied the Viscountess. 'The man has such a carrying voice it is impossible to ignore him. Most likely he developed it shouting orders at his poor crew.'

'Horrible man!' muttered Clarissa. 'How can he be so smug, so complacent—'

'I know, it is unforgivable.' Lady Gaunt soothed her. 'But I have been working on a way to pay him back. No, no questions now, Clarissa. Wait until Emily and Georgiana are here.'

Clarissa was intrigued, but her companion refused to say more and Clarissa went off to talk to her stepmother, who was

looking decidedly anxious.

'I cannot help it,' complained my lady, when Clarissa remarked upon it. 'Dorothea says I am to encourage Lord Ullenwood's attentions tonight, but I cannot even think of the man without shuddering.'

Clarissa considered the matter.

'Well, I suppose you will have to make him believe you will keep your word, Mama-Nell. But he knows how reluctant you are, so he will not expect you to fall into his arms.' She patted her hand. 'You must be brave, my love. I do not like this subterfuge any more than you, but it is only until you have the letters. You could defy him, you know, tell him to publish, if he so wishes.'

The gentlemen came in at that moment and Lady Wyckenham's eyes travelled across the room to rest upon her stepson.

'No. Impossible. Such a scandal would ruin William. And I have you and Anne to consider, my love.' She smiled, a little sadly. 'There is nothing I would not do to protect you, darling. Oh look: Emily and Georgiana have arrived.'

Clarissa turned.

'We had best tell them the day is set.'

'No need,' sighed Lady Wyckenham. 'Dorothea is there before us. I will go and join them, and find out from Dorothea if there is any member of the Club who does *not* know. Oh this is a wretched business!'

'Poor Mama-Nell, are you wishing you had never started the Belles Dames Club?'

'Yes! Well, no. It *has* been fun.'

Clarissa laughed. 'That sounds as if it was all at an end.'

Lady Wyckenham did not reply, merely patted her arm and walked away.

Clarissa saw Julia Norwell coming towards her and she said with a smile, 'I had little chance to talk to you at dinner.'

Julia shuddered. 'Do not mention that meal!'

'Poor Julia, was it dreadful for you, sitting between Captain Shirley and Alresford? I fear their opinions are very different.'

'Yes indeed, but I was much too frightened to agree with either of them.' She dropped her voice. 'And is it true, are we to – you know – on Saturday?'

'Yes. Dorothea is arranging everything and enjoying herself hugely. I believe she has a penchant for adventure.'

Clarissa realized Julia was not listening to her. Following her gaze she saw that Sir Howard Besthorpe had come in.

'Julia?'

Mrs Norwell jumped.

'I beg your pardon. It – it is that man.'

'I thought as much. Poor child, you look like a rabbit locked in the same room with a fox.'

'He – he has not come near me since that night at Norwell House, but I cannot help but be afraid . . . it is very silly of me.'

'Yes it is,' agreed Clarissa. 'The secret is to laugh at him: you cannot be afraid of someone if you think them ridiculous. Put your mind to it, Julia. Picture his riding away from Norwell House, breechless, with his shirt flapping out behind him.'

Julia concentrated. She watched Sir Howard parading across the room in his hedgehog wig and green corduroy coat. Clarissa saw her smile grow. It was unfortunate that Julia chose to giggle just as Sir Howard was passing them. He did not glance their way, but his reddened face and furious frown told Clarissa that he knew he was the object of their derision.

'Well, do you feel better for that?' asked Clarissa.

'You were right,' said Julia, still chuckling. 'I shall try the same on Lady Norwell, when she is in her gorgon mood, but I shall make sure that *she* does not know I am laughing at her.'

'I did not expect him to come quite so close,' admitted Clarissa. 'He certainly did not like being laughed at: I vow he

was so angry those blue ribbons around his knees positively trembled with his rage!'

'And what is it that you ladies find so amusing?' demanded Barnabus, coming up at that moment. 'Your servant, Miss Wyckenham.'

'Clarissa has been teaching me not to be so timid,' said Julia, smiling up at him.

Barnabus took her hand.

'As long as she doesn't teach you to disregard me.' He grinned. 'Now come along Ju, Mrs Leighton-Kettering wants to hear us sing.'

He led his wife away and as they moved off Clarissa realized that Lord Alresford was standing behind his friend. There was less than six feet between them and she felt sure he would speak. He took a small step towards her but a sonorous announcement stopped him.

'Sir Gordon and Lady Medway, and Miss Medway.'

The hand that had been reaching out was withdrawn and, with a stiff bow, the earl turned on his heel and walked away.

Disappointment stabbed Clarissa. He would have spoken, she was sure of it, if Florence Medway had not arrived, and now he was going to greet her – but he was to be disappointed, William had reached her first. Never before had Clarissa been thankful for her brother's punctilious attention to duty. She watched Lord Alresford hesitate, then he turned and went to stand against the wall near the pianoforte. Clarissa hoped his angry scowl would not impair Julia's performance. Instantly she upbraided herself for being childish: Lord Alresford's countenance was as impassive as ever. If anyone was displaying an angry scowl, it was herself. Clarissa took a deep breath and schooled her features into what she hoped was a more pleasant expression, determined to be on her best behaviour for the rest of the evening.

CHAPTER THIRTY-TWO

Lady Wyckenham sighed and wondered how soon she could make her excuses and go home. Lord Ullenwood had arrived while Julia and her husband were singing a very pretty Italian duet. This had provided an excuse not to speak, but the way the marquis had squeezed her fingers when they met had made her blush with the memory of past intimacy, and now Sir Robert Ingleton had come up, seen at a glance that she was not happy and demanded to know the reason. She had sent him off to procure a glass of wine for her, but her poor brain felt too tired to concoct an excuse that would satisfy him. She knew the marquis was watching her, and that made her even more nervous. As Sir Robert came back across the room she wondered what she was going to say to him.

'Shall we sit down?' he said, nodding towards an empty sofa. 'I believe the Greynards are going to sing next.' He waited until she had made herself comfortable and disposed her skirts gracefully before handing her the glass of wine.

'Thank you. I think you will enjoy their singing, Sir Robert: Lady Alicia is very good, and her husband is a splendid baritone.'

She tried to concentrate on the singing but was painfully aware of Sir Robert sitting beside her, one arm thrown negligently along the back of the sofa, his fingers drumming lightly on the silk-covered padding in time to the music. His nearness made the hair on the back of her neck prickle. How pleasant it would be to sink back against him, to feel that arm tighten protectively around her. But it could not be. Tears threatened and she could only pretend to sip at her wine, for her throat was too tight to swallow.

A smattering of applause greeted the end of the song and the couple were begged to sing again. Sir Robert put down his glass.

'Helen, what is wrong, my dear?'

'What sir?' she spoke with brittle gaiety. 'I do not understand you: there is nothing amiss.'

She met his eyes, only for a moment, and saw that for once there was no smile lurking in their depths.

'You are ill at ease. Have I offended you?'

'No, of course not.'

'Then tell me what is troubling you. I am your friend, you know.'

Lady Wyckenham blinked rapidly.

'La, sir. You must not be imagining anything is wrong every time I am a little quiet. A lady cannot forever be chattering, you know.'

He seemed to pull back a little.

'Why do I feel you are fencing with me?' She took a sip of her wine and did not answer him. At last he muttered, 'By Gad, you are in a strange mood tonight, madam. I hardly know you.'

'You do not know me at all, sir!'

'That is not true.' He reached out, 'Nell—'

'Don't!' She snatched her hand away as if she had been burned, and his look of hurt and surprise made her want to cry. Instead she forced herself to say coldly, 'I am not in the humour for a flirtation, Sir Robert.'

He stood up.

'Perhaps you are not in the humour for my company.'

Her heart sank at his sharp tone and it took all her willpower to maintain her haughty demeanour.

'No, sir. I find you extremely tedious.'

She dare not look up, but she was aware of him watching her, and could imagine his bewilderment.

'Very well. I will relieve you of my – tedious – company, my lady. Goodnight.'

He walked off and she had the dubious pleasure of seeing him accosted by Emily Sowerby and her sister. She was too far away to hear their conversation, but Georgiana's strident laugh reached her, and she had no doubt that they were flirting outrageously. Abruptly she rose, wanting to be alone, but the door was on the far side of the room and to leave would involve explanations. Instead she retreated to a window embrasure, thinking she could hide in the shadows provided by the heavy curtains. Too late she realized her mistake, for Lord Ullenwood followed her.

'You are not enjoying the music, my lady?'

'Yes, yes, of course I am. It – is a little cooler here, that is all.'

He stepped closer.

'Is it? I can discern no difference.' He reached up to rest the back of his hand against her cheek. 'Your skin is quite cool.'

She tensed but did not reply.

'I believe our hostess has announced supper – would you care to eat?'

'Thank you, I am not hungry.'

'I saw you talking to Ingleton.'

'You mistake, sir. *He* was talking to *me.*'

'A subtle difference.'

'But significant, my lord.'

'It does not prevent me objecting to it.'

'You will have seen, sir, that I sent him away.'

He took her hand and lifted it to his lips.

'Very wise, my love.' She turned from him and would have walked away but he stopped her with a hand on her shoulder. 'I wish it were possible to carry you off tonight,' he murmured. 'You are so damned beautiful.'

Lady Wyckenham swallowed.

'Saturday will be soon enough, sir.'

She felt his breath on her neck, then his lips. The curtains and the deep alcove screened them from most of the company, but as the marquis bent to kiss her neck my lady saw Sir

Robert standing on the far side of the room, watching them. Slowly, deliberately, she brought her hand up to touch Ullenwood's cheek. A look of distaste flickered across Sir Robert's countenance, then he turned away and strode out of the room.

'Sally, have you seen Mama-Nell?' Clarissa came up, a slight crease in her brow.

Lady Sarah shook her head.

'Perhaps she has gone into the supper-room. I was on my way there when Lady Gaunt asked me to join her in the little book-room. She was looking for you too Clarissa, and Julia – ah, Julia, love, over here: Lady Gaunt wants to see us.'

'And where are we to go? Where is this little book-room?' asked Clarissa.

'She said to go past the supper-room and it is the first door in the passage to the right. She said it is never used and we can be quite secret.' Lady Sarah giggled. 'Trust Dorothea to know of such a room!'

'What do you think she wants now?' asked Julia.

Clarissa chuckled.

'We had best go and find out. Julia, pray do not look so anxious, I am sure it will be nothing dreadful.'

They slipped out of the salon and instead of following the other guests into the supper-room, they went on towards the passage. As they turned the corner Lady Sarah, who was leading the way, collided with a serving maid hurrying in the other direction. The maid, blushing furiously and with her cap awry, bobbed a curtsy and begged a hasty pardon before scurrying away.

'Well I never!' Lady Sarah stopped, fanning herself vigorously. 'Is this the room?' she asked, pointing to a door.

'Dorothea said the first one,' affirmed Julia. 'Pray go first, Clarissa – but do knock, in case someone should be in there.'

It was indeed a small, book-lined room. Candles burned in

the wall brackets and although no fire had been kindled, the curtains had been pulled across the window, giving the room a cosy, intimate atmosphere. The ladies went in.

'I hope Lady Gaunt will not be long,' said Julia in a hushed voice.

'She said she was going to find Emily and her sister.' Lady Sarah moved to a chair and sat down. 'Perhaps she has more news.' She looked up as the door opened again to admit Lady Gaunt with Georgiana and Emily. 'Dorothea, what are you planning now?'

Lady Gaunt closed the door softly behind her.

'A little amusement,' she drawled, her eyes gleaming with mischief. 'And a way to help Mr Sharp's cause.'

'Tell us,' demanded Georgiana.

'Well, the men's riding dress I had made up for you was delivered today.'

'Dorothea, you didn't order it yourself!' breathed Georgiana, awed.

'Of course not: Grantham handled everything. He is proving to be such a treasure, I shall be sorry when I have to let him go. But that is by the by. I thought it would be shameful to have had all the trouble of finding coats and boots and breeches for just one occasion.'

Emily clapped her hands.

'You want us to wear them to a masquerade!'

'No,' said Clarissa, frowning. 'How would that help Granville Sharp?'

'Not at all. But the ill-gotten fortune of a slave-trader could be put to good use in his campaign.' Lady Gaunt's piercing gaze swept over them. 'Well, have none of you guessed? We shall intercept the gallant captain on his way to Bristol tomorrow!'

CHAPTER THIRTY-THREE

Lady Sarah gave a little shriek and clapped her hands to her mouth.

'Dorothea! How dare you even jest about such a thing.'

'No jest, my dear. We were all mightily affected by Mr Sharp's talk the other night, yet not one of us has done anything to help his cause.'

'That is not true, Dorothea: you have sent little Samuel to school,' said Emily.

The Viscountess dismissed this with a wave of her hand.

'That is an insignificance.' She leaned forward. 'The good captain said at dinner that he returns to Bristol tomorrow. You may remember Augusta telling us that he presented letters to the bank to take money out: I would wager my diamonds that he will have a small fortune with him when he leaves tomorrow. I think it would be better if that money went to Mr Sharp's campaign.'

'That would be highway robbery,' breathed Georgiana, her eyes widening.

'Are you afraid to join me?' asked Lady Gaunt.

Georgiana looked at her sister. She giggled nervously.

'No-o, but it is very dangerous.'

'Only if we are caught,' retorted the Viscountess. 'I made it my business to discover how the captain means to travel, so the risks are minimal.' She lowered her voice. 'I have already ascertained that Captain Shirley pays off his outriders once they have crossed Hounslow Heath. He will have only his driver, and perhaps one guard.'

'I would dearly love to join you,' said Lady Sarah, 'but Toby's mama has summoned us to dinner tomorrow night, and I cannot cry off.'

'No matter, Sally. We will manage without you.'

Clarissa put up her hand.

'No, ma'am, pray forget this scheme. It is madness.'

Lady Gaunt looked at her.

'Why?' she said coolly. 'What is so different between this and our original plan?'

'Yes,' agreed Emily. 'In fact, is this not a much nobler scheme? It could help to save thousands from slavery.'

Clarissa looked helplessly at the excited faces around her. Only Julia Norwell seemed anxious. She tried again.

'Should we not consult the others?'

'I have deliberately not asked them to join us, my dear,' said Lady Gaunt. 'Your stepmama has enough to worry her at the present time, Letitia and Alicia are not happy about our original scheme and Augusta – well, the captain is her cousin, so it would be out of the question to involve her.' She gave her thin smile. 'No, this will be a secret for just the six of us. We will consider it a dress rehearsal for Saturday.'

Minutes later the ladies departed and the room was silent again. For five minutes more nothing moved save the shadows thrown by a guttering candle. Then the curtains over the window twitched, and a stockinged leg emerged from the velvet hangings: a stockinged leg adorned with blue knee-ribbons.

Nothing could be more decorous than the riding party that gathered outside Lady Gaunt's Grosvenor Square mansion the following day. There were only five ladies present, and after waiting a good half-hour for Julia to arrive, the viscountess decided that they would have to set off.

'Perhaps she is ill,' suggested Lady Sarah.

'Or lost her nerve,' remarked Emily. 'She was not at all happy about this venture.'

'Well, we cannot wait, or we shall miss our quarry,' said Lady Gaunt. She signalled to Grantham to throw her up into the

saddle and moments later, the little group set off. Clarissa looked over her shoulder.

'Why Grantham, and not your groom, Lady Gaunt?'

'We need only one servant with us, and Grantham is – ah – most discreet.'

'Quite,' murmured Miss Wyckenham, her eyes twinkling merrily. 'And just what is your plan for today, ma'am?'

'The good captain should be leaving town in just under the hour – I found that out from Augusta last night: thought it would be useful to know.'

'Undoubtedly.'

'The captain told me he pays off his escort at Colnebrook, so we will ride past there and lie in wait for him.'

'And the men's clothing?'

Lady Gaunt smiled.

'Grantham took everything in a wagon early this morning, including the men's saddles that we shall need. I am glad to see that you all heeded my advice to bring horses with no distinctive markings – so much easier to avoid detection.'

Clarissa laughed.

'Dorothea, you were born to be hanged!'

'Thank you, my dear. I will take that as a compliment.'

With the town behind them they quickened their pace, through Kensington and Hammersmith, across Turnham Green and bearing right at Hounslow and across the Heath to Cranford.

'We had best leave the road here and travel across country,' said Lady Gaunt. 'It would not do to advertise our presence here. Grantham will lead the way.'

They swung north, cutting across fields and through woods to pick up the Great Western Road again between Colnebrook and Slough. A stretch of open ground led down to the road, and apart from a small copse, the land towards Colnebrook had been recently cleared, although dozens of felled trees lay

untidily along the length of the road.

'What a desolate spot!' declared Emily, shivering.

'Then it is perfect for us,' said Lady Gaunt. 'Grantham has left the wagon up there in those trees. Come along: we have to change.'

Seeing the others in their men's attire, Clarissa wished that she too was masquerading. The dark riding jackets and buckskins fitted well, but disguised their feminine curves. Satin masks covered their eyes and woollen mufflers could be pulled up over the lower part of the face to give an almost total disguise. Each lady wore her hair tucked up securely under a tricorne hat and when they turned to Clarissa for her opinion, she applauded them enthusiastically.

'I wish I could join you,' she said, watching them swagger up and down in front of her.

'We need you here to keep watch,' said Lady Gaunt. 'You have a good view of the road from here in both directions.' She beckoned to Grantham, who handed each of them an elegant pistol. 'Be careful, Grantham has already loaded them.'

'What are we to do with these?' asked Georgiana, holding her weapon nervously before her.

'Tuck it in your waistband for now – you need not worry, it won't go off unless you cock it. Clarissa, you must have one too.'

'But I have never fired a pistol, Dorothea.'

'You must use it to warn us if anyone approaches while we are relieving the captain of his money. Now, Grantham will take the carriage to Grosvenor Square – it will be dark by the time we return so we can ride back in disguise.' She took out her watch. 'You had best be going, Grantham, it is nearly five: even allowing for slow horses, the captain should be here soon.'

They settled down to wait within the cover of the trees. The cloud grew thicker and a chill wind sprang up, rustling through the trees and making the horses stamp and snort nervously. In the next hour they saw only one lumbering farm-cart and a

clergyman riding a tired-looking nag.

Emily coughed nervously.

'You are sure we have the right road, Dorothea?' she said. 'He should have been here by now.'

'Of course this is the road. Perhaps he was delayed getting away, or he may have stopped at an inn.'

'So close to London?' said Clarissa. 'That is not likely, is it, ma'am?'

'No, I admit it is not.' Lady Gaunt took out her watch again. 'It's past six. The light is already fading. Damn this cloud!'

'Most likely he was delayed,' said Georgiana, the most optimistic of them all.

'Well,' said Emily, 'if he doesn't come soon—'

Clarissa waved her hand.

'Hush, someone's coming, from Colnebrook.'

They all followed the line of her pointing finger: a coach pulled by four sweating horses was coming towards them.

'It's the captain!' cried Emily, jumping up and down.

Lady Gaunt stared down at the road.

'I believe it is. Mount up, ladies!'

They waited until the coach reached the open ground then at a signal from the Viscountess they went cantering down the slope to intercept it.

Clarissa moved to the very edge of the wood to watch. A shot rang out: Clarissa suspected it was Lady Gaunt who had stationed herself in the road, forcing the coach to stop, but the failing light made it difficult to see. As the 'highwaymen' closed in, a man climbed out of the carriage, waving his arms as if to remonstrate with the attackers.

A movement on the far side of the road caught Clarissa's attention. A light rain had started to fall and Clarissa had to strain her eyes to pierce the enveloping mist. The fallen trees and gorse bushes could not conceal riders, but – another movement caught her eye and cold, panicky fear chilled her. There

were men crawling amongst the felled trees. She knew she must warn the others and her right hand reached for the pistol, but before she could pull it free from the pocket of her riding jacket, she found herself caught in a vice-like grip, and a large hand was clamped over her mouth.

CHAPTER THIRTY-FOUR

'Don't scream.' A low voice sounded close to her ear. 'No noise, and I'll let you go. Understand?'

Quaking, she managed a slight nod. The hand came away from her mouth, but the steel grip remained on her arm. Slowly she turned her head, and found herself looking into the dark eyes of the Earl of Alresford. He let her go and nodded towards the men hiding amongst the fallen trees.

'We need to pin them down.' He took out his own pistol. 'Shoot over their heads.' Clarissa was still reeling with shock, but she tried to concentrate.

'What – what if I hit someone?'

He looked at her.

'Have you ever handled a pistol before?'

'No, never.'

'Don't worry, your chances of hitting anything at this distance are remote.' He raised his arm. 'Ready? Fire!'

Two reports sounded. The noise and recoil sent Clarissa staggering back, the pistol flying from her hand. Lord Alresford did not turn: he was staring down at the road.

'Good. They've taken cover: that will give your friends precious seconds to get away.'

Coming up beside him, Clarissa watched as the 'highway-men' wheeled their horses and set off along the road.

'Where are they going? They are heading the wrong way.'

'As long as they are riding away from here that is all that matters for the moment. Don't worry about them – our friends down there have seen the flash from the muzzles, look.'

Horrified, Clarissa saw a group of riders appear from the small copse. The earl caught her arm.

'We must go.'

She ran to her horse. The earl threw her into the saddle and scrambled up on to his own black hunter.

'This way.' He led her through the woods at a canter. Although the trees were not yet in full leaf, the light in the wood was poor and Clarissa struggled to see the way as she pushed her horse on, keeping as close to the earl as she dared. Then they were flying across open country and although the going was easier, she trembled as she heard a shot ring out behind them. Suddenly Alresford veered to one side and plunged into another belt of trees.

'Cover,' she muttered to herself. 'We are safer under cover.'

Once within the shelter of the trees he drew rein and waited for her to catch up. As she brought the bay mare alongside his horse she blurted out the question that had been nagging at her since they had started their flight.

'What are you doing here – how did you know of this?'

'Julia. She was so nervous about this whole business that it became apparent even to Barnabus that something was wrong. He coaxed the story from her and persuaded her to stay at home.' There was a hint of a smile as he glanced across. 'She would not have been much use to you.'

'No,' agreed Clarissa. 'Poor Julia having hysterics could only have compounded our problems today: I suppose Barnabus told you everything.'

'He did, but I would not have interfered – your mad-cap schemes are none of my business, after all – but I was driving

through St James's Street last night after he had told me the whole. I saw Besthorpe talking to Captain Shirley. Knowing what I did, I thought it was odd, so I followed Shirley when he left town. Fortunately I was keeping to the trees up here on the ridge, and came across you in time to raise the alarm.'

'I suppose I must thank you.'

His severe look fled, replaced by something very close to a grin.

'Much as you hate to do so!'

She could not resist an answering smile.

'You are right, I hate to be beholden to you. But it must be done, and I will do so graciously.' The look that passed between them turned Clarissa's insides to water, and she was obliged to grip the reins to combat the dizziness that threatened her. She was relieved when he looked away.

'Very well, ma'am. We had best press on, and quickly, for they saw us enter these trees and will surely search here.'

The flight seemed endless. They crashed through the undergrowth, emerging on open ground where the earl kicked his horse on to canter up the rise before dropping down the other side into a green lane. Sounds of pursuit had faded and the rain stopped, but still they pressed on until Clarissa was exhausted and her bay mare labouring to keep up with the earl's powerful hunter. And all the time it grew darker.

At last the pace slowed. They had entered a small copse, disturbing the nesting rooks who took to the air, protesting noisily. The earl stopped.

'I think we've lost them.'

'Have we lost ourselves?' she murmured with a flash of spirit. 'Where are we?'

'I am not sure: we have been travelling north mostly, so probably nearing Uxbridge. We haven't crossed the river, though.' He jumped down as nimbly as if he had just enjoyed a quiet ride in the park. 'You look tired, Miss Wyckenham. Let's rest

here for a moment. He came across to help her dismount and she slid into his arms. His hold tightened as her knees buckled.

'Thank you.' She tried to laugh, but found her voice shaking. 'I do not think I can stand.'

His grip did not relax and it seemed the most natural thing in the world to lean against him, her head resting on his shoulder.

'I take it this mad-cap scheme was Lady Gaunt's idea?'

Clarissa could not deny it.

'She wanted to take the slave-trader's money and give it to the abolitionists.' Now that the excitement was over, she felt the tears prickling against her eyelids. 'It was very wrong of us and I am grateful that you came to our rescue, even though you must be very angry.'

To her surprise he threw back his head and laughed, a full, deep laugh that rang through the trees.

'Angry? No, not angry. No one appears to be any the worse for this adventure and if Captain Shirley's complacent bubble has been pricked, so much the better.'

She turned her face up to look at him. The laughter had banished his usual austerity and the smile that lurked in his eyes as he looked down at her made her heart turn over.

'Are you . . . *enjoying* this?' she asked him, her voice hushed with amazement.

'Flying cross-country in the rain, pursued by armed men? Yes, yes I am. Are not you?'

He looked at her, inviting her to share his merriment. Clarissa's breath caught in her throat.

'I don't understand,' she managed at last. 'I thought, I thought. . . .'

He grinned, and her words died away completely.

'When I first saw you I had the oddest feeling that you carried the sunshine with you.' He shrugged. 'It was as if I was living in some huge dark mansion, and every time we met you threw open another window, letting in more light.'

'Oh.'

His arms tightened about her.

'You have taught me to laugh at life again, Clarissa.'

His dark head came down and she instinctively raised her face to his, meeting his lips with her own. The touch made her senses reel. She had read of the experiments with electricity, where the power crackled between two points, and now she felt she was experiencing just such a phenomenon. Her skin tingled, her body seemed to meld itself to his. She wanted to climb inside his very skin in her efforts to be close to him.

At last he broke free. He held her away from him, his breathing very ragged.

'We had best get on. We cannot go much further tonight and we need a shelter. Can you ride a little more?'

Dumbly she nodded, still dazed from the shock of his kiss. What did it mean? She asked herself the question once she was in the saddle again and following Lord Alresford out of the copse. She had seen her father embrace Mama-Nell in just such a fashion when one of his horses had won at Ascot. He had lifted her off her feet and swung her round in the exuberance of the moment. That was all it could be. The earl had been brimming with excitement from the chase and it needed an outlet. That did not explain his words, of course. Gradually Clarissa found that the disturbing effects of his kiss were giving way to a much softer but equally frightening idea: that he truly liked her.

CHAPTER THIRTY-FIVE

They had left the copse behind them and were now riding along a narrow ridge with the land falling away gently to one side. Clarissa brought her mare closer to the black hunter.

'My lord, how long will it take to get back to town?'

'Too long to reach it before dark. If my memory serves me correctly the river is over in that direction. We can cross it at Uxbridge, but then it is still more than an hour's ride.' He pointed down the hill. 'There is a small building in the field down there, a shepherd's hut, most likely, and a stream. Water for ourselves and the horses. We can shelter there until it is light.'

He did not wait for her to comment but pushed on again in the failing light: to the west, a purple-black bank of cloud was rising, bringing with it the promise of a black, wet night. They crossed the field in silence and after a rapid look around to make sure there was no one in sight, dismounted by a small wooden hut.

'This is not big enough for the horses,' muttered the earl. 'We will risk letting them run free.' He pushed open the door and Clarissa followed him inside. Two slits high in the walls, just below the eaves, allowed in a little light and once her eyes had grown accustomed to the gloom she saw that it was bare save for a pile of straw in one corner and a horn beaker on a ledge. A small fireplace had been built into one wall, with sticks and wood lying ready.

'Stay here while I see to the horses.'

'I will help you.' She moved back to the door. 'It will be done in half the time if there are two of us, and the light is almost gone.'

He did not smile; she heard no word of thanks, nothing more

than a curt nod, but she felt she knew him well enough now to be satisfied with that. They removed the saddles and stacked them just inside the hut.

'Heaven knows how we shall untangle this,' said Clarissa, dropping the harness on top of her saddle.

'It will be easier in the daylight.'

'If we still have horses. What if they wander off?'

'They won't go far in the dark, and there looked to be a stout hedge around the field on three sides, and the stream across the bottom. Talking of which,' he picked up the beaker. 'Would madam care for a little refreshment before we retire?'

She followed him down to the stream.

'Was that a jest, my lord?'

'I suppose it was.'

'I vow I did not think you had it in you.'

'I have said before, you do not know me, Miss Wyckenham.'

She smiled, but made no reply. The sound of water was very close and soon Clarissa could see the white froth tumbling past them. Lord Alresford was bending low over the water.

'There's a rocky bed. We must hope it is clean.' He reached forward and washed out the beaker before filling and raising it to his lips. 'That's sweet enough.' He refilled it and handed it to Clarissa. 'It's not champagne, but it will do.'

By the time they started to make their way back it was so dark the hut was only a full-black square against the grey-black night. The earl reached for Clarissa's hand.

'I don't want to lose you,' he said shortly.

The hut was warm after the fresh breeze.

'Why don't you push the straw up into a mattress?' he suggested. 'I'll light a fire.'

Working mainly by feel, Clarissa scraped the straw together, trying not to imagine what might be nesting there. By the time she had finished, Alresford had kindled a blaze which he was feeding with more sticks. The flames threw a welcome glow

over the little hut. He glanced up at her.

'It will warm up soon. You had best take off your wet jacket and lay it over the saddles to dry.'

'What of your greatcoat?'

He took it off. 'I shall spread it over the straw: the rain did not soak through, so it will serve. There, would you like to try your bed, my lady?'

She sat down carefully on the makeshift mattress. 'Very comfortable – what about you?'

He continued to stack logs around the fire.

'I'll contrive.'

She shook her head.

'You know very well there is nowhere else to sleep.'

'There's always the grass.' He rose to his feet and leaned against the wall, gazing down at the smoky fire.

Even as he spoke. the rain began to drum heavily on the roof.

'Impossible,' said Clarissa. 'There is plenty of straw, and your greatcoat is wide enough for the two of us.'

'I think not.'

Clarissa stood up.

'If you will not rest, then neither shall I!'

'Don't be absurd,' he growled at her.

Clarissa turned away, smiling to herself. Outside the storm raged, occasional gusts of wind making the door rattle. She thought she should be frightened, or nervous, but she felt strangely calm. The hut was a self-contained little world, quite removed from reality. She reached out and took his hand, saying softly, 'Come and lie down, sir. We cannot remain on our feet all night.'

For a brief moment he resisted, then with a sigh he threw himself down upon the makeshift bed. Clarissa sank down beside him, moving closer until her head was resting against his shoulder. She closed her eyes, remembering the feel of his arms about her. She ached for him to hold her again. She snuggled closer but he turned his back to her.

'I'm cold,' she murmured.

Silently he sat up, removed his jacket and tucked it around her.

'And now what will you do?' she asked, as he lay on his back, straight and still beside her.

'I shall manage.' To Clarissa it sounded as if it he was speaking through clenched teeth. 'You need not move closer, madam.'

She ignored him and moved her head against his arm. He groaned and turned away. Clarissa tentatively put her hand on his arm.

'It is so much warmer if we lie together, sir.'

'Remove your arm, madam. You do not – you cannot understand.'

Clarissa ignored him. Her hand travelled down his arm until she could lace her fingers with his. Sighing, she rested her cheek against his shoulder. He was so reassuringly solid.

'Don't, Clarissa.'

The aching inside was too much to bear. A small sob escaped her.

'Ah, don't push me away!'

In one swift, violent movement he turned. She found herself pinned beneath him.

'I – must – push you away!' The words came out on a sigh. 'Good God, don't you know how dangerous this is?'

Clarissa blinked.

'Dangerous? *This* is not dangerous – being chased across country by armed men is *dangerous*.' She spoke lightly, but it was an effort. She exulted at his closeness, breathing in the intoxicating mix of spices and man, anticipating the salty taste of his skin beneath her lips. She reached up and pulled his face down to hers. He did not resist and the touch of his lips was even better than before. This was no tentative, exploratory touch, it was raw hunger. Her arms tightened about his neck as he kissed her and she responded, instinctively pushing her body against his.

173

'No.' He lifted his head, gently easing himself away from her. 'I will not do this. I will not seduce you.'

She stared up at him, her breath coming in uneven gasps. Hot waves of remorse flooded through her as she realized how much she wanted him to take her in his arms again. She turned away, pressing her fist against her mouth.

'I am sorry,' she muttered. 'I am to blame! I should never . . . what must you think of me!'

'I think you are brave, and spirited, and adorable. If only—' He sighed, then she heard him rise. 'I think the rain has stopped. I am going outside.'

She lay rigid and tense as he left the hut, then strained her ears to listen to his footsteps whispering over the grass. Soon there was only silence and with a sob she turn her face against the rough cloth of his greatcoat and cried herself to sleep.

CHAPTER THIRTY-SIX

Clarissa awoke to a grey dawn and the sound of birdsong. She lay very still, trying to recapture her strange dream, but gradually she realized it had been no dream. Lord Alresford's greatcoat was beneath her, smelling of damp wool and musty straw. Her fingers clutched at the superfine cloth thrown over her shoulders – the earl's riding coat. A slight sound made her turn her head and she found the earl sitting on the edge of the straw, watching her. Her heart lurched at the sight of him, dressed only in his shirt, waistcoat and breeches.

She said, uncertainly, 'My lord?'

He smiled, dispelling her unease and replacing it with an inexplicable conviction that all would be well.

'I must get you back to town, if we are to avoid a scandal.'

'And if I said I didn't care?'

'I would not listen, because I would care for you.'

'Would you?' she looked up at him, suddenly shy. 'Would you, truly?'

'Yes, truly.' He leaned forward and kissed her lightly on the mouth. 'What made Dorothea Gaunt put you all in so much danger yesterday?'

Clarissa sighed and lay back, considering.

'She was incensed, I think, by Captain Shirley's arrogance, and she was more affected by Mr Sharp's talk than she would admit.'

'But there are other ways of helping to abolish the slave trade – better ways.'

'I know, but she thought it would be a good idea to try out our. . . .' Clarissa hesitated, then decided she would trust him. 'You see, we had already planned to hold up a coach.'

'Indeed?'

'Yes. If I tell you, will you promise it will go no further? It is a great secret, you see, and not really mine to tell, but I want to explain it to you.'

'You may be assured of my secrecy.'

She sat up and handed him his coat.

'We plan to hold up the Marquis of Ullenwood, to retrieve some letters that my stepmother, Lady Wyckenham, had written to him.'

'And why is it so important to recover these letters?'

'Because Lord Ullenwood is threatening to publish the letters if Mama-Nell will not run away with him. She believes that if he does so, it will ruin my brother William's career: he wants to enter politics, you see.'

'But does Lady Wyckenham have a *tendre* for Lord Ullenwood?'

'No. I believe she fancied herself in love with him for a short time, but that was long ago.'

'I thought her not indifferent to Sir Robert Ingleton.'

'Have you seen it, too?' She smiled up at him. 'I am so glad, because Mama-Nell will not admit it, but I am convinced that she loves him, and he certainly loves her, do you not think?'

'Undoubtedly. So why does she not ask Sir Robert to get her letters from the marquis?'

'Because she thinks he will despise her for having been so foolish. So . . . we – her friends – came up with the plan to rob Lord Ullenwood.'

'But how do you know the marquis will have the letters on him?'

'Well, Mama-Nell has arranged to run away with the marquis, on condition that he gives her the letters as soon as they set off. We will be following and when she gets out of the coach to destroy the letters, we will ride up, pretending to be highwaymen, and . . . and carry her away. Are you laughing at me, sir? I assure you it is a very good plan.'

'Slightly better than your last one, I admit, but still fraught with danger.'

'But we must get the letters back! Mama-Nell can have no peace until they are destroyed, surely you see that.'

'Yes, I do, but I am not convinced you are going about it the right way.' He rose. 'It is time we were moving.'

She allowed him to pull her to her feet. He turned to pick up her riding jacket.

'I hope this is dry enough for you,' She did not move, and he cocked an eyebrow at her frowning countenance. 'What is it, my dear?'

'Last night.' She flushed, looking down at her clasped hands. 'What I did – it was very wrong of me, I'm sorry.'

She risked looking up at him and the way he smiled at her sent her stomach spiralling through the floor.

'Don't be: I have wanted to make love to you since that first

day we met, in the woods.'

'You have?'

He nodded. 'That is why I was so angry that you were unat-
tended. You were quite unaware of the danger you were in.'

'And I thought you merely disapproving – you always look so
severe.'

He reached out and caught her fingers with his free hand.

'I know, 'tis my way, but I could change, if you would help me.'

'How?'

'You must teach me to laugh, Clarissa. Show me how to
laugh at the world, as you do.'

'Do you not think me too frivolous?'

He tossed aside her coat and pulled her into his arms.

'I know there is a serious side to you, but you choose not to
show it readily.'

'With good reason, my lord.'

He stilled, aware of her changing mood.

'How so? Tell me.'

'In my first season in town, I thought I was in love.' She did
not look at him. 'James Marlow and I were to be married, the
date was set but before the announcement was made Papa
had a stroke. It was very sudden, and Mama-Nell thought it
would be better to take him back to Wyckenham Hall. He
died there a week later. James came to the Hall, to support
us, he said. However, two weeks after the funeral he left
suddenly – eloped – with my best friend.' She bit her lip.
'They had met when she came to town to help me buy my
wedding clothes, and since she lived close to Wyckenham
Hall it was only natural that she should call upon us when
we brought Papa home. I did not realize then why she came
so often.'

'My poor girl. He ran off with her, while you were in such
distress?'

'Oh they did not get very far. The carriage overturned. J-
James broke his neck; *she* was unharmed, and went back to

177

her family in the country. It was hushed up, of course.' She drew a breath and looked up at him, her eyes bright with unshed tears. 'I doubt if anyone in town even knows the story.'

'And . . . your smiles – they were to hide a broken heart?'

His tone was harsh. She reached up to stroke his cheek.

'No, they were my armour to keep the world out. I did not want to risk being hurt again.'

He leaned forward to kiss her, a light, butterfly touch. Her hands crept about his neck. He muttered into her hair: 'You are not helping me to protect you, Clarissa.' With a groan Alresford gently pushed her away. 'I will not compromise you any more than I have done already. Here, put on your jacket, Clarissa. We must be on our way.'

Recognizing from his voice that he would not be moved, she obeyed. Conflicting thoughts and ideas raged within her: at one moment her heart sang, but then her spirits would tumble and some vague disquiet would seep through her. She knew he was right, they must be moving, but something wild and decadent within her wanted him to throw her down on to the hard, uncomfortable straw and make love to her. The disquiet returned. Had she offended him, she wondered, by her forward behaviour? She had certainly not acted as a lady. The thought troubled her for a moment then the earl turned and smiled, and all her doubts fled away.

'Let us see if we can find the horses.'

Shrugging on his riding jacket he strode to the door, picking up the harness as he went. She could hear him calling to his horse and by the time she pinned on her hat and went outside, both horses were tethered to a nearby tree, waiting to be saddled.

Half an hour later they had crossed the River Colne and were riding through Uxbridge. 'Thank goodness there is no one to see us,' murmured Clarissa, glancing around her. 'With no glass

to help me, I have no idea how I look.'

'Charming,' grinned the earl, 'if a little tousled. Once we have cleared the houses, I suggest we push on with all speed. The earlier we reach London the less people there will be to see us.'

'By all means. I am ready for my breakfast.'

By the time they reached London the street vendors were in full cry, milk-maids with their pails, the knife-grinders, pie-men and flower-girls, all competing with each other to make most noise and rouse the gentry from their beds. Lord Alresford stopped when they reached a small market cross.

'This is as far as we can go together. There is an inn around that corner: you will be able to hire a hackney carriage from there to take you home. Tell them your mare went lame and you had to abandon her. I will send her back to you later. Do you have enough money?'

She nodded, feeling for the purse in her pocket.

'Good.' He dismounted and went over to lift her down. 'You must walk through the passage over there – it leads directly to the inn yard. Come, I'll show you.'

He tethered the horses at the railing and walked with her across to a narrow alley. It was deserted and as he stepped inside he pulled Clarissa to him, pinning her against the wall. He kissed her once, roughly. Then he released her.

'Go,' he muttered. 'I will watch you from here – you will be quite safe.'

Mutely she looked up at him, but there was no comfort in his stern, forbidding face. He scowled at her.

'Go home, Clarissa.'

'You – when will I see you?'

'Tomorrow.' The corners of his mouth lifted. 'Your step-mama has invited me to her party. I will be there, you have my word.'

She nodded, then turned and hurried away through the narrow passage to the inn yard.

CHAPTER THIRTY-SEVEN

Clarissa arrived in Charlotte Street to be greeted by an anxious-looking Simmons, who informed her that Lady Wyckenham was in the morning-room.

'Lady Gaunt is with her, miss,' he added. 'She arrived only ten minutes ago.' Clarissa nodded. 'I will go to her. Pray have Becky lay out some fresh clothes for me – and send up hot water for a bath – you will see from the state of me that I have been obliged to spend the night in the open, having got lost in the dark. I did not enjoy the experience!'

Simmons responded with a fatherly smile.

'Well, we are very glad to see you safe back, miss, if I may be so bold as to say so,' Clarissa hurried to the morning-room, where Mama-Nell greeted her appearance with a shriek and flew across the room.

'My love – thank goodness!' Lady Wyckenham hugged her ruthlessly. 'Thank heavens you are safe.'

Clarissa glanced over her stepmother's shoulder at the Viscountess who was standing by the window.

'Helen knows everything.' Lady Gaunt spoke for once without her usual drawl.

'When we were separated last night and had to return without you, I thought it best to tell her.'

Clarissa nodded.

'And the others, they are safe?'

'Yes, all of them. We rode back into town at dusk last night and when I had seen them all safe to their homes I came immediately here, to Charlotte Street. It was too dark to do anything more last night, but at dawn I sent Grantham out looking for you.'

Lady Wyckenham gently pulled Clarissa towards a sofa. 'Sit down, my child, you look worn out. Do you feel strong enough to tell us what happened to you? We have told the servants that your horse bolted and you were separated from the others.'

Clarissa suddenly felt very tired, but she managed a smile.

'I have said as much to Simmons, too.'

Lady Gaunt sank into a chair opposite.

'What happened, Clarissa?'

'I had to fire the pistol, to warn you that the captain had a small army of men with him.'

'Oh heavens!' exclaimed Lady Wyckenham, her cheeks growing pale at the thought. Lady Gaunt gave a tight little smile.

'We escaped, Helen, but unfortunately they decided to follow Clarissa. I take it you out-ran them?'

'Yes, but became hopelessly lost. My mare went lame and I took shelter for the night in a deserted hut. This morning I walked to an inn and hired a hackney carriage to bring me home. The mare should be returned later today.'

'Never mind the horse,' declared Lady Wyckenham, blinking rapidly. 'You are safe, my love, and that is all that counts.'

Lady Gaunt sighed.

'Pity of it is that we came away empty-handed.'

'And thank heavens for that!' declared Lady Wyckenham looking as severe as it was possible for her to do. 'How *could* you think of resorting to highway robbery, Dorothea? I cannot credit that you could do such a thing. And to be leading the others into such danger. . . .'

'I know, and I am vastly sorry for it,' responded the viscountess gravely. 'I agree it was most irresponsible – a momentary madness, brought on by boredom.'

'Yes, well, it is too bad of you, Dorothea. It must not happen again.'

'You are quite right, Helen, and after Saturday I promise I

shall not involve you in my schemes again.'

Lady Wyckenham stared at her.

'You do not mean to continue with that plan, after last night?'

'But of course.'

'Mama-Nell, I agree that yesterday's escapade was unwise, but Lady Gaunt is right: we must go ahead with our plans to recover your letters. How else are we to free you from Lord Ullenwood's power?' Clarissa returned her stepmother's gaze steadily, and Lady Wyckenham transferred her attention to the viscountess, biting her lip in frustration when she realized that they were both determined to act.

'Very well,' she said at last. 'But there must be no more such schemes, In fact,' she added after a short pause, 'I think it would be best if we disbanded the Belles Dames Club.'

'I agree,' said Lady Gaunt. 'It has been an enjoyable distraction, Helen, but I think you are right: our little club is no longer a secret, and that was a considerable part of its charm. Besides, Gaunt wants to take me to Derbyshire next week, and from there I think I shall accompany him to the Continent.' She smiled at Clarissa. 'I am so glad you are returned safe, my dear, and I am more sorry than I can say that you were put into such danger. I will let the others know, although I am sure they will want to talk to you about it tomorrow night.'

Lady Wyckenham threw up her hands. 'Well, I do not want to talk of it: I cannot even *think* of it without shuddering! My poor Clarissa, to be alone and unprotected all night – I am quite distraught.'

Clarissa had to turn away. Despite her tiredness an irrepressible dimple threatened to peep out. What would they say if they knew the truth? She quelled the thought: it must not be discovered. She looked up suddenly.

'Where is my brother, does he know?'

Lady Wyckenham shook her head.

'William was out when Dorothea called last night, and he went straight to his room when he came in. We have not told him.' She looked a little guilty. 'I suggested to Simmons that as long as you returned safely today, it would be better if we did *not* tell him. It is not that I do not value your brother, Clarissa,' she went on, colouring slightly, 'but if there is no harm done, then it would be pointless to upset him.'

Clarissa smiled at that.

'Of course, Mama-Nell. If the servants believe I lost my way last night, they will think it only natural that I do not wish William to know of my folly.'

'Good.' Lady Gaunt stood up. 'If you can keep Lord Wyckenham from knowing anything about this until we have you and your letters safe, Helen, I think it would be best. Now, I must go. Clarissa, we meet again on Saturday, ostensibly for another riding party.'

'Perhaps the others will not want to take part in another such scheme, after what happened yesterday?' asked Lady Wyckenham not unhopefully.

'No, we are agreed,' said Lady Gaunt. 'And we will be much better prepared this time. Now, Helen, you are not to worry: only play your part and we will do the rest.'

Clarissa looked up.

'Will you not be at Mama-Nell's party tomorrow, ma'am?'

'Alas my dear, no. Gaunt is coming and I want to be at home for him – unfashionable I know, but I am really very fond of him.' She smiled as she moved towards the door. 'I hope Grantham has returned by now, and I can tell him you are safe, Clarissa. I suppose I will have to let him go now Gaunt is returning, but have no fear, my dears, he shall be well rewarded for his – ah – exemplary services.'

'Well!' exclaimed Lady Wyckenham, when the viscountess had left, 'I do not know whether to be most shocked or amused by Dorothea. She is a very good friend, but a dangerous one. And

not fit company for a single lady,' she added.

Clarissa felt that after the last twelve hours she was in no fit state to comment upon Lady Gaunt's behaviour. Pleading exhaustion, she fled to the seclusion of her bedchamber.

Her maid pounced upon her as soon as she stepped through the door, and Clarissa was at pains to repeat the story she had agreed with Lady Wyckenham: conjecture would be rife below-stairs, but she hoped they would trust Becky's account of what had happened to her mistress. To escape her maid's fussing, Clarissa bathed quickly then took to her bed. She was soon asleep, waking several hours later to find her stepmother leaning over her.

'Did I disturb you? I am sorry.' Lady Wyckenham smiled.

'What time is it? I must get up for dinner. . . .'

Mama-Nell gently pushed her back against the pillows.

'I shall send your dinner up to you, my love. You need not think that I shall be lonely, for William is dining at home tonight. I have told him you are indisposed, by the by, and, being a man, you may be sure he will not enquire too closely.'

'Then perhaps I should come downstairs to sit with you after dinner. . . .'

'No, no, for I have to go out for a while.'

'Oh? Do we have an engagement? You will have to give my apologies—'

'No, it is nothing like that. It – I have heard from an old friend who is in town and I wish to make a brief call. I shall not be late, I promise you.' She leaned down to press a scented kiss on Clarissa's cheek. 'You must rest, my dear, for I want you in your very best looks for my party tomorrow night.'

Clarissa entered the breakfast-room the following morning to find both her brother and stepmother had arrived before her. She cast an enquiring look towards Lady Wyckenham and caught the faintest shake of her head, which she took to mean that William knew nothing of her escapade. A few moments'

reflection convinced her that this was quite possible. Lord Wyckenham was a rare visitor to Charlotte Street and it did not surprise her that out of loyalty to their mistress, the retainers chose to withhold information from his lordship, and from his lordship's very superior valet.

With a pleasant good-morning, Clarissa took her place at the breakfast-table. Lord Wyckenham did no more than glance at her before continuing to read his newspaper, a habit that Lady Wyckenham deplored but which her stepson refused to give up, saying with ponderous humour that it was the only part of the day when he was at liberty for such an indulgence. Frowning at this lamentable behaviour, Lady Wyckenham turned to her stepdaughter, enquired after her health, then began to talk about her plans for the evening party. Clarissa buttered a piece of bread and nibbled it while Mama-Nell chattered on.

'I do not think I have had more than two refusals,' she declared. 'It will be the most shocking squeeze, which is most gratifying. And William has agreed to be here all evening, is that not so, my love?' She had to repeat the question before eliciting a response from Lord Wyckenham and, as he returned to his newspaper, she smiled roguishly at Clarissa. 'Of course, to persuade William to honour us with his company I have added several names to my list, dull and worthy people who will wish to talk of politics with him all night, but that need not concern us.'

'And Sir Robert, is he coming?' asked Clarissa, pouring another cup of coffee.

A shadow crossed Lady Wyckenham's lovely countenance.

'No, I had a note from him yesterday to say he is engaged elsewhere.'

'Oh, but I thought—'

'Good God!'

Clarissa jumped as her brother's cup crashed into its saucer,

and Lady Wyckenham looked up, alarmed.

'William, my love, whatever is the matter – oh dear, you have spilled your coffee.'

'What? Oh, oh yes. Most careless of me.' He rose quickly. 'My apologies, Mama-Nell. I – er – I had quite forgot the time. I have an appointment. I must go.' He rushed out of the room, leaving Lady Wyckenham staring across the table at her step-daughter.

'It is most unlike William to be late for anything,' murmured Clarissa.

'He does so pride himself on his punctuality.' Lady Wyckenham sighed. 'I hope it does not put him in a bad skin for this evening.'

Clarissa was looking towards the newsheet lying on top of William's breakfast plate.

'I wonder if there was something in the *Gazette* – perhaps a report about Captain Shirley.'

Lady Wyckenham looked even more nervous.

'Oh not so soon, surely.'

'No, of course,' said Clarissa, pulling the newspaper towards her. 'That would not have made William leave so suddenly.'

She quickly scanned the paper. Her eye alighted on an announcement bordered with a black line and the world seemed to tilt a little. She blinked, trying to read the words, the heavy black type began to dance before her eyes:

Notice of the marriage of the Earl of Alresford to Miss Florence Medway, daughter of Sir Gordon Medway Bart. of Devizes, Somersetshire, in June (date to be announced shortly).

CHAPTER THIRTY-EIGHT

'Clarissa, Clarissa my dear – what is it, what have you found?'

Clarissa folded the newspaper.

'Nothing. Nothing that could signify.' She was surprised that her voice was so normal. 'If you will excuse me, Mama-Nell—'

'Pray do not run off, Clarissa. I made sure you would help me. There are a thousand things to do before tonight's party.'

Clarissa heard herself asking if it could not be left to Simmons and received such a look of silent rebuke that she dragged up a smile, giving up any thoughts of escape.

'Of course, Mama-Nell. Tell me what you want me to do.'

Clarissa concentrated on carrying out the errands that Lady Wyckenham set for her, resolutely crushing all conjecture on what she had read in the newspaper. She felt her head would burst with the thoughts that kept welling up. Her heart screamed at her that it could not be true, that it was some awful mistake, but how could it be? As she walked the length of the house with an armful of linen she told herself there could be no mistake. She had seen the earl with Sir Gordon Medway and his family often enough to know that he was a close friend. Even Lady Gaunt had told her that Florence Medway was just such a good, pious creature as the fiancée Alresford had lost.

The memory of their night together in the shepherd's hut came back so strongly that she stopped in one of the long corridors, and had to remain there for several minutes, leaning against the wall while she fought down a great desire to weep at the thought of her actions. She had thrown herself at him in the most wanton manner – he had been a saint not to take

advantage of her. Hers was the blame, and she would have to live with it.

'Foolish girl!' she muttered fiercely, starting forward again. 'Foolish, headstrong girl!'

The youngest housemaid, coming out of one of the bedrooms at that moment, paled at being thus addressed.

'I'm very sorry, miss,' she stammered, dropping a nervous curtsy. 'Very sorry, I'm sure.'

Clarissa stared at her, then hurried on, closing her lips tightly lest anything more incriminating should escape her.

By the time she returned to her own room Becky was already laying out her dress for the evening.

'I thought you would want to wear the new cream muslin with the long sleeves, miss.'

Clarissa looked at the gown her maid was holding up and felt slightly sick. Alresford would not come – he could not. Then she remembered he had promised her. How would she face him? Clarissa gestured to her maid.

'Pray go away, Becky. I have the headache, and will lie down for a while.'

'Ooh, miss, I am sorry – shall I fetch you some lavender water to bathe your forehead, or perhaps my lady has some laudanum. . . .'

'No, nothing, thank you. I just wish to be quiet for a while. Come back in an hour.' She saw the maid's dubious look and summoned up another smile. 'Off you go: it will pass more quickly if I rest.'

'Very well, miss.'

The maid left, closing the door softly behind her and for a long time Clarissa did not move. At last she walked to her dressing-table and sat down, staring with unseeing eyes at her reflection in the glass. There seemed to be an argument raging in her head, one voice insisting that the notice was an error: Alresford would come tonight and explain it all to her. How could he? scoffed the other voice The notice was clear, they

were to be married in June. One month's time. Alresford must have known of it: he had not planned to be alone with her and he had made her no declarations of love, no promises. She could not claim he had broken faith with her. *Wait until you have seen him, spoken to him,* said the first voice. *Don't give up hope.*

When Becky returned an hour later Clarissa allowed her to dress her in the new cream muslin, caught around the waist with a wide lemon sash and under Becky's skilful hands her hair was persuaded to fall in soft curls to her shoulders, caught back from her face with another lemon ribbon, and a number of pale yellow rosebuds cunningly placed amongst her curls.

'Ooh, miss, you look as fine as fivepence, if I may say so,' declared Becky, fastening the single string of pearls about her mistress's slender neck. 'You will wear the pearl ear-drops too? Good . . . there, now let me look at you: you look a picture, although 'tis a pity you won't let me powder your hair – so thick it is, why there's many a lady has to resort to padding and false hair pieces to produce such thick curls! And perhaps a little rouge for your cheeks, miss, for you are still looking a little pale. . . .'

Clarissa waved her away.

'No, Becky, no rouge. It is time I joined Lady Wyckenham. Our guests will be arriving.'

An hour later Clarissa was wondering if she should have pleaded a migraine and kept to her bed. She stood beside Mama-Nell at the head of the wide staircase and greeted the steady stream of arrivals with her usual grace and charm. She smiled, laughed and chattered away, but had no idea what she said. Her face felt taut with the effort of constantly smiling: she was determined no one should know her inner turmoil and she was thankful that Lady Wyckenham was too occupied with

her duties as hostess to give her more than a cursory glance. William, too, seemed preoccupied and gave her very little attention. She turned so that she could look into the drawing-room, where her brother was conversing with a group of sober-looking gentlemen: probably he was too busy trying to ingratiate himself with the two cabinet ministers Mama-Nell had been at such pains to invite. Lady Wyckenham's voice cut through her reverie, bringing her back to the present with a jolt.

'Sir Gordon, Lady Medway – how delightful. . . .'

She spun around in time to see Sir Gordon bowing over Lady Wyckenham's hand. His wife stood at his side but seemed reluctant to smile, as if torn between gratification at being invited and disapproval of the opulence around her. Clarissa scolded herself for being so uncharitable. She gave her brightest smile to Florence, who was standing slightly behind her parents and was rewarded with a cool nod.

'Miss Medway – you are looking very well, and such a pretty gown.' Lady Wyckenham did her best to draw her out. 'Such an unusual shade of blue – how well it matches your eyes.'

Miss Medway looked non-plussed, uncertain how to respond to my lady's kind words. Her father gave a fat chuckle.

'Yes, a new gown, and we persuaded little Florence to choose something other than the sober colours she likes so well. After all, we have something to celebrate, do we not?'

Clarissa saw the colour mount in Miss Medway's cheeks as she felt it drain from her own.

'You look puzzled, ma'am,' Sir Gordon continued. 'Perhaps you have not heard: our little girl is to be married to Lord Alresford. The notice was in the newspapers today.'

'N-no, I had not heard.' Lady Wyckenham looked towards Clarissa, who felt as if she had been turned to stone.

'I am sure my lady has been too much occupied with her little party.' Lady Medway gave a thin smile.

'Well, it is delightful news,' said Lady Wyckenham, making a

recovery. 'You are to be congratulated, Miss Medway.' As the happy family moved away she hissed at Clarissa, 'Did you know of this?'

'I – I saw something. . . .'

'I cannot credit it!' muttered my lady, tapping her fan against her hand in agitation. 'I had thought – but never mind that now. Alresford! Well, he is always so severe and she is invariably Friday-faced, so they are made for one another, don't you think?'

She did not expect an answer and Clarissa was grateful, because at that moment she felt so miserable she could not speak. There could be no doubt now about the announcement. Clarissa raised her head and fixed an even brighter smile: she would not spoil Mama-Nell's party with her megrims.

CHAPTER THIRTY-NINE

Once the stream of guests coming up the stairs had thinned to a trickle, Mama-Nell dismissed Clarissa from her post at the top of the stairs and asked her instead to look after her guests in the drawing-room. Lord Alresford had not appeared, and Clarissa told herself she was glad he had not come, yet she continued to watch the door. When Sir Howard Besthorpe came in, she glanced across the room at Mrs Norwell, but Julia was happily engaged with a group that included her husband, and Clarissa was confident that Barnabus would not allow Sir Howard to approach his wife. Her spirits dipped when Lord Ullenwood's tall figure appeared, but she realized that Mama-Nell had been obliged to invite him, if their little scheme to

retrieve her letters was to work. She tried to concentrate on her guests and was soon approached by Georgiana Flooke and her sister, who wanted to know everything of her flight from the Heath, but even as she talked to them she was aware of every new arrival, and at last she was rewarded: Lord Alresford walked in.

Clarissa swallowed. There seemed to be some constriction in her throat and her heart was beating so hard she was afraid those standing near would hear it. The earl's frowning glance scanned the room and came to rest upon her. Clarissa's spirits, dipping so badly a moment earlier, now soared: had he been looking for her? There was no change in his expression, but he inclined his head a little to acknowledge her, then deliberately turned away.

Clarissa put up her chin and snapped open her fan, upbraiding herself for hoping for anything different. He could not approach her: no one must have any suspicion that they were anything more than acquaintances. Clarissa made her way through the crowded drawing-room, her smile fixed, eyes unnaturally bright. If he could behave so coolly, then so could she. At some point he would come to her and explain himself, she was sure of it, but that was impossible in such a gathering as this. As the heat and the noise grew ever more oppressive, Clarissa's head began to pound. The guests had spilled out on to the landing, but next to the drawing-room, the door to Mama-Nell's sewing-room had been thrown open and the candles lit, providing a quiet retreat from the crush of the party. Clarissa slipped into the empty room, thankful for a moment's solitude. She crossed to the window and threw up the sash, allowing in the cool night air. A noise behind her made her turn, and she found Sir Howard Besthorpe standing in the doorway. He came forward and made her a bow. It was perfectly executed, but she found the gesture insolent.

'I did not think to see so many of your little club here this evening, Miss Wyckenham.'

She returned his venomous glare with a haughty one.

'I do not know what you mean, sir.'

'After your – ah – adventure on Hounslow Heath on Tuesday I expected at least some of you to be clapped up.'

A cold chill ran through Clarissa. She put up her chin, determined not to admit to anything. Her silence goaded him to continue and he leaned forward, spitting out the words.

'I overheard your little plans at Lady Maramond's the other evening.'

A sudden memory of that night came into her mind. She was again walking towards the little book-room and saw the maid coming out, looking flustered and adjusting the kerchief around her neck as she hurried away.

Clarissa's lip curled.

'Can you go nowhere without finding some poor female to persecute? You have sunk so low that not even the housemaids are safe from you.'

His little eyes snapped.

'She was willing enough for a tumble, and what I learned once she had left, and I had hid myself behind the curtains, was enough to foil your little plans. Damme but you were so foolish. Did you—?'

'Well, well, 'tis Sir Howard.'

Clarissa jumped as Lord Alresford's deep voice cut across Sir Howard's waspish tones. The earl strolled into the room, Mr Norwell beside him. Sir Howard stepped back and offered them a small, stiff bow.

'I think you can have nothing to say to me, my lord. If you will excuse me—' He went to step past Lord Alresford but the earl put out a hand.

'Not so fast, Sir Howard. I have lost patience with you. Whenever I see you I am sorry for it. I do not think we can tolerate your presence any longer. What say you, Norwell?'

'Oh I agree, Alresford. I think we should do something about it.'

'I fail to understand you.' Sir Howard's voice was high and querulous.

The earl stepped in front of him.

'Let me explain it to you: I think it is time you left town, sir. Norwell, will you act for me?'

'With pleasure,' was the prompt reply.

'Very well. Besthorpe, my man will call at your lodgings at noon tomorrow. If you are still in residence, he will deliver my challenge and we will meet on the heath on Saturday morning.'

'But that is preposterous!' spluttered Sir Howard. 'I will not be bludgeoned into leaving.'

Lord Alresford gave a slight shrug as he turned away. Watching, transfixed, from the corner of the room, Clarissa thought she had never seen him so menacing.

'That, of course, is your choice, Sir Howard.'

'Wait! You – you have no cause to call me out!'

Lord Alresford stopped.

'Cause?' he said slowly. 'Your whole being offends me. That is cause enough, is it not?'

'By Jove it is!' Mr Norwell grinned. 'Damme, it offends me, too.' He took Sir Howard's arm, while that gentleman opened and closed his mouth in silent fury. 'Come along. You will want to be getting home, I don't doubt, for you have preparations to make. If you are determined to meet Alresford, then you had best set your affairs in order, for he's a devilish good shot, you know. . . .'

He propelled Sir Howard out of the room, and Clarissa was left facing Lord Alresford.

CHAPTER FORTY

Lady Wyckenham stifled a sigh and prayed that no one would guess she had the headache. Her rooms were overflowing with guests and there was no time to relax. She glanced around her: William was doing his duty, talking to the Medway girl. If only he would smile more! Her eyes travelled across the room to where Clarissa was talking with Emily and Georgiana. She was looking a little pale, but that was understandable after the shocking prank – Lady Wyckenham could not forgive Dorothea for embroiling her stepdaughter in such a dangerous escapade. She saw her laughing at some remark Emily had made and her heart turned over at the sight of her lovely countenance. How beautiful she was: Clarissa deserved to marry well. Lady Wyckenham would not allow any hint of scandal to ruin her chances.

She moved about the room, a word here, a smile there: Lady Wyckenham was all graciousness, her guests would want for nothing and she would confirm her reputation as a notable hostess.

'Helen.'

Lady Wyckenham started. She turned, schooling her features into a smile.

'Lord Ullenwood.' She held out her hand to him and he raised it to his lips.

'You are lovelier than ever tonight, Helen.'

She drew her fingers away, flushing at the passion she read in his face.

'You cannot monopolize me tonight, sir. I must attend to my guests.'

'I would not dream of it.' He looked amused. 'A glittering

evening, my dear. I cannot wait to see you play hostess in my houses.'

She could not suppress a shudder, but rather than be offended he laughed and leaned forward, saying softly, 'I will make you love me again, Helen.'

Lady Wyckenham stepped away from him, her cheeks flaming.

'Please, Elliott, not now. Let me enjoy my last evening here.'

He bowed.

'As you wish, madam. I can wait a few more hours.'

She turned and hurried away from him, fighting down a great desire to burst into tears.

In the sewing-room, Lord Alresford looked steadily at Clarissa.

'You have seen the *Gazette*?'

She nodded. Risking a look at him she saw more than the forbidding scowl: he looked desperately tired, but she dared not allow herself to feel sorry for him.

'Yes,' she said brightly. 'Congratulations, my lord.'

He put up his hand as if to ward off a blow.

'Clarissa, believe me – I did not know, was not aware . . . nothing had been agreed. As soon as I got back yesterday I went to Mount Street to tell them – but it was too late, Sir Gordon had already sent the notice.'

She stared at him.

'He could hardly have done so without your consent.'

Alresford sighed.

'I had not – that is, I must have given him some reason to believe. But we had not. . . .' He looked up, anguish in his dark eyes. 'Clarissa, I am sorry.'

She clasped her hands tightly before her to stop them shaking: she was amazed how calmly she could speak.

'Thankfully there will be no repercussions from Tuesday night. Your . . . circumspection saw to that.' Only at the last did her voice betray her, and he flinched at the bitterness in her

tone. Her lip curled. 'Perhaps that was your intention, to make sure there could be no proof of your iniquity.'

'No, I never meant—'

She said bitterly, 'I was merely a diversion, is that it?'

'No! No, Clarissa.' He sighed and said quietly, 'What would you have me do?'

'Nothing,' she whispered. 'It has been announced, it cannot be refuted. There is nothing to be done.'

They stared at one another, so much more to say, so much that must not be said.

'There you are, Alresford.' Florence Medway stood in the open doorway. 'We have been looking for you everywhere, my lord. Mama is ready to leave, and you are to escort us. . .'

Lord Alresford looked at her blankly for a moment.

'Yes, of course.' He turned back to Clarissa and bowed, his face expressionless. 'Miss Wyckenham.'

She inclined her head.

'Goodbye, Lord Alresford.'

He turned away and walked to the doorway where Miss Medway was waiting. As she placed her fingers on his arm she gave a last, triumphant look at Clarissa.

The Earl of Alresford felt the noose tightening around his neck. He had slept little, disturbed by dreams that included a vivid scene where he choked the life out of Sir Gordon Medway. This gave some relief to the torment of emotions raging within him, but it was short-lived. He rolled to the edge of the bed and threw back the hangings. The house was still quiet but daylight pushed in around the curtains at the window. With sudden decision he climbed out of bed. He would not lie there and be prey to the guilt and anger that had ravaged his sleep. He dressed quickly in the buckskins and cloth coat thrown over a chair, knotted his neck cloth with a carelessness that would have shocked his valet and tugged on his boots. Perhaps a walk would clear his head. He let himself

out of the house and set off across the square and into the fields beyond.

He remembered his shock when he learned that Sir Gordon had sent the notice to the *Gazette*. Sir Gordon had been all bluff good humour.

'Well, my boy, thought we had waited long enough – after all, we had talked of it, had we not, and little Florence was pestering me to make the announcement – and you know I cannot refuse her anything! You were out of town, but I thought, what's the harm, we all know it is going to happen, so now it's done, all right and tight.'

No, not all right but definitely tight, thought the earl, running a finger around his neck cloth as he marched along.

He crossed Tottenham Court Road where a few traders' wagons were beginning to make their way into the town and found himself on the corner of Charlotte Street. It had not been his intention – after all one could not make a social call at five o'clock in the morning. He carried on to the corner and was surprised to see a carriage pulled up outside Lady Wyckenham's house, and even more so to see the lady herself emerge, wrapped in a large travelling cloak. As the lackey held open the carriage door for her, the earl saw the Ullenwood crest emblazoned on the black panel. He stepped back as the carriage came towards him, sweeping past at a smart pace. He followed it into Oxford Street, then, as it drew away from him, he began to run. He turned into Wardour Street, where his frantic knocking at the door of one of the rented houses finally brought a sleepy servant. A few terse sentences and he was shown into a small parlour, where he paced the floor until the master of the house came in.

'Alresford! What the devil do you mean by coming here at this hour?' Sir Robert Ingleton entered wearing a garish dressing-gown and a very dark frown.

'I would not have done so if I had not a good reason.' The earl stopped his pacing. 'I have just seen Lady Wyckenham getting

into Ullenwood's coach.'

Sir Robert's frown deepened to a scowl.

'So, what is that to do with me?' he said harshly. 'The lady has made her choice.'

'I do not believe it was a choice, Ingleton. I think 'tis blackmail.' Quickly the earl told him everything Clarissa had divulged about Lady Wyckenham's letters and the plan to retrieve them. 'I cannot tell you my source, but it was thought that Ullenwood would be taking Lady Wyckenham out of town on Saturday.'

Sir Robert shrugged. 'That may have changed.'

Lord Alresford frowned. 'Possibly, but I think it much more likely that the lady deceived them: she did not want her friends to risk so much for her sake.'

Sir Robert slammed his fist into his palm.

'Damnation, why did she not come to me?'

Lord Alresford studied the toe of his boot. He said carefully, 'I understand that she did not want you to know of her foolishness. The letters were written soon after she was widowed, when she was alone, distraught and friendless.' Marius saw Sir Robert wince and added quietly, 'She thinks by sacrificing herself she can save her stepchildren from scandal.'

'Well she shan't sacrifice herself,' declared Sir Robert, striding to the door and shouting for his man. 'More to the point,' he added, directing a straight look at the earl, 'she shan't sacrifice me! Will you come with me?'

'Of course, if you will send a runner to the stables for my horse. We will save time if we leave from here.'

'It shall be done. Which way were they going?'

'The last I saw the carriage it was turning south off Oxford Street. Ullenwood has a property in Wiltshire, I believe.'

Sir Robert nodded.

'He will be heading out on the Bath road, then. We shall catch him at Hounslow and stop him on the heath, if necessary

– does that amuse you?'

'No, merely I am becoming quite familiar with the place.'

Sir Robert did not waste time asking for an explanation. Instead he looked at the earl, his eyes narrowing 'You are taller than I, but it should not be a problem: I will look out a hat and a greatcoat for you – I am not sure how we will proceed, but we may need disguise.'

Alresford nodded, his lips curling into a reluctant smile.

'Very likely – and you might like to take a brace of pistols, too.'

Sir Robert did not flinch but went off to issue his instructions and to dress, leaving the earl to curb his impatience as best he might.

A half hour later they were riding out of town. Neither gentleman had said more than a few words but now Sir Robert turned to Alresford.

'So why are you taking such an interest in this family?' He cocked an eyebrow at his companion. 'If I might hazard a guess – Miss Wyckenham?'

Lord Alresford hoped his countenance did not give him away. 'I would do as much for anyone.'

Sir Robert laughed. 'Including breaking the law? I doubt it.'

The earl felt the flush creeping into his cheeks. Sir Robert said gently, 'Come man. You have trusted me thus far – will you not admit you have a fondness for the girl?'

'It is true,' said Marius, his voice not quite steady. 'But I am not free: I hope by helping Lady Wyckenham I can atone somewhat for what I have done.' He read sympathy in Sir Robert's face, and said harshly, 'We have reached open ground – we should press on.'

CHAPTER FORTY-ONE

In the Marquis of Ullenwood's elegant travelling carriage, Lady Wyckenham sat on the very edge of her seat, her hands clasping and unclasping nervously in her lap. Lord Ullenwood lounged in one corner, watching her with a faint smile curling his thin lips.

'Madam, you should take your ease. We have a long journey, pray, rest yourself.'

She hesitated, then sat back, leaning against the fat, padded squabs. Unwilling to meet the marquis's amused glance she looked around her at the luxurious interior. The carriage smelled of new leather: a carriage pistol rested in a tooled leather holster next to the door. Thank heavens the Belles Dames Club had false information about her flight: Ullenwood was reputed to be deadly with a pistol.

'What are you thinking, madam?'

'That you have a well-appointed carriage, my lord. Do we travel far today?'

'We will breakfast at Maidenhead and put up at Marlborough overnight. Tomorrow I shall take you to your new home at Clevedon Bassett.' His paused. 'You are still nervous, my lady.'

'Of course I am nervous. I have come away with you with nothing more than a small portmanteau, as you instructed. I have only the clothes I stand up in.'

He smiled.

'I think you will find I have provided everything you require, including several gowns. A seamstress will be waiting at Clevedon Bassett to fit them for you.'

'I need more than elegant robes, sir.'

'Do you think I have no experience, my dear? There is a trunk strapped to the back that contains the very finest chemises, petticoats and furbelows, as well as a very fetching nightgown which I am sure will – ah – enhance your natural charms. I chose it myself.'

She flushed at the thought and they drove on in silence. As they approached Hounslow Heath my lady said, 'When will you give me my letters?'

He reached into his pocket and pulled out a bundle of papers tied with a scarlet ribbon.

'Whenever you wish.'

He held out the bundle and she took it, quickly counting the neatly folded packets.

'You need not worry, they are all there. I play fair, my love.'

She put up her chin, blinking to clear the tears that threatened to spill over.

'So do I, my lord.' She took a couple of deep breaths to calm herself. 'We are nearing the nine-mile stone on the heath: pray ask your man to stop there for a moment.'

The marquis looked mildly surprised, but he pulled the check-string and the carriage came smoothly to a halt. Lady Wyckenham stepped down and looked about her. Despite the sunshine the heath looked bare and desolate, and she could not repress a shiver. She walked toward the shallow, stagnant pool beside the road, opened the first letter and dropped it into the dark water, which quickly distorted the black writing until it was nothing more than grey smudges on the paper. The other letters followed suit and, as the last one touched the surface, my lady stooped to pick up a stone and place it on the paper. With no more than a few bubbles the stone and the papers disappeared into the black pool. She straightened up to find the marquis standing beside her.

'Well, Helen?' Gently he turned her towards him, putting a finger under her chin and forcing her to look up at him. 'I have no hold over you now: will you take the first opportunity

to leave me?'

She forced herself to look at him, her little chin tilting up proudly as she said, 'No, Elliott. I have told you: I play square.'

'But I do not.'

'What the devil—' The marquis jumped back and Helen turned, open-mouthed to see Sir Robert Ingleton standing on the far side of the road, a serviceable pistol in his hand. A second armed man, mounted on a black horse, was keeping watch on Lord Ullenwood's servants, who remained motionless on the carriage.

'The fools were too busy gawping at you to keep watch on the heath,' grinned Sir Robert. 'You should turn 'em off.'

'I should indeed,' replied Lord Ullenwood evenly. His cold glance flickered to Lady Wyckenham. 'Is this your idea of playing square, my dear?'

'No, no,' she said, quite dazed. 'I knew nothing of this.' She blinked and stared at Sir Robert and his companion, who were both wearing caped greatcoats and dark tricorne hats. 'You look like highwaymen.'

'I think that is the idea, my dear,' drawled Ullenwood. 'They have come to steal you from me.'

'The lady is not your property,' retorted Sir Robert. 'She is here under duress.'

'You think so?' The marquis curled his lip. 'Perhaps we should ask the lady.'

Sir Robert grinned.

'Oh no,' he said. 'I shall not give you the chance to appeal to her sense of honour, Ullenwood.' He whistled, and his long-tailed bay came trotting up. 'Come, Helen. You will ride before me.'

My lady hesitated, and Lord Ullenwood spoke quietly.

'Go, my dear – if your conscience will allow.'

'Conscience be damned,' said Sir Robert cheerfully. 'If you don't come with me, Nell, I'll put a bullet through his black heart.' He dropped the pistol into the pocket of his greatcoat

and held out his hand. 'Come, madam.' He threw Lady Wyckenham up on to the saddlebow and climbed up behind her. She felt Sir Robert's arms tighten around her as he gathered up the reins. 'I am sorry if this is not very comfortable for you, Nell.' His voice was warm and comforting in her ear and she leaned back against him, revelling in the feeling of security that had suddenly enveloped her. He lifted his head. 'Are you ready, Alresford, shall we go?'

She stifled a gasp as she recognized Sir Robert's accomplice, but she was still too overwhelmed by events to speak. They moved off, gradually picking up speed, and Lady Wyckenham clutched at her travelling cloak, which had begun to billow out around her. She risked a glance up at her rescuer. Sir Robert was intent on keeping up with the earl's black hunter, but despite the look of concentration, there was an upward curve to his lips, and when he glanced down at her she saw the familiar devil-may-care gleam in his blue eyes.

'Don't worry, sweetheart, you are safe now.'

She leaned against him, smiling. It was quite nonsensical, she knew, but now at last she really did feel safe.

As the two horses galloped away, Lord Ullenwood's coachman scrabbled for the shotgun.

'Leave it,' the marquis barked out. 'You should have been ready with that when they were approaching.'

'My lord, they are still within range. I could—'

'No.' The marquis watched the riders gallop away. 'No, let them go. It is over.'

CHAPTER FORTY-TWO

'We must find a chaise or something to carry you home. We were in such a hurry to set out that I had not time to arrange it.'

Lady Wyckenham sighed happily and leaned her head on Sir Robert's shoulder. Once they were sure they were not being pursued they had slowed to a walk.

'I am very comfortable here,' she murmured.

'Aye, sweeting, but have some compassion for the poor horse, having to carry the two of us.'

'Mayhap we should have taken Ullenwood's carriage,' suggested the earl.

Lady Wyckenham raised her head and looked in surprise at Lord Alresford.

'My lord, I had always thought you the very model of respectability.'

Something almost like a grin softened the earl's severe features. 'So I was, ma'am, until I came off my horse in a wood near Tottenham: I think it gave me a brain fever. But Ingleton is right, my lady: we need a carriage to take you home.'

'And I suppose I must take you back to Charlotte Street. My lodgings are not suitable for a lady.'

She gave a little cry.

'Oh goodness! I left a note!'

He rolled his eyes.

'What woman does not? Be still, sweetheart. We may yet get you back before any of the family have left their rooms.'

Realizing there was nothing else to be done, Lady Wyckenham turned her thoughts to the events of the past few hours.

'But Robert, how did you know what was happening, who told you?'

'Alresford saw you getting into the carriage.'

'At five o'clock in the morning?' She looked at the earl. Returning from some gaming hell, she supposed. 'But what made you go to Sir Robert?'

A pair of strong arms tightened around her.

'Everyone knows we are desperately in love, Nell.'

'They – they do?'

Sir Robert was smiling down at her in a way that put all rational thought to flight.

'Yes, they do! Now be quiet and keep your eyes open for anyone who might have a vehicle we can use.'

An inn was soon reached and the landlord produced a very shabby gig that he agreed they could have at what Lady Wyckenham considered an extortionate fee. Once the transaction was completed, Sir Robert tied his horse to the back of the gig and climbed up beside her. Lady Wyckenham turned to the earl.

'Will you ride with us, my lord?' She hoped her warm smile would draw some response, but he merely bowed.

'If you will excuse me, I will leave you here. You have no further need of my services.'

'I hope not,' agreed Sir Robert, gathering up the reins. 'Goodbye, Alresford – and thank you.'

With a final salute the earl trotted off and was soon out of sight.

'Well, I cannot understand that man,' declared my lady. 'Always so correct and yet he was willing to come with you on this escapade. If only he would smile more – one cannot but think he is carrying some great unhappiness.'

'Very likely,' agreed Sir Robert, driving out of the inn yard. 'He is certainly not about to marry the love of his life, as I am.'

'Oh!' My lady blushed. 'Robert, pray do not say such a thing.'

'Do you think I have gone to all this trouble to have you refuse me?'

'Oh no, of course not, but—'

'But what?'

She began to pleat the edge of her cloak between her fingers.

'You have not asked me,' she said quietly.

'Is that all? Well, madam, will you marry me?'

She did not look up, but a dimple appeared in her cheek.

'Yes, Robert, I think I will.'

'Good. Then it is all settled.'

My lady gave an indignant little cry.

'No, it is not all settled! There is much to be considered, like – like Clarissa, and William.'

'Clarissa I agree we must consider. She will have a home with us, if she so wishes, but please do not ask me to think about William. I find him a prosy bore, do not you?'

'Oh stop it!' she cried, torn between indignation and laughter. 'You know what I mean – this is all so sudden.'

'No it is not. I have loved you for years, Nell, and if I hadn't been sailing on the other side of the world when Wyckenham died I would have made sure you didn't get involved with a man like Ullenwood.'

'Oh.'

'That was foolish beyond belief,' he said severely.

She hung her head.

'I know it, and I have always regretted it.'

'And all this business with the Belles Dames Club. I can see that it was very diverting for you, but highly irregular.'

'But no one was supposed to know about that.'

'Impossible to stop the servants from gossiping. Before you know it, tales are being spread all over town.'

'You are right, of course. News of it even reached William in Bath, which is why he came to town to put a stop to it.'

'Well, for once I have to agree with him. I have no objection to you trying your skill at dice and cards, and for your visits

to Vauxhall and Ranelagh I have no doubt that you were masked but . . . wrestling matches in your drawing-room, Nell?'

'We only did that once, Robert, and – and it was very entertaining.'

His lips twitched.

'I can imagine. Who thought of that little diversion?'

'Well, Dorothea. . . .'

'Lady Gaunt; I should have known! The sooner Gaunt comes back to take her in hand the better. I suppose the idea of holding up Ullenwood's coach was hers, too.'

'You knew about that? Well, at least I was not prepared to allow them to go ahead with that hare-brained scheme. And how can you criticize,' she said, turning to him, 'when you have just done the very same thing yourself?'

'Not at all the same thing,' he said firmly. 'When we are married, I think I shall carry you off to Newfield Hall out of harm's way. You need not be bored; there will be plenty to do. I will set up a studio for your painting and if you grow tired of drawing plants and landscapes and have a desire to try a life study you will have to make do with me for a model.'

The thought of Robert lying naked on a couch made Helen's insides liquefy. She peeped up and found that he was looking at her, his blue eyes twinkling wickedly.

'As a matter of fact, I quite like that idea,' he added.

My lady resolutely turned to stare at the road ahead.

'Be quiet and drive,' she said severely. 'You had best let me recover my composure, Robert, for I really would like to arrive at Charlotte Street with some degree of decorum.'

CHAPTER FORTY-THREE

Clarissa was in the morning-room with her brother when Lady Wyckenham and Sir Robert were shown in. Clarissa jumped up.

'Mama-Nell – I thought – your letter!'

'Yes,' Lord Wyckenham waved a sheet of paper. 'My dear madam, what is all this nonsense?'

'Just that, nonsense,' said Lady Wyckenham, untying her bonnet and casting it aside. 'You will burn that note, if you please, William.'

Sir Robert came forward.

'Perhaps my lady should explain.'

'What have you to do with all this?' demanded William. 'This says Lord Ullenwood—'

'You have already been told to ignore that letter,' Sir Robert cheerfully interrupted him. 'I have come to inform you that Lady Wyckenham and I are to be married, as soon as possible.'

'Married!' exclaimed William.

'Oh I knew it!' Clarissa ran to her. 'Oh, Mama-Nell, I am so happy for you. But I thought—'

My lady gave her a warning glance.

'I will explain everything later, my love,' she murmured, squeezing her hands. She looked up. 'I was foolish enough to get embroiled with Lord Ullenwood, resulting in my going off with him this morning. William, you will not ask for more details, if you please. It is all over now and far too sordid for you to hear. Thankfully Sir Robert came to my rescue.'

'Embroiled – married? What . . . I do not understand,' Lord Wyckenham spluttered and frowned.

Sir Robert smiled at him.

'All very simple, Wyckenham. I am off to arrange a special licence, so that we can be married as soon as maybe. Now, why don't we step into the library to discuss settlements? I am sure you will want to know something of my circumstances.'

'But I don't want you discussing my affairs with William!' objected Lady Wyckenham.'

Sir Robert took her hand and kissed it.

'No, I am sure you would rather deal with all that yourself my love, but you must see that as head of the family, Wyckenham will want some say in the matter. You stay here with Clarissa. I am sure you will have much to talk about.' With a reassuring smile he turned and ushered Lord Wyckenham out of the room.

When the gentlemen had gone, Clarissa and her stepmother looked at each other in silence for several minutes.

'You told us the wrong day, Mama-Nell,' said Clarissa reproachfully, sinking down on to a sofa.

'I am sorry.' Lady Wyckenham came to sit beside her. 'I could not have you all risking yourselves for my sake. I went to Ullenwood and made him change his plans.'

Clarissa nodded.

'And you told Sir Robert. I cannot be sorry, he clearly dotes on you.'

'Yes; but I did not go to him: I had made up my mind to go with the marquis. It seemed the only way to protect you and William. I remembered what Dorothea had said about the pool so I made Ullenwood stop and I destroyed the letters. It was there that Sir Robert and Lord Alresford appeared.'

Clarissa stared.

'Alresford! What was he doing there?'

'He told Sir Robert I was being abducted. I do not know how he came by such an idea, but I am very glad he did, and that he called on Sir Robert to help him.'

Clarissa hugged her, blinking rapidly.

'It does not matter how he knew. All that matters is that you are safe.'

'Thank you. And' – Lady Wyckenham looked closely at Clarissa – 'you do not object to my marrying Sir Robert?'

'Object? Of course not, I think it is just what you need, Mama-Nell. The two of you have been making sheep's eyes at each other ever since he came back to town.'

'Clarissa, how can you be so vulgar! We have done nothing of the kind.'

Clarissa laughed at her stepmother's outraged countenance.

'Admit it, you are very much in love with him.'

'Well, yes, I am, but I hope we know better than to wear our hearts on our sleeves.'

Clarissa's eyes twinkled but she did not reply, and Mama-Nell continued, 'Robert says that you are to make your home with us, Clarissa, if you would like that. I cannot see that you would want to live in Devon with William.'

Clarissa threw up her hands in horror.

'Oh heaven forbid! We should be ready to murder one another within the first week. I could go back to live with Anne for a while, of course, but,' she paused, wondering if it was too early to disclose her plans, 'I am thinking of going abroad, Mama-Nell. You and Sir Robert will want to have some time to yourselves. Augusta Maramond and Lady Alicia are planning a trip to Rome this winter: I thought I might go with them.' She saw the surprise in Mama-Nell's face and hurried on, 'I have always wanted to see Rome, and Augusta says they will be engaging a courier, and will have an escort, so it will be perfectly safe.'

'Yes, my love, I am sure but – Augusta and Alicia are so much older than you. Surely you would prefer to go with someone more your own age?'

'Rome will look the same, whatever the company.'

Lady Wyckenham touched her cheek.

'That is not quite true, my love,' she said, smiling. 'I think

211

you should be with young people.' She hesitated, then blurted out, 'You are too beautiful to remain single!'

Clarissa froze. Something of her despair must have shown in her face for Mama-Nell was looking at her with concern and she quickly veiled her thoughts.

'Well, plenty of time to think of that,' she said with forced brightness. 'For now I am too excited about your wedding to think any further ahead.'

She encouraged Lady Wyckenham to talk about Sir Robert and her plans for the future, and the subject kept them occupied until the gentlemen returned. Sir Robert took his leave, promising to join them for dinner and when William went off to his study Clarissa persuaded Mama-Nell to lie down for a few hours. Only then was she free to pursue her own thoughts. The knowledge that Lord Alresford had been involved in the morning's events gave her some comfort: she had been regretting taking him into her confidence, but she had no doubt it was the reason he had sought out Sir Robert. The little clock outside her room chimed the hour. Twelve o'clock. She wondered if Sir Howard had left town or if he intended to meet the earl. The thought made her grow cold with fear. Mr Norwell had said his friend was a crack shot, but things could go wrong. Her apprehension grew as the day wore on. She scribbled a hurried note to Norwell House, but although Julia replied by return she could give her no comfort: Barnabus had told her nothing of the matter.

By dinnertime Clarissa was in such a state of anxiety that she could barely eat. A few seemingly careless questions to Sir Robert elicited no information other than he had not seen the earl since that morning. Unfortunately this gave Lord Wyckenham the opportunity to lecture them on the dangers of travel. The servants had withdrawn and Sir Robert was the only guest at dinner, so Lord Wyckenham did not scruple to comment upon Sir Robert's nomadic existence.

'You may rest easy,' Sir Robert said, with a reassuring glance at Lady Wyckenham. 'I have already told Sir Joseph that I shall not be going on any more expeditions. My travel from now on will be confined to these islands.'

'But even that is not without its dangers,' objected William. 'All the roads from London are beset by highwaymen; no one is safe, even in daylight. Why, Maramond was telling me only yesterday that his cousin – you know the one – the sea captain we met a couple of times when he was in town recently. Well, he was set upon on Hounslow Heath earlier this week—Mama-Nell, did you speak?'

'No, my dear, it was a piece of nut caught in my throat,' replied my lady, reaching for her wineglass.

'Was that reported in the newspaper, William?' asked Clarissa.

'No; Maramond said his cousin had some warning of what was planned and had men waiting to surprise his attackers. Dashed villains, it's the gallows for their kind!'

'And do they report duels in the paper?' said Clarissa, pursuing her own thoughts.

'Duels, Clarissa?' Lord Wyckenham looked down his nose at her. 'Yes, I suppose they might. Mostly if the authorities find them out and prevent 'em.'

'Why ever should you want to read about such things, Clarissa?' Lady Wyckenham broke off her conversation with Sir Robert to enquire.

Sir Robert winked at her across the table.

'Perhaps there is some young man fighting for her honour.'

Clarissa tried to smile at the jest, but it was Lord Wyckenham who replied, saying testily, 'My sister would not be involved in anything so ill-bred, Ingleton. I would thank you to remember that.'

'I suppose you consider what happened this morning was shocking, also,' retorted Lady Wyckenham, disliking William's tone in replying to her beloved.

William lifted his napkin to dab at his lips.

'We will not talk of that, if you please,' he said heavily. 'Although how you could think that going off with a man of Ullenwood's stamp could possibly save the family from scandal—'

'I think it was a very noble thing to do!' cried Clarissa.

'So do I,' said Sir Robert, raising his glass to Lady Wyckenham, who blushed fierily.

Clarissa giggled, and Lord Wyckenham looked revolted by this display of affection at the dinner-table.

The gentlemen did not linger over their brandy once the ladies had withdrawn, and Clarissa excused herself before the tea-tray was brought in, pleading a headache. Since William retired soon after, saying he had papers demanding his attention, Lady Wyckenham found herself alone with Sir Robert.

'What an obliging family you have, ma'am,' he remarked, coming over to sit beside her and pulling her into his arms.

She opened her mouth to protest and found herself being ruthlessly kissed. It was the most delightful sensation and she responded immediately, allowing him to push her back against the sofa before she remembered where they were. With a little groan she tried to push him away.

'Oh Robert, no more, stop. William might come back.'

She struggled to sit up as he released her.

'Are you going to make me wait until we are married before I can touch you?'

She began to straighten the muslin kerchief, keeping her eyes lowered.

'No-o, but we must be discreet. I will tell Simmons to have the guest-room prepared for you for the night: it adjoins my dressing-room, and I have keys to all the doors – I have learned *something* from Dorothea Gaunt.'

He met her twinkling glance and laughed.

'You are a darling!' he said, kissing her again.

A discreet knocking at the door made her jump away. She looked at Sir Robert in horror, but he merely adjured her to straighten her cap.

A footman entered to announce that a delivery had arrived for my lady.

'A – a delivery?' she repeated, looking blank. 'At this time of the night? What is it?'

'A trunk, my lady. The carrier has instructions that he is to deliver it to you personally.'

She looked at Sir Robert, who shrugged.

'I suggest you let them bring it in.'

With much huffing and puffing two of the footmen carried in a large corded trunk, which Sir Robert directed them to set down before Lady Wyckenham.

'Thank you,' she said, 'that will be all. Pray ask Simmons to pay the carter for his trouble.' The footmen withdrew and she looked down at the trunk.

'Well,' said Sir Robert, 'it is not locked. Are you going to open it?'

Slowly she unfastened the clasps and lifted the lid to release a waft of delicate perfume. The trunk was lined with blue silk, and seemed to be filled with silver tissue. She drew aside the top layer of fine paper and lifted out a length of filmy muslin, gossamer thin and decorated with blue ribbon.

'Robert,' she breathed, wide-eyed. 'It-it is a bed-gown!'

Sir Robert lifted the material: even through two thicknesses of muslin his hand was visible. He looked up at her, his eyes dancing.

'Nell, have you not guessed yet? Look at the crest on the side.'

She stared at the trunk and her eyes widened.

'It is from Lord Ullenwood,' she gasped. 'He said he had bought me – oh! How dare he do this!'

'It seems he dares very much,' grinned Sir Robert. 'He has

215

sent you a wedding gift.'

With that he threw back his head and laughed.

CHAPTER FORTY-FOUR

By eight o'clock the following morning Clarissa could bear it no longer. She would call on Lord Alresford. She had heard him tell Sir Howard that he would meet him Saturday morning and now she was desperate to know if he was safe. In under an hour she was dressed and ready to leave the house. The butler looked up in surprise as she descended the stairs.

'Miss – are you going out? Will you not step into the breakfast-room first?' With an agitated hand she waved him away and was out of the door before he had time to tell her of the note Lord Wyckenham had directed should be given to her at breakfast.

The footman who opened the door of Lord Alresford's mansion in Bedford Square showed no surprise at finding a heavily veiled lady requesting to see the earl so early in the morning. He allowed her to step into the marbled hall, where a second, equally impassive footman showed her into the morning-room while a message was sent to the earl. Clarissa breathed a sigh of relief. At least he was not dead, then. A quarter of an hour later Lord Alresford entered, dressed with all his usual neatness in biscuit-coloured small clothes and a coat of blue superfine. Another relief, no sign of any injury. He stood by the door, regarding her with his impassive stare.

'Madam?' She lifted the veil and saw the look of surprise on

216

his face as he recognized her.

'I had to come,' she said quickly. 'Forgive me, I had to know if you had met Sir Howard.'

'What? Oh . . . no. He had left town when Norwell called yesterday.'

'Oh thank heaven.' She sank down on to a chair.

'Miss Wyckenham.' He was staring at her, as if trying to memorize every detail. 'You should not be here.'

'I know it; I am sorry.'

'You are very pale, let me get you something to drink—'

Her heart ached when she observed him: he looked as miserable as she felt. With a jolt she realized how wrong she had been to come: it added to his pain, as well as her own. She summoned up every shred of resolution.

'No, I am sorry. I must not stay. I-I wanted to . . . to thank you for helping Mama-Nell.'

'It was nothing.'

'That is not true,' she cried. 'Ullenwood is very powerful—'

'I did it for you.' He gave a short laugh. 'I had not realized how incredibly dull my life had become before we met.'

Tears welled in her eyes. She rose.

'I must go.'

She ran for the door, but he caught her and pulled her to him.

'Not yet. Tell me, tell me what you are going to do.'

She could not look at him: just the touch of his hand was enough to set her pulse racing so fast she thought she must faint.

'I – um . . . oh, this is dreadful!' she cried. 'I wish I had not come, I wish I had never met you!'

She tried to pull away, but his grip was too strong.

'Don't say that,' he muttered. 'Tell me you don't mean that.'

She found herself being pulled into his arms where she subsided against his chest, sobbing.

'No,' she swallowed convulsively. 'No, I could never regret

knowing you.' With an effort she pushed away from him, drawing on her pride to help her through this ordeal. 'Lady Wyckenham and Sir Robert are to be married, is that not wonderful?' She managed to walk away a few steps. 'They have offered to let me live with them, but they will want some time alone first, so I shall return to my sister Anne for a few months and then . . . then I think I shall go abroad, to Rome. I have always wanted to see Rome.'

'I believe the antiquities are fascinating.' He was following her lead. 'There will be plenty to divert you.'

Not enough to make me forget you! She closed her eyes as tears threatened again. He walked to the window.

'If you have the opportunity you should travel to Florence. You would like that. I was there— Good God!'

She started. 'What is it?'

'Sir Gordon Medway. He is coming in.'

Even as he spoke a distant bell jangled and there was the sound of voices in the hall. Clarissa stared at him.

'He must not find me here!'

Sir Gordon's booming voice could be heard clearly.

'In there, is he? No need to announce me!'

'Quickly.' He hurried her towards a door in the far wall. 'Wait in there.'

She found herself in a small, book-lined room. The earl pushed the door shut just as Sir Gordon entered the morning-room.

'There you are, Alresford!'

Clarissa noticed with alarm that the door to the little room had not closed properly. She heard the earl walking away but she dared not pull the door in case Sir Gordon should notice and discover her. She bit her lip, disliking the role of eavesdropper.

'I am glad I find you up, sir,' declared Sir Gordon. 'I've distressing news. Come, my lord, we must be off at once.'

'Off, Sir Gordon?' Alresford's deep voice came clearly to her.

'I do not understand you. Where are we to go?'

'To the border, sirrah!' There was the rustle of paper. 'Read that, sir, read it! My little girl has run off with Lord Wyckenham!'

CHAPTER FORTY-FIVE

Clarissa thrust her gloved fist into her mouth and bit hard to prevent herself from crying out with surprise. William and Florence Medway? Her heart seemed to be trying to leap out of her chest, and it was a struggle to hear the earl's quiet reply above its heavy drumming.

'What would you have me do about it, Sir Gordon?'

'Do? Why, man, we must catch 'em, and bring her back. From her note I know they left at midnight. If we set out now we shall catch up with them before nightfall and this whole sorry business can be hushed up.'

'But, Sir Gordon, if she has run off rather than marry me. . . .'

'Bah! The girl doesn't know her own mind.'

'Pardon me, Sir Gordon, but I have always had the impression that Miss Medway is very strong-minded.'

'She has been dazzled, sir, that's what it is. Dazzled by Wyckenham.'

Hysterical laughter threatened and Clarissa was obliged to bite hard again on her glove. That anyone should be dazzled by her prosy brother!

'You have been too patient with her, Alresford,' grumbled Sir Gordon. 'Not enough of the lover. Well, that can change.'

'I do not wish for an unwilling bride, sir.'

'She ain't unwilling, my lord, you have my word for it. No, the notice has been sent to the papers – think of the scandal if we have to revoke it. It must not be. My carriage is outside, we must be off—'

'Let us not be hasty about this.' Lord Alresford's measured tones broke in. 'You know, sir, that Lord Wyckenham is a wealthy man—'

'Not as wealthy as you,' came the swift reply.

'Perhaps not, but he is destined for parliament.' Alresford paused to let that sink in. 'I believe he is standing at the next election. Think how that would help you in your good works, Sir Gordon.'

There was a long silence. Clarissa longed to shift her position, but dared not move. At last Alresford pressed home his advantage.

'Miss Medway is cut out to be a political hostess: she was most disappointed to learn that I have no real ambition in that direction. Wyckenham is an honourable man, Sir Gordon. That he has taken the step of flying to the border shows that his affections are deeply engaged. Go after them by all means, sir, but tell them that you come with my blessing: I will not stand in the way of their marriage.'

'But – the announcement—'

'I will attend to that, Sir Gordon. I shall draft a notice today. I think you will find that it will explain everything most satisfactorily. There will be no hint of disgrace attached to your daughter.'

'Hmmm, I suppose it might do.'

There was the sound of footsteps, and a door opening.

'Then I suggest you move with all speed to overtake your daughter, sir. Tell her I bear her no ill-will. Indeed, I wish her every happiness with one who, I believe, is ideally suited to be her life-partner.'

A silence.

'Very good of you, my lord. But, will you not come with me? I—'

'Sir Gordon, my presence could only complicate matters. It is better that you go alone.'

'Aye, aye. Well, I'll be away then. Good day to you.'

'God speed, Sir Gordon, and good luck.'

Clarissa was still standing by the door when the earl pulled it open.

'You heard everything?'

She could only nod. He took her hand and led her back in to the morning-room.

'William,' she said at last. '*William?*'

He grinned.

'When you introduced them at Holborn you could not have guessed how it would end.'

'It begins to make sense,' she said, a tiny crease in her brow. 'His remaining in London, the trips to Mount Street.'

'Your worthy brother has met his match.'

'And I am very happy for him but . . . *William*, elope?'

His arms were around her.

'Love is a very powerful emotion, Clarissa. We cannot always control it.'

He reached up and tugged at the ribbons of her bonnet.

'What are you doing?' she asked

'I cannot kiss you while you are wearing it. It is in my way.'

With a laugh she removed the offending bonnet and veil and dropped them to the floor.

'Is that better?' she asked, looking up shyly.

'Much.' He kissed her. 'How soon can we be married?' he murmured, nibbling at her ear.

She shivered deliciously.

'As soon as possible, if you please.'

He kissed her again, then dropped on to the satin-covered settee and drew her on to his knee.

'Very well, and I shall take you to Rome for our honeymoon, then Naples, and Florence.'

'Mmm.' She leaned against his shoulder. 'And when we return, will you continue your support for Mr Sharp and the anti-slavery campaign? I should very much like to help.'

'I don't see how we can avoid it, if my brother-in-law is involved.' He bent a frown upon her and said severely, 'Is that why you are marrying me, ma'am? For my wealth and influence?'

She pulled his head down towards her. 'No,' she murmured, 'because I cannot live without you.'

'Nor I you.' His voice was unsteady, and his burning look sent her spirits soaring.

'I love you, Clarissa.'

With a sob she threw her arms about his neck and kissed him. When at last he released her she leaned against him, her head resting on his shoulder, listening to the beat of his heart.

'That night, in the hut,' she said slowly, 'when you turned away from me, I thought. . . .'

'What?'

'I thought you did not . . . want me.'

He shifted his position so that he could look at her.

'Not want you!'

He gently pushed her aside and got up to walk to the door. She watched him, frowning.

'What are you doing?'

'Locking the door.' He said. 'I don't want us to be disturbed.' He walked back and dropped on his knees beside her. 'Now,' he smiled, 'let me show you just how much I want you.'

The following week all the major newspapers carried the announcement of the marriage of Lord Wyckenham, of Wyckenham Manor in Devonshire, to Miss Florence Medway, only daughter of Sir Gordon Medway of Devizes. At the same time Marius, ninth Earl of Alresford would be married to Miss

Clarissa Wyckenham, sister to the above Lord W., the marriages to take place in a double ceremony at St George's Hanover Square, on Tuesday se-ennight and would be followed one week later by the marriage of dowager Lady Wyckenham to Sir Robert Ingleton (Bart), renowned scientist, explorer, and member of the Royal Society.

T- 2011

CN ✓